I0681391

High praise to a powerful new author!

"Being a writer of traditional westerns, I couldn't imagine what the combination of vampires and cowboys could be like. Well, I just finished Colin Webster's book and now I know. Solid, never ending action with a twist at every corner. A refreshing change, I must say."

– Will Riley Hinton
Author of "Lonely are the Hunted" –

"Colin has done something that is very rare, and very special these days. He's written a good Western that you can sink your teeth into like a nice thick beef steak seared over the open flame of a camp fire. You can smell the desert sage and feel the grit carried by the wind and it makes you squint your eyes as you read. But this isn't your Dad's Western, some surprise elements are going to grab you. By the time you finish the book, you'll be wearing a cartridge loop belt to work. This is a great story and I am eagerly looking forward to the sequel.."

– George Hill
Author of "Uprising USA" and "Uprising UK"–

"*Blood and Tequila* doesn't just bend the mold of a traditional western, it shatters it. Great characters combine with a fast-paced plot to form a solid debut novel. And, c'mon. Cowboys and vampires--vampires and cowboys. This ain't your pappy's Saturday afternoon read!."

– Josh Clark
Author of "The McGurney Chronicles" and "Dakota Divided" –

"In Colin Webster's book, *Blood and Tequila*, the author has done something I didn't think was possible. Skillfully, he has managed to blend two conflicting genres, the Western and Sci-Fi. With Webster's strange but riveting mixure of cowboys and vampires, perhaps the book should have been called, The Quick and the Undead."

– RG Yoho
Author of "Death Comes to Redhawk" –

"Cowboys and vampires, what a combination, and Colin Webster does it with flair. *Blood and Tequila* is a rip-roaring read. This book is just plain fun."

– JK Jones
Author of "In Due Time" –

Acknowledgements

I would like to thank the folks at White Feather Press for making this happen and helping Clay and Maria come to life with excellent design, editing, and story input, and the excellent group of fellow writers at wethearmed.com for all their encouragement and criticism.

COLIN WEBSTER

Published by White Feather Press, LLC
www.whitefeatherpress.com

ISBN: 978-1-61808-106-3

Printed in the United States of America

Cover design created by Ron Bell of AdVision Design
Group (www.advisiondesigngroup.com)

White Feather Press

Reaffirming Faith in God, Family, and Country!

This book is dedicated to
my mother, Pamela Webster,
for everything that she does for me and
for teaching me how to read and enjoy
books at an early age. Without that, it
would be awfully hard to write them!

CHAPTER 1

I LOOKED OVER THE SIGHTS OF MY RIFLE AT THE man I was about to kill. I hesitated, just for a moment. I won't tell you I felt any kind of pity for him. I didn't have that kind of emotional investment in anything anymore, and hadn't for a long time. Most likely, I never would again.

He just didn't look like the type, that's all. He stood tall and erect, unshaven but with a strong, open sort of face and clear, intelligent eyes. The paper in my breast pocket said he was the one responsible for the fact that a woman and her three children were dead, but I had my doubts. He didn't look like the sort of man to do such a thing, but you never could tell with a body, and if I were to let misgivings get in the way of doing my job, well, I wouldn't be eating much.

Rick Grange was the name on the paper, and he'd manage to escape the county jail down south, mere hours before becoming the guest of honor at a gallows affair. He'd protested his innocence all the way through the trial, but he'd been covered in the victims' blood when they found him, and that was enough for the court. Still, he'd already been found guilty, and like I said, it didn't make much difference to me anyway.

The paper I had in my hand promised a reward of a thousand dollars, dead or alive. Since the result was to be the same, I decided the former option would save me time and trouble. I took a deep breath and let it out again, watching the sights settle back down onto his torso. I'd guessed the range at no more than two hundred and fifty yards, which with this rifle, lying down behind a log, was an easy shot. I'd had plenty of time to prepare and could take my time choosing when to fire.

I'd gotten into position that night, gone without my fire while he'd cooked and ate his supper over a big one, either not caring or not having the sense to figure someone might just be chasin' after him. I loaded a long .45-70 cartridge into the Sharps and settled down for a long night, watching and waiting. I'd already taken the leather strap, which I'd hung from the barrel, and tied it snugly to my left upper arm, allowing me to hold the rifle steady as a rock even if I had to make a standing shot at that distance.

I was amazed at his nonchalance when he rose up without even looking around, rebuilt his fire, and started making coffee. He'd probably long since figured he'd given the good folks of Idaho Territory the slip, and indeed he had. I'd rode his trail for the last week, but I'd hung back, thinking the easy way he'd been riding was surely an attempt to set me up for an ambush. But the whole time I'd been studying his trail, I noticed he didn't veer off once to double back or even give much of an effort to hiding his tracks. It was almost too easy, and that's what had me worried.

After a week of this cat and mouse game, I'd finally figured he really just wasn't given to carefulness and probably lacked the skills to do much at all to obscure his passing. His last job had been as some kind of hotel manager, but out west that didn't mean much. Folks out here held all kinds of jobs during their lifetimes, and this one could well have been riding the cow trails for years before deciding to settle down to a quiet town life.

Many men would have looked down on what I was about to do, backshootin' a critter like this, but that didn't bother me none. In fact, my methods already tended to earn me the disdain of more than a few lawmen I'd dealt with. I looked at it as a business. Giving some reprobate a fair chance or an even draw was a sure way to go out of business fast. In short, the much-vaunted code of honor dime novelists attributed to western men didn't apply to me one bit. I didn't shoot because he was moving around the little camp, making coffee and frying a side of bacon. It smelled pretty good, and I resolved to take the shot before he ate all of it.

I'd been mighty low on funds when I'd started after him, and I'd run low on chow. I waited for him to set down on the fallen log he was using for a bench and took aim again. I had a good shot at his side, and I lined it up to send a four-hundred-grain chunk of hot lead through both lungs and hopefully, the heart. One good shot will put down a buffalo, so as long as my aim was true, I didn't plan on having to take another. Just as my finger tightened on the trigger, I let up again. Damn it all, his horse walked right behind him.

If I shot now the heavy bullet would surely pass through my man and hit the animal. And he was already loading the sizzling meat onto a tin plate, licking his lips with relish. If I didn't shoot him soon, I'd be out my chance for a hot breakfast. The horse stayed where he was, cropping grass. There was no way I was going to risk hitting the horse.

Despite having a bit of a soft side for animals, the main reason was that the horse was mine by right after I'd killed its owner. Well, it was more like there weren't any kind of rules on that sort of thing. I didn't have to turn it over with the body, and he wouldn't be needing it anymore. Besides, I'd have to use the horse to bring him in for the bounty, my own being overloaded as it was with guns and ammunition. There.

The gelding finally trotted out of the way. I let out another breath and sighted in just beneath his armpit as he reached for another strip of bacon. The last strip. Squeezing the trigger, I felt the long rifle buck hard, then looked over the sights to see the fallen log bereft of its occupant. I didn't see my target anywhere, just his horse cropping grass as calmly as you please, not even lifting his head to see the cause of the disturbance. Loading another long cartridge into the sharps, I cat-footed my way through the brush up to the campsite, stopping well back to sit and observe. If I'd missed him clean, he was waiting in the brush or trying to make his way around to the gelding so he could leap on and ride away.

I wasn't going to let that happen. Often I'd found patience had saved my life, so I waited and watched from a good spot behind the stump of a lightning-charred tree. No movement came, and after half an hour, I was sure this tenderfoot, if that's what he was, would have broken cover and made a try for it by now. On the off chance that he was still lyin' in wait for me, I circled around the camp to come from the opposite end, figuring he'd be looking toward where the shot came from. After I'd made it around, I waited and listened for a while longer. The horse just sort of wandered around then crossed the camp to the log where the man had sat and sniffed at something just beyond it.

Slowly, I crept up and peered over the log. The first thing I saw was a boot. Its owner lay still on the cool ground, a massive hole still leaking blood out the left side of his chest. He was going to be a mess to get up on the horse. I noticed with disdain that the whole rasher of bacon had disappeared over the log with him and was now soaked in blood. I was hungry, but not that hungry.

I took my time getting his gray gelding saddled, then heaved the body up and over across the leather. I tied his hands to his feet so he wouldn't fall off. The coffee was still on the fire and starting to burn, so I took the tin pot off the flame and set it down next to the log where he'd been sitting. Going through his saddlebags, I found two boxes of .44-40 cartridges, a silver flask of whiskey, and a few stacks of bills, forty dollars altogether. That would be a nice addition to the thousand dollars offered for his return. The rest of the odds and ends I threw away and checked the other side. A big grin broke out on my face. There was an extra slab of bacon!

Another hour and I was mounted on my own steel dust stallion. He never made me welcome with any stable hands, but he was a one-of-a-kind horse, and I knew it. Ornery to the extreme, he'd kick or bite if anyone else tried to ride him, and I don't think he ever came across a mare he didn't try to mount. It was a good thing I rode alone. With a full belly and a pocketful of cash, I set my course for the nearest town. Having followed this fellow for the last week or so as he fled north, I'd been guessing I was somewhere in the Wyoming Territory. Cattle was the booming business here, though there were plenty of mines as well. Still, most of the country was wild and untamed, and Indians were around in force.

There was some noise about the territory becoming a state, but I didn't figure it to happen for a few more years. I rode all day and part of the night before making camp. I hadn't stopped to do any hunting, so I chewed some jerky after making camp, which pretty much consisted of throwing my bedroll on the ground and unsaddling the horses. I'd packed the sharps and my shotgun in the dead man's saddle and took my colt lightning to bed with me. I loved that rifle. I'd had it for nearly four years now and used it to save my hide more than a few times.

Most folks carried lever guns, but the slick pump action lived up to its name. It was lightning fast, and I could rack the slide and shoot it faster than any cowboy could work a lever. It originally came with a long twenty-four-inch barrel, but I'd cut it down to eighteen inches, which still let me hold ten rounds in the tube and one in the chamber. I'd taken to keeping it well-oiled and clean, and I'll be damned if that thing wouldn't shoot the eyes out of a turkey at a hundred yards.

The wind was blowing pretty hard, but the air was dry, so I lay under the stars and drifted off, listening to the coyotes howl and yip their nightly song. I didn't dream often, but when I did it was usually bad. I was walking through a darkened primeval forest, with nothing but my knife and a heavy club of wood. Something prowled in the shadows beyond, large but lithe and agile. I couldn't see what it was but knew somehow that it was out to get me. I kept hearing it behind me, but I whirled around to see nothing but blackness.

Finally I panicked and started running through the pitch-black woods, hearing the crash and crackle of branches as the shape chased after me. I turned and slashed at the air, but again there was nothing there. Something moved in the corner of my vision, and I spun around just in time to see a flash of large white teeth headed for my face.

I sat up in a cold sweat and realized I'd been thrashing

around in my sleep. The sky was just beginning to lighten in the east. The wind still blew, but much more softly now, and it was gentle and warm on my face. I was a few feet out of the bedroll, and twigs and leaves stuck to the sweat on my face and arms. Brushing myself off, I started to rise and then went stock still.

Out there in the darkness, something moved! Something big. Something that was sniffing and huffing deeply, so I could hear it easily, like a huge pair of bellows being worked behind the brush pile where I'd seen it. If I squinted I could make out the silhouette of something large, round, and shaggy snuffling about. I figured it must be a bear.

If I had meat around I would have taken pains to tie it up in a tree well away from where I slept, but I hadn't thought much about the dead man propped up against a tree on the other side of the camp.

I'd have been happy to let the grizzly (and from the size I knew that's what it had to be) take him, except for the fact that I'd need the body to collect my reward. Darting for the rifle, I grabbed it and rose up just as the huge bear broke cover. When he saw me, he stood up on his hind legs and roared. He was either trying to get a better look at me or showing me how big he was. If he was trying to impress me, it worked. The animal looked enormous just standing there, not fifty feet away.

I must have looked awful tiny to him, and I felt it at that moment. I had some experience with bear, mostly black bear, but I'd never hunted grizzly. That looked like it was going to change in the next few seconds, and I was about to be fighting for my life. I did know that bears could soak up a tremendous amount of lead, and could keep going even with their heart and lungs all but turned into confetti by bullets. Experience told me the only reliable way to stop man or beast instantly in a fight was to hit him in the brain or the heart, or at least a heavy bone.

I was going to have to go for the brain. I stood my ground, hoping the griz would just decide to go and look elsewhere. A low whine as he opened his mouth to show me his teeth told me I was going to be disappointed. It really was very gentlemanly of him to give me the option of fleeing, and I was determined to return the favor by killing him quickly. Or so I'd hoped when I snapped up the rifle and took a bead on that gaping mouth. The next second his head disappeared just as I squeezed the trigger.

I didn't know what had happened, but as I pumped the slide to bring the muzzle back down I saw him charging me, and I touched off another round. He didn't even wince, and was now only a few yards away. I've heard tell a grizzly can run down a horse over short distances, and I believe it. I'm not a fast runner, even by human standards, and there was no way I was going to outrun this bear or even make it to some kind of cover in time. I pumped the rifle again and fired, digging a deep furrow in the top of his skull, but it looked like the round kind of slid off rather than penetrated the thick bone. I was out of time.

Throwing myself to the side, I felt a tremendous impact send me further on my way than my legs could have managed. I hit the ground tumbling, and felt the rifle catch on something, tearing away from my grasp. Coming to my feet as the bear turned, I ripped my Colt single action army revolver from its holster. Or at least I would have if it had been there. A quick glance showed me it was lying near my bedroll, probably fallen out at some point during my thrashings in the night. I was in the habit of slipping the thong off when I slept so I could get at it in a hurry if I needed to.

As the bear charged again, I dug in my pocket for my derringer, hoping my two shots could be made to count for all their worth. I stuck it out like I was pointing at the bear's eye and fired. His head was bobbing up and down as he ran though, and the bullet went high, burying itself along his spine. As I fired the second shot the bear's hind legs collapsed, but his momentum carried him forward, sending us both tumbling as he bowled me over.

I was in a full-on panic as I rolled, expecting any second a massive paw to tear my head from my shoulders. I finally slammed hard on my back, the breath knocked out of me by a very poorly placed rock, at least from my point of view. I had no idea where the second bullet had gone, but my empty derringer wasn't any good to me at this point, so I grabbed for my bowie, which thankfully hadn't been dropped, snagged, or otherwise lost so far.

While I was pulling the long blade from its sheath, the bear was pulling itself toward me. Its fangs looked huge. It was dragging its rear legs behind it, but that didn't seem to slow it down much. I struggled for my feet gasping for air. I made it just as he reached me and hooked at me with those big claws. They caught hold in my boot and he dragged me in. I was determined not to go quietly.

Staring into that gaping maw, I raised my blade and brought it down hard on his muzzle. The edge skidded off and cut a long gash down the side of his face, earning me an angry bellow for my trouble. In response to my antics, he grabbed me with his other paw and pinned me to the ground, dragging his jaws toward me while I thought the pressure would pop my eyes out.

I heard, rather than felt, two of my ribs crack and I slashed with the knife again, landing a cut across his wet, black nose. He drew his head back, and this bought me a second to come up with some kind of plan. I didn't have much to work with, so I stabbed the knife down hard into the paw that pinned me to the ground. The claws spread and jerked back, and I rolled away, leaving my boot in the beast's grasp.

Jumping to my feet, I almost made it out of his reach before I felt the claws dig into my back and swipe down. I still would have made it away if his talons hadn't caught in the leather of my belt.

Brought down to the ground again, and seconds from death at the hands of an angry bear whom I had not molested, I became angry. When I get mad sometimes I don't think entirely straight. Some people might tell you I even seem to lose my mind a little. It was so with me now, and a black and red haze swelled up in my head.

Instead of trying to escape from the bear, I attacked it head on. Throwing myself at the animal, I felt the claws tear free and I sailed up and onto its back. I gripped one arm around its neck and with the other I plunged the knife in again and again under it chin and through the loose, fatty skin at its throat. I howled something incomprehensible, and the bear tried his damnedest to reach me with his paws, but the angle wasn't right. He raked me a few times, but couldn't get hold of me, and I kept stabbing.

I couldn't tell you how long it was, but eventually his struggles grew weaker and he slumped forward, unmoving. I staggered to my feet and picked up my revolver, walked back to the bear, and put two shots into his head both to make sure and because it made me feel better.

***

THE NEXT THING I KNEW I WAS STARING UP AT AN evening sky, the darkness already gathering. I didn't know when I'd passed out, but I was lying next to the bear and there were ravens circling around us. Everything in my body was pain, my ribs, my head, every muscle, every patch of skin. I looked like I'd gotten into a one-sided fight with a razor blade, and it was hard to tell where the cuts stopped and where they began.

I knew the dangers of infection as well as blood loss, so I made myself rise. It hurt. Bad. I was already stiff and sore, to say nothing of the white-hot pain whenever my skin stretched and moved, breaking open the cuts where the blood had thickened into wet scabs.

I managed to get a canteen out of my saddlebag and build a fire. My canteen was all metal, so I just put the loop over some propped-up sticks and sat down in front of the fire. I dragged my rifle over to me, cradling it in my lap for reassurance. I even managed to get my shaky hands to thumb cartridges into it to replace the ones I'd fired.

I was weak from the blood loss and whatever other injuries I'd sustained and needed to bathe my wounds in hot water and find a place to rest safely. In the high mountain country there was less likelihood of infection for some reason. I didn't know why this was, but it was so. Many had noticed how wounds didn't seem to fester and healed faster and cleaner than in other places. Still, scratches and bites from carnivorous animals were troublesome, due to the traces of flesh and blood that rotted and decayed on them.

When the water was hot enough, I used it to bathe my wounds, wincing when the steaming liquid touched my bare skin where it was not laid open and gritting my teeth to keep from screaming where it was. If nothing else, it would help. I was sure there were plants around that might have been used in a poultice, but I knew little of such things. I couldn't just hole up somewhere and wait to heal completely. I knew I needed to try and seek help if it was nearby, but if I waited too long the dead body I was carrying would either get eaten by something or swell and decay until it was unrecognizable. Either way I wouldn't be getting my bounty.

It was imperative that I got saddled up and on my way as soon as possible. I didn't see any reason not to have a fire, and so I stumbled around, painfully gathering up dry branches and seasoned wood to stack around the fire, hoping to keep it going as long as possible. I dragged the body over near it, practically passing out from the pain that caused. I reckoned the fire would keep any more animals away, and on the chance that anyone came looking to take advantage, they'd shoot an already-dead body instead of me. That done, I turned the horses loose to graze, and gingerly made my way deeper into the woods with my rifle and bedroll. In the gathering darkness I tripped and fell.

Cursing my sudden weakness and inattention, I discovered I was staring into the mouth of a small cave. It would be a safe place to spend the night, should any more bears, wolves, or catamounts be attracted to the smell of blood and death that now permeated the camp. I rose to my feet with a great effort, and limped back to the fire. It only took a few moments to make a torch with a stick of wood and a few strips of cloth torn from the dead man's clothes. Heading back to the mouth of the cave, I entered slowly and cautiously, hoping nothing had taken up residence here. There were a few well-chewed bones inside, but they looked old. The torch didn't give off enough light to see around me, but somehow I could sense there wasn't a lot of space, though the ceiling was high enough to stand up straight and then some. I dropped my bedroll and gently lowered myself onto it as the torch guttered out. I don't know if I passed out or fell asleep, but darkness washed over me with the dying of the torch.

***

GRADUALLY I BECAME AWARE OF MORNING SOUNDS, the chirping of birds and the chittering of squirrels. The warmth on my face told me it was light out, and the sun was well up in the sky. Usually I was an early riser, but given the events of yesterday I could definitely make exception. I wanted nothing more than to stay exactly where I was, but I knew it was urgent, maybe even a matter of survival, to move on.

Cursing softly, I opened my eyes and nearly jumped out of my skin when they focused. I was looking into a grinning skull, with open eye sockets and not a whit of flesh left on the face. Glancing around, I saw the cave was small but high, as I'd thought the night before. The skull before me looked straight at me with its empty eyes, as if in greeting. Suppressing a shudder, I looked over the skeleton beyond it, tatters of clothing still hanging from the bones. It looked like someone had died sitting down in the cave, and time had slowly withered the skeleton away until the skull had fallen off to land in its lap. The bones rested against a depression in the wall, a sort of natural alcove. My temporary refuge suddenly felt a lot less comfortable and inviting.

The thing that was most strange about my apparent

bedfellow was that he'd been huge in life, as he still was in death. The skull was much larger than mine, and either of its hands would have made two of mine. I'm a big, strapping fellow, standing over six feet tall in my stockings, and this man looked like he would be at least a foot and a half over that if I'd stood him up. The bones were not just long but thick, and he looked to be powerfully built. I didn't know what to make of it. Some of the Indians I'd seen were big men, but they were the exception rather than the rule. Moreover, the features on the skull indicated a high forehead and prominent cheekbones, which was different than any Indians I had seen. Recessed into the pit where the stomach used to be, a low gleam caught my eye. An ancient leather sheath housed a blade with a horn handle. Actually, it looked quite a bit like ivory, though where an Indian would get that I didn't know. Something told me the skeleton, and therefore the knife, was very, very old.

I'm not a superstitious man, but I thought about it for a while before I reached out and took hold of the blade. Slipping it from the sheath, I admired the soft sheen. It was made of metal, which was obviously out of place here. Holding it up to the light, I could have sworn it was made of silver, though I couldn't explain that either. If these remains were as old as they seemed, they would date to a time well before the pioneers had made it this far, bringing tools of iron and steel with them. I'd read enough history and heard enough from the Indians though to know there had been others here well before Europeans had traveled west, at least the current crop of Europeans anyway.

I sat for a time, looking at the bones and wondering who they might have belonged to. My steel dust wandered over to the cave entrance and sniffed, undoubtedly following my scent. I called softly to him, and he nodded his head up and down as horses do and ambled away in search of more grass. If anything, the pain and stiffness were worse now, and I took my time getting to my feet. Before leaving the cave something else caught my eye. Off in the corner near one of the bony hands was a set of beads on a leather thong that looked like they had been carved from bone. I picked them up and stuffed them in my pocket; I could examine them later. The body had been left undisturbed, and for this I was glad. It was, however, beginning to smell, and the former owner's horse didn't like it one bit when I heaved him up and onto his back. I felt the cuts on my back open up and nearly passed out from the pain.

Riding my horse and leading the other, I headed off to the east. There was a thin plume of smoke rising toward the sky, and I set my course for it. I was high up, and by heading down to the valley beyond I would reach it before a few hours had passed.

I was feeling tired already, and so I let my mind wander, and trusted to my horse's keen senses to alert me to any danger. I felt cold, but my brow was damp, and I knew a fever was already coming on. I reached the town well before sunset, and for that I was glad. I'd no desire to spend another night in the woods, and I could probably use the services of a physician, if the town had such. It looked to be small, with a single main street and two rows of buildings that were saloons, gambling houses, or hotels. The cattle business was booming in the Wyoming Territory, but most of the business was done at the end of long droves to the south and east, and so the area was still a little less than ... cosmopolitan.

I drew stares when I rode into town, but whether it was because I was a stranger or the fact I was leading a horse with a body slung over it I couldn't tell. All I knew was I was tired, and I wanted to get my business here done and over with as soon as possible, so I could have a hot meal and climb into a warm bed.

I would have enough to stay here for a while if I chose, and I would at least need to stay long enough to heal up before I made any kind of decision. There was usually work for someone in my profession anywhere in the West, and even this small town would be no exception. I passed by the sheriff's office, and found what I really wanted right now. A saloon. The sheriff would come to me before long, I was sure of that. I climbed down from the saddle and hitched the two horses at the rail before entering.

Normally I'd stable my steel dust first, but I still had business to attend to, and more than once I'd found out quickly that I had worn out my welcome in a town and had to ride on in a hurry. Sometimes, when you ride in with a dead man, you get a chance to meet some of his friends, who are all too eager to introduce themselves to you. Conversations tend to be loud and short, and accompanied by thick smoke.

I pushed my way through the batwing doors, trying to appear unhurt and at ease, though I was covered in blood so there was no telling how convincing I was. I sat down heavily at the bar and asked for whiskey. The bartender was a short man, run to fat but with short, efficient movements. He glanced from the blood still on my face to a spot behind the bar, so I knew where he kept the scattergun.

He poured me a tall glassful, and I told him to leave the bottle. I would use the rest of it later to pour on my wounds, something I was not looking forward to in the slightest. Given how the hot water had felt, I decided to drink a good portion of it and dab the rest on as gently as possible. I hadn't been seated five minutes when I heard heavy footsteps enter the saloon, and all the eyes around me went to the door. You've got to like an efficient lawman. I spun around slowly to meet his eye, since I'd be the man he'd want to talk to.

He was as tall as I was, but slim, wearing a suit and tie and rather dapper bowler tilted on a head of thick, brown hair. His moustache was waxed and curled slightly on the ends. He wore hand-tooled black leather boots that looked expensive, and a silver star pinned to his left lapel. He might have looked like a dandy, but the way he wore his gun tied low on his hip and the look in his icy green eyes told me this was no tenderfoot.

"You there," he said, which I thought was unnecessary, since he was already looking right at me.

I didn't respond, just raised my glass and tilted the rest of it back, hoping I could get my business done as fast as possible. I didn't feel good at all, and I wanted to hunt a place to sleep.

"You the one rode in with that body?"

"That's right," I answered, glad he was direct and to the point.

"Want to tell me what happened?" He was frowning as he looked me over, and I had to agree with his assessment: I looked terrible. Getting mauled by a grizzly will do that to a man, so I'm told.

"Not really, but you can read this if you like." I wasn't in the mood to give anyone an explanation.

Maybe I had a problem with authority, or just maybe I

was in a foul mood, but I didn't feel like sitting here and jawing about the circumstances; the wanted poster I produced from my shirt pocket explained all the pertinent details anyway. I'd noticed railroad tracks running past the town, and I was hoping they could ship the body that way, which would save some time. I sure wasn't riding back with the body; it smelled bad enough already.

The sheriff eyed me suspiciously, but he took the poster and looked over it carefully before handing it back to me.

"That him?" he said, jerking his head in the general direction of the corpse outside. "Sure is," I replied with a nod. "If you can wire the Idaho governor's office, they should send the reward straightaway. They'll be asking you to confirm his identity."

Fortunately there was a very good and recent photo on the poster. The body had started to swell, but I was confident they'd be able to recognize him and get me my money in a timely manner.

"Heard of this one," the lean lawman said suddenly, looking me in the eye. "We'd had a telegraph saying he might come through this way. I know what he did down there, and I'm glad to see you got him. I've got to say Mr ..."

"Carlson, Thorn Carlson."

"Mr. Carlson. Dodge Garrett, I'm the sheriff here in Elk's Run. I don't have any love for your profession, but I'm glad to see he's caught. You can expect our cooperation and assistance in this matter."

With that, the lean lawman spun on his heel and walked out. As he left, I noticed two deputies who'd been waiting outside turn around and leave with him. This was much different than what I was used to. Most sheriffs acted like the big bull on the farm, and seemed to be anxious to let you know it. This man seemed fair, tough, and competent. He also seemed to be the man to fork his own broncs, as people liked to say. Most lawmen I knew would have had the deputies come and bring me down to the office right off, which in the past had ended up with more than one broken jaw, none of them mine.

Well, things were going smoothly enough, so I threw back another shot of the whiskey and settled down on the stool. My initial meetings with the local law were usually less than cordial, and I already knew the name of the town, so I felt I was making progress. Actually, I felt a little light-headed, and I reminded myself that I'd lost a lot of blood and was running a fever. I threw back one more and started for the door, feeling a little bit dizzy. I needed to get a room, bathe my wounds, and maybe have a bite to eat before I slept for a good, long time. There was a stable across the street, and it would only take a moment to get the horses bedded down for the night.

As I walked toward the door, a burly young cowhand with a red face and straw-colored hair got up to bar my path. "You're Thorn Carlson?" he drawled, and by smelling his breath, I thought I'd taken another shot of whiskey. He was swaying slightly, but I noticed he'd slipped the thongs from his guns. He wore one on each hip, and I noticed he was the only one doing so at the bar. The local tough, no doubt. I noticed he was swaying slightly, feeling his liquor, and I briefly hoped he merely wanted to tell me he was a fan of my work. Alas, it was not to be so.

"Don't look s' tough t' me," he slurred. I didn't feel like dealing with any trouble, so I decided to get this over with quickly.

"Why don't you just sit down and have a drink, friend," I said, giving him a smile and starting past him. He shot out a hand, rather quick given his condition, and leaned in so I could smell his breath even stronger.

"You brought in Shamus McMasters, right?" His eyes narrowed, but didn't appear to focus all that well. I nodded, noting the position of his feet. "He was a friend of mine!"

I could hear the anger in his voice, and I knew where this was heading. I shot out my foot, kicking a leg out from under him, the one he'd been resting his weight on. As he fell, I grabbed him by the belt and smashed three short, wicked rights into his jaw, one after another. Letting go, he dropped like a sack of flour and lay still on the floor. Ignoring the sudden silence in the bar room, I stepped over him and headed for the stables. Only when I was out of sight of the saloon did I bend over and try to catch my breath, and will the spots swimming before my eyes to go away.

I was glad I'd remembered to tuck the bottle into my back pocket, especially since I seemed to have opened up all of my wounds with the short flurry of activity. When I could stand straight, I untethered the horses and crossed the rest of the way to the stable. A boy of no more than twelve came running out.

"Can I take your horses, mister?"

The young man looked all industry as he helped me with the saddles and led the horses into the stables. My steel dust usually put up a fuss, but he was docile as a sheep when the boy took the reins. Horses have a way of telling about people, and I felt he was in good hands.

"Hey, kid," I said, when he set to brushing the horses immediately.

"Yes, sir?"

"You buy saddles here?"

"We do, sir. Which are you looking to sell?" I held up the one belonging to the former convict. It was a good saddle, but I already had one, and I could sell the other horse in the next few days, once I was up on my feet.

"I could give you twenty dollars for it," the kid said, studying his feet. He looked a little embarrassed; probably that was the price he'd been told to offer, and it was remarkably low.

"I'll let you have it for thirty," I offered, and I saw him look up, surprised. Saddles were worth quite a bit, and he was most likely used to people being insulted when he offered the set price. I wondered who owned the stables.

The kid had an open, honest face, but he wore threadbare, homespun clothes, and was barefoot. I figured whoever did was either dirt poor, or mighty cheap.

"I can take that for you, sir. Would you mind ... picking up the money tomorrow?"

"Sure, I can do that. Take good care of those horses now."

"I will, sir! And thank you for your business!" He ran off and started filling feedbags full of oats.

Truth be told, I didn't mind letting the saddle go for so little. It wasn't like I had paid for it ... just a bonus on top of my reward. If it made the kid's day easier to have gotten a good deal for his employer, well, at least I could sleep knowing I'd done a good deed, which had been few and far between in my lifetime. I stopped at the first hotel on the left, and laid down a wad of dollars on the counter.

"Will this cover me for a few days?"

"Most certainly, sir!" said the clerk, and he looked perfectly suited for his job.

"Is there a doctor in town?"

"Why yes, sir." He smiled apologetically. "But he'll be gone for a few more days, taking care of a wounded man out at the Bar K."

I figured that was one of the local ranches. I'd fixed up a gunshot wound on my own before without the services of a doc, so I figured I could deal with this too if necessary. I've got a strong constitution, and I'd survived my share of injuries of all kinds. This one would only make me a little uglier, that's all.

I'd walked with a limp for the better part of last year, after having my leg broken when my horse was shot out from under me. I'd been shot several times, knifed, had my skull cracked with an axe handle, and even lynched, though a timely rescue had gotten to me before my neck muscles had given out. I still had scars on my neck from it. I hobbled up the stairs, making a solemn resolution not to look in a mirror if there was one. Opening the door to my room, I saw it was efficient and tidy, if not luxuriant. I dropped the saddle, my rifles, and shotgun in the corner.

I'd taken the dead man's pistol, a Colt in the same caliber I used, and set it on the stand next to the bed. I slipped my own gun under the pillow. I slid off my boots for the first time in days, wiggling my toes and enjoying the sensation. Nothing, I mean nothing, feels better than taking off your boots after a long time on the trail.

The exhaustion of the last few days swept over me as I disrobed, stripping down to my bare skin. I did have to use the mirror after all to bathe the wounds on my back. My scars would be extensive, but that didn't matter much to me. I had four long claw marks on the left side of my face, running across my cheeks. My eyes were bloodshot and had dark circles underneath. I looked like hell itself had chewed me up, decided it didn't like the taste, and spat me out again.

I took another swallow of the burning liquid and then poured some on a clean cloth and bathed my wounds. My eyes teared up something fierce. The stinging was unbearable, but I knew it was necessary to disinfect the wounds. I probably needed stitches. My clothes were caked with the blood that had been seeping through them for the last two days. I had a sewing kit in my saddlebag, but I needed the right kind of material to close the wounds up. I could use thread if I had to. I'd worry about it tomorrow. Keeping my derringer in hand, I lay down on the bed and passed instantly into sleep.

CHAPTER 2

MORNING FOUND ME WITH A RAVENOUS APPE-
tite, and feeling somewhat better. My fever had broken, and
I'd only bled a little on the sheets. Buckling on my gun belt,
and stowing the derringer in the pocket of my one clean set
of clothes, I fell to on a plate of bacon, fresh eggs, and strong
coffee. I only caught a glimpse of the old woman who'd
made my breakfast, but I decided if she were maybe forty
years younger, I'd marry her just for the cooking. When the
doughnuts came out, greasy, hot, and rolled in sugar, I decided I may just have to marry her anyway.

I ate two plates of the best vittles I'd come across for a
time, and decided I'd picked the right hotel for sure. The
name of it was King's Nest, and though it sounded preten-
tious, to me it was a little slice of heaven. I watched a young
gal go upstairs to change out my linen, and though I didn't
know if that was the regular service or because I'd soiled the
sheets with blood, nevertheless I was impressed. I'd been in
many a place where the linen was far less than fresh when I
got it.

The food strengthened me, and brightened my mood
considerably. A look outside showed the town coming to
life, though it was not quite seven in the morning. Across
the street from the hotel was a general store, and I made up
my mind to stop there first. I needed supplies, being poorly
outfitted when I'd gone after Grange.

Crossing the dusty street to the general store, I made an effort to walk as if I was in no pain. In any western town, a stranger was already ripe pickings for the local cutthroats and ne'er-do-wells, and every town had them, though Elk's Run seemed to be thriving and full of honest, hardworking folk. Once you'd scratched the surface though, there was no telling what you'd find.

I entered the general store, which was neat and tidy. Could have been just about any general store I'd ever been in; I'd swear there's some sort of floor plan they all share and follow. A slim man with a crisp white shirt and hair to match greeted me when I entered.

"How do, sir, what're you looking for today?" I perused the wares on the clean wood shelving. I picked out two extra sets of clothing, a new leather belt (mine had suffered greatly at the hands of the bear) and a pair of blue bandanas. You could never have enough of them, and I'd already soaked my last one with blood, having thrown it away on the trail when it began to smell.

I also selected a pouch of tobacco and cigarette paper. I'd run out a few days into my hunt for Grange, a fact which hadn't improved my mood any.

There were odd knickknacks from out East, watches and pens, sheaves of paper, and books. A man in my position had to travel light, and I was already carrying more than most did, and most of that was in the form of weapons and ammunition. I had plenty of those already, but I had a fancy for firearms, and so I always stopped to browse, and tried to think of an excuse to buy another.

"What's that over there?" I pointed to a large-barreled lever action on the wall behind the store keep. "That right there is the new cat's meow my friend, another product designed by Browning for Winchester. This here's the latest in scatterguns, a ten-gauge lever action, thirty-two-inch barrel, full choke, and guar-an-teed to blow a hole the size of your fist clean through any critter God ever made."

He took it down with a sense of reverence and handed it over to me. The magazine tube was so large they'd just sandwiched a bit of wood for the forend in between it and the barrel. It had good lines, for sure, and the receiver was huge. It looked like it would hold six shells with one in the chamber, and that was four more than any double barrel. It was awfully long, but I could lop off the barrel down to twenty inches without affecting the capacity any, and it would give me a wider spread. It was a gun for close work at any event, and it suited me just fine.

Guns are tools, and it helps to have the right tool for the job. Most cowhands carried a rifle and a pistol in the same caliber, and I did the same. It helps to only have to use one kind of ammunition. Gunplay was a part of my job though, so I never hesitated to pack an extra tool that might save my life someday. I might just keep the extra horse and use it to stow my extra goods on. I'd always used just the steel dust, but with two horses I could switch out and run down my quarry faster, not to mention having a backup if one horse happened to get shot or break a leg, both of which had happened to me in the past. One does not want to be left afoot in the West, particularly if there's someone out there with you, interested in your scalp or just the contents of your purse.

"I'll take it." I wasn't going to fight this one, so I just plunked down the money for my purchases, and the old man threw in two boxes of shells free of charge. I thanked him and left the store.

Returning across the street to my room, I stowed my purchases in my saddlebags. I'd practice with the shotgun some before I actually had to use it, but I loaded it full after working the action a few times and getting a feel for the way it handled and pointed. The lever had a long angle of travel, but in any case I'd be able to chamber and fire it much faster than I could reload the coach gun. I'd get another scabbard for it, and set it just beneath the one for my colt lightning. With those two and my six-guns, I'd be pretty well set for whatever came my way.

Going back down to the street, I sat down on a bench outside and took in the sights. Folks were coming in on wagons and pulling up to the general store, and more than one stopped by the saloon first. The calendar inside the hotel had indicated it was Friday, and further told me there was to be some kind of event tomorrow, with horse races and a dance. I didn't plan on attending, though I'd made money in the past riding the steel dust to victory. He was an odd mix of horse, that's for sure, but he had speed and staying power to beat any I'd seen yet.

I took out the makings and rolled myself a smoke, inhaling the pleasant smoke and enjoying the sun on my face. I was already feeling tired, and thinking about going back to bed. I saw a familiar figure walk out of the saloon, with the side of his face all purple and blue, and one eye swollen shut. It was the fellow with the straw-colored hair from last night. I hoped he didn't hold a grudge, and it had just been the drink talking. A man was smart not to make enemies if he didn't need to. It's a truth though, that one can pick one's friends, but not often one's enemies. They seem to pick me, sure enough.

The angry glance the young cowhand threw my way told me he hadn't forgotten about what happened last night, and once he got over his hangover, he'd be back for more. Oh well. I was quite a hand with my fists if I do say so myself, and I'd try to keep relations at that level if I could. A shooting here in town wouldn't win me any friends, and I was thinking about staying a while. At least long enough to heal up.

Someone was yelling over by the stables, and I was reminded of my promised thirty dollars for the dead man's saddle. I decided to go and collect, since my new shotgun had taken up most of my cash until the reward came in.

When I approached the stables, I saw the boy there hard at work feeding and caring for my two horses. He had a fat lip and a welt on the side of his face. He looked at me, then down when I entered.

"You been fightin'?" I asked him. "No, sir," he said, but didn't offer any further explanation. Not my business, I reckoned.

"I've come for the thirty dollars," I explained, and he studied his feet for a while before answering.

"Uncle Bartlett says you'll have to talk to him about that. He said the price is twenty dollars and not a penny more." "And where is Uncle Bartlett anyhow?"

"You'll have to wait until afternoon, when he gets up. He's usually dead drunk until then."

"Where's your parents, boy?" "Dead, sir, Uncle Bartlett takes care of me." I had a feeling it was the other way around. I had a soft spot for kids, as I suppose most everyone does, and I already didn't like "Uncle Bartlett," not one bit. It looked to me like he kept the boy busy running his stable night and day, while he did little else other than get drunk. I didn't object to physical punishment, but I suspected this was doled out in a harsh manner and for no other offense than not being able to talk me down to a ridiculous price for my saddle. I was going to have a little talk with Uncle Bartlett sooner or later, that's for sure.

"What's your name, son?" He looked up at me as if no one ever asked him that. "Billy," he stammered, then corrected himself and stood up straight. "I mean, William Sherman Harris, sir."

So he had dignity, despite how he'd been treated. I took a shine to him right then. "You get paid here, William?" He shrugged. "Room and board."

"Well, it looks like you're doing a fine job with my horses, and that's appreciated. Tell you what, I'll keep the saddle for now. Here's something for your efforts."

I stuck a dollar bill in his shirt pocket, and smiled at his embarrassment. "Yes, you can take it. Get some candy or whatever it is kids want nowadays, and keep up the good work. If you hear anything around town that might be of interest to me, be sure and let me know."

It wouldn't hurt none to have an extra set of ears about town, for you never knew what to expect, or what would develop. I was a stranger, or worse, nearly everywhere I went, and I'd long learned it was wise to prepare in advance. I didn't expect trouble here, outside of the usual way, but it often found me in the most unlikely places.

I took the saddle with me, and sold it to the general store for fifty dollars, which wasn't much of a price either, but I didn't feel like haggling, and I made more than I would have on it anyhow. Tired as I was, I took a stroll down the street anyway, just to get a look at the town. There were a few houses behind the rows of shops and stores on the street. You never know when the lay of the land may be the factor that determines life or death, so I made a careful study of the buildings and outlay of the town. I had entered the town from the south, and on the north end there was a railway stop, the tracks swinging in wide from the east to pass west, where they turned south again, no doubt to go around the mountains that jutted up into the sky. This was high country, and the cool, brisk air felt good. It was dry here, but there was plenty of green on the hills and mountains, considering.

I sat down on a bench to rest, and rolled another smoke. A wagon came bucking and rolling into town at top speed, the two horses in a lather. A heavyset man sat on the buckboard, a shotgun across his lap. Two riders, cowhands by the look of them, were positioned on each side of the wagon. They dismounted in a hurry, and lifted a man out of the back. I couldn't see what was wrong with him, but there was a lot of blood. He looked like I imagined I must have after being mauled by the bear, and my mind was turned again to my wounds. There was a lot of shouting and yelling for the doctor, and I saw they had pulled up alongside a one-story storefront with a sign reading Jonas Sterling, MD.

The wounded man looked to be barely conscious as they carried him inside. A sort of crowd gathered in all the windows up and down the street, and a few even stepped outside to stare and gawk. I didn't figure anyone would appreciate it if I went over to look, so I just sat on my bench and stubbed out my smoke to roll another.

"Someone fetch the doctor!" one of the men holding the wounded cowhand cried.

"I'm here," said a calm voice, full of assurance but with an edge of fatigue.

The voice belonged to a tall man, astride a horse, dressed in a tweed suit and carrying a fine leather case under one arm. He had a strong jaw and flinty blue eyes, and despite the suit, looked more like a western man than an eastern college boy. He was young, perhaps in his twenties, but you couldn't tell by the way he carried himself. He dismounted swiftly and led the cowhands into his practice.

"Set some water to boiling," he told someone, "I'll have to disinfect my equipment." The wounded man cried out something fierce as they maneuvered him onto a table. I had a lot of pity for him, whatever had happened, because I had been in his shoes, more or less, in the past two days. What I saw of his skin and clothes showed me long claw marks, not much different from the ones that had raked me. I hoped the doctor had experience with such things, and I figured bear attacks were probably not uncommon in this country.

There wasn't a lot to see, just a lot of noise and thrashing about, the wounded man inside putting up a tremendous fuss as they cleaned and worked over his wounds, not that I could blame him any. At least the doctor was back in town. He was obviously busy at the moment though, and my wounds were doing well enough, so I decided to leave him be and visit him again, that night or the following day for a look-see. I flicked the remainder of my cigarette into the street and limped my way back to the hotel.

The sun was high in the sky now, and I was already feeling like I had been out and about too long. My fight with the bear had taken a lot out of me, and I needed rest. The hotel seemed far away now, but it was most likely only a hundred yards off. I passed the barber's and unconsciously began scratching the growth on my face. I would have liked a shave and a hot bath, but both would have to wait until my wounds healed up some.

Finally, I made it back to my hotel. The clerk flagged me down as I entered. There was a message left for me. It read:

"Mr. Carlson, arrangements have been made to transport the body of Patrick Grange to Idaho, whereupon identification of same, the bounty will be available for withdrawal by yourself, from Morgan and Rockwell bank in Elk's Run. Signed, Dodge Garrett, Sheriff"

Well, the sheriff wasn't one to waste time, and for that I was glad. Content that all was well and I'd be getting my bounty soon, I made my way up the stairs and stretched back on the bed. The sheets were fresh and clean, so I made sure to kick my boots off before stretching back for a long nap.

The sound of gunfire awoke me. I snatched my colt from its holster and pointed it at the door, ready for whatever was coming. After a few tense moments, I realized there was laughter and shouting outside in the street, accompanied by more gunfire. I turned over in the bed and held the pillow over my head for a moment, then realized I was ravenous.

Sitting up gently, so as not to risk opening my cuts again, I slipped my boots on and went downstairs to see what was for dinner. The clerk informed me the hotel served breakfast only, but recommended the diner across the street. When I went outside, everything seemed chaotic. The sounds of singing and stomping feet drifted out of the saloon, along with some terrible piano playing. Horsemen were galloping up and down, firing off their six-guns in the air. Cowboys from the surrounding ranches had come into town, apparently determined to blow their week's pay all on Friday night. There was a group of them clustered in the street, shooting at tin cans placed about fifty yards off. They weren't hitting many, though the way they were guzzling down liquor, it wasn't surprising.

As I crossed the street, the group called to me. "Hey, Stranger, come join us, we're taking bets."

I didn't want to be disturbed, but I also didn't want to be unfriendly. I'd have to be in town a few more days; besides, I could always use the extra cash, and where I thought this was heading, it seemed like a sure thing.

"What's the bet?" "The first one to knock over all three cans with three shots gets the pool, ten to buy in." It was a long, lean cowboy that spoke, and he seemed good-natured enough. Just a bunch of cowpokes having some fun on payday. I'd be glad to take their money. There were seven of them, and that meant seventy dollars.

"Sure, here's ten." I fished the dollars from my pocket and stuffed them in his hand.

The cans were small, and pretty far for a pistol shot. I could see why these had been at it for a while. But I'd been practicing with my firearms for years, and I knew exactly where they'd shoot, and at what distance. Most people in the West had a good deal of proficiency with weapons, but I'd spent days on end training with all my guns, knowing that I was sure to get into fights and preparing accordingly. I wasn't a trick shooter, though I could accomplish some of their feats of skill.

I trained for mortal combat with firearms, that was my way. I'd practiced both fast and slow-aimed fire, could hit a man-sized target in the chest by just pointing, rather than aiming my weapon from a good distance, and I'd spent hours loading and reloading my weapons as fast as possible. That was the edge I counted on to keep me alive in my profession.

They stood to the side while I studied the distance and the target. Sometimes it's good not to show your skill with a weapon; at other times making a point of it can save you further trouble. Since I'd already bought in, I decided to make a show of it. I'm not given to bravado, but I wanted to make a statement that would warn off troublemakers, like the one I'd met last night.

This area wasn't given to the traveling gunfighter, usually young men out to make a name for themselves in the most useless kind of way. I'd drifted on from plenty of places before in an attempt to avoid just that kind of reputation. Kill a man or two in a gunfight, and the next thing you know you have people you've never even met gunning for you, hoping to make your name a notch on their guns.

I lined up the distance, and walked through the process, seeing it in my head before it happened, seeing each can fly up when I hit it, seeing my pistol move from target to target.

I drew and fired, three quick shots, and when I reholstered in one smooth movement, not a can was left standing. A low whistle went through the crowd.

"Well shucks, mister, you made short work of that ... ," the lean one spoke again. The rest of them looked awed and disappointed at the same time. Impressed with my shooting, yes, but also realizing they'd just lost a sizable chunk of money.

I didn't want hard feelings, so I took the money and gave each of them five dollars back. "I haven't been drinking," I explained. That seemed to cheer them up considerably, and I watched as they disappeared into the saloon to part with the rest of their paychecks.

When I looked down, William was staring up at me.

"Mister, would you teach me how to shoot like that?" he asked with wide eyes.

"If we find time. You ever shoot a gun before?"

"No, sir. Well ... there was a couple times when Uncle Bartlett was dead drunk, and I took the rifle out to the woods and fired it a few times. I didn't hit much ... ," he explained, digging in the dust with his toes.

"Tell you what, William, you find time when you can get away from the stable, and let me know. I'll teach you the basics, but it's up to you to master them."

"Gee, thanks!" He beamed at me, and took off running. I had been much younger than William when I first learned how to hold a rifle steady. It had been longer than me at the time, and my father, God rest his soul, had impressed upon me the importance of learning how to use it well. He died during the Civil War, a member of the Iron brigade called up from Wisconsin, who'd earned a name for themselves as the crack troops of the north. I'd been far too young to enlist at the time, too young to even have a hope of lying about my age.

I was older now, thirty, and long past the time when I should have settled down and started to raise a family. I'd punched cows, worked as a buffalo hunter for the railroads, even tried my hand at mining time and again. It wasn't 'til a few years ago that I'd realized the only thing I was much good at was hunting men.

The bounty hunter is almost universally despised, even though the service he provides is a good one, or at least desirable in the eyes of the community. Disliked by lawmen, citizens, and outlaws alike, demanding constant travel and risk, I'd found it hard to set down roots anywhere, even if I'd wanted.

Perhaps it was time to change all that. I decided to leave deep thinking to a time when I felt better, or at least had a full stomach. Making my way into an establishment with a sign that proudly proclaimed Ma's Kitchen as the finest meals west of the Mississippi, I grabbed a table near the rear door and sat down.

A lot of folks liked to sit with their back to the wall, but I thought it more important to be out of sight of the windows if possible, and be near an exit, usually the back one. It was a lesson I'd learned the hard way, after the first time I'd been shot. I still carried the .45 slug somewhere in my abdomen, though I couldn't feel it. The doctor said scar tissue would grow around it, after he'd done his best to dig it out of me. I'd drunk a lot of whiskey that night, both before getting shot and after, as the old Civil War sawbones had made a bloody mess of my insides going after that bullet with dirty tools. I'd nearly died from what a real doctor had later called "the sepsis", and from that day on I either made it a point to see a bonafide professional or do my own doctoring.

A pretty young lady came to the table, with plenty of Indian in her features. She took my order with plenty of significant glances and coy smiles, but I knew enough of womenfolk to know it wasn't so much directed at me in particular as to raise business. I'm sure Ma's diner was plenty popular with the young cowboys, Indian blood or not.

A plate of beef, thick dark bread, and gravy was brought out to me in no time, and I set to with a vengeance. I listened to the conversation all around me as I ate, and tried to ignore the hasty glances at the cuts on my face. At the table next to me sat a young woman and man, well dressed, and I was given to understand the woman worked in the capacity of a nurse for Jonas Sterling, doctor of medicine. She was a pretty thing, and I made up my mind to engage the services of the doctor first thing in the morning.

She was relating the circumstances under which the wounded man met his accident, as she'd called it. He didn't have much to say, being half out of his mind with fear and pain, but he had mentioned teeth and claws, and babbled on and on about yellow and green eyes all around him. His companions said he'd been riding the fence line at night; apparently their ranch, the Bar K, had been suspecting rustlers of carrying off their stock. Sounded to me like he got jumped by a catamount, or some other predator. I'd seen one man tore up something fierce by one of the big cats, and he hadn't lived long afterward.

She told her dining companion that the blood loss had been too great, and the young cowpoke had passed on before the good doctor had a chance to do much to get the wounds closed. It was a shame, but such things happened often in this part of the country, and I was walking, breathing proof of that.

After finishing my meal and paying, I stepped outside and rolled a smoke. The saloon was bustling, and the occasional drunk cowboy was stumbling out to vomit in the street before climbing onto his horse and heading back for the home ranch. I looked up at the sky to study the full moon. It seemed awfully big and close here in the mountains, and a luminous white. Some said there were mountains on the moon, and I'd always hoped to get a chance to look through a telescope at it and see if that was true. If I was going to stay awhile, I could at least talk to the general store about ordering one. Such a device could come in handy in the course of my employment, so I was able to justify the thought as something other than an entirely frivolous purchase. A hard voice broke in on my reverie.

"You," was all the voice said, which usually didn't indicate a friendly conversation was about to follow.

I looked to my left to see the straw-colored hair of the man I beat up last night, only this time he was flanked by two others. One was rather short and wiry, but the third was a half a foot taller than me and looked to weigh fifty pounds heavier. All three were wearing guns. I put my hands on my hips and faced them, trying to appear uninjured. In reality I felt like nothing more than going to sleep after the heavy meal, and my wounds were hurting from all the movement of the day, but I couldn't afford to show it.

"This the one who took in my brother?" said the big man, and I knew there was going to be trouble whether I wanted it or not. Still, if it was at all possible, I wanted to avoid a gunfight. In my present condition, and at this range, a bullet or two might end up killing me even if it didn't reach a vital spot, and the odds were I'd catch at least one.

"Yes," I said, "that would be me, so long as your brother's name is Shamus McMasters. You should thank me really, I took him in alive, when it would have been easier just to kill him. As it was, I'd whipped the tar out of him, and trussed him up like a calf. You looking for the same treatment?"

The big man scoffed, and cracked his knuckles. I'd just given him a challenge, and as large as he was, I probably seemed like easy prey.

"Don't make no difference to me," he barked," I'll kill you with my fists just as easy as with a gun."

Others had gathered around now, and it would seem like he was afraid of me if he didn't fight me himself, alone. He was confident, laughing as he stripped off his gun belt and shirt before stepping out into the street.

William came running up, so at least I had someone to stand for my second. I didn't unbutton my shirt, because I didn't want him to see the long, barely closed cuts all over my body. He'd surely target them, 'cause that's what I would do. This was going to be a painful affair. I handed William my guns, knowing I had my derringer in my pocket if it came to foul play.

William whispered to me, "Careful, mister, I've seen him fight, he whips everybody."

"How does he fight?"

I wanted to know some sense of his style before encountering him head-on. "He mostly just whallops a feller, and then he falls down, He's awful strong!"

William looked worried about me. Frankly, I was worried about me too. I'd beaten big men before, and I'd picked up something of boxing here and there. I'd fought for money in my younger days from time to time, and I knew I could soak up, as well as give, one hell of a beating.

In my weakened condition, though, I didn't know how much I could stand. It was comforting to note the sheriff out of the corner of my eye, standing outside next to the saloon. He made no move to stop the fight. It was to be a fair, one-on-one match after all, but thought I could count on him to keep one of the big man's companions from back-shooting me, which left me free to worry about other things.

One of those things was a massive fist already sailing straight at my head. While I was looking around, Shamus's brother had charged in, swinging a wild haymaker. That's what I'd been expecting, so I was able to duck my head quickly to the left and smash a right cross into his nose. It burst blood and ran down the big man's face, but as he staggered back, he was laughing. This was going to take a while. I already felt hot fluid running down my back, and I knew the wounds had opened up again. Ignoring it, I stepped in, and when he swung again, I ducked and hammered both fists into his gut. He took the blows and walloped me across the top of my head with his left. I saw stars.

Bellowing, he threw another looping right, and I stuck an arm up to block it, opening my palm to smash it up under his chin. His head flew back and he staggered, but he ran right in again swinging. I pivoted out of the way quicker than you'd think I could and managed to lay one on him as he sailed by. As he turned I leaped at him and drove a hard right into his mouth. He wrapped me up in his massive arms and threw me to the ground like a toy, but I popped back up and threw a vicious uppercut into his belly before smashing him across the face with my left, then another right. He wrapped me up again, but before he could throw me, I reared my head back and slammed my forehead into his nose, which definitely broke it. I felt his grip loosen and he fell back. I followed after, determined not to give him a moment's rest. I felt like I had no strength left already, and in my condition I knew I couldn't keep this up for long. Driving my fists into his face, I knocked him to his knees, then slammed my boot heel into his temple. He hit the ground, began to rise, and then stretched out in the dirt, unconscious.

Angry now, I shouted a challenge to the other two. "Which one of you is next?" I shouted, but both shook their heads, amazed that their champion had fallen.

I staggered back to William, with blood seeping out of my clothes all over the place. He handed me the gun belt, and I smiled at him, expecting to see him looking proud that his man had won the fight. I was pretty proud of myself, but William just looked worried. I heard him start to say something, but his voice sounded unnaturally deep and far away. My eyes rolled back into my head, and darkness washed over me.

The first thing I was aware of was a pounding pressure in my head. The room seemed awfully bright, and I was laying down somewhere. When my vision adjusted, I heard a female voice say, "He's conscious," which seemed like a blatantly obvious statement to me at the time.

I was looking up at two faces I barely recognized, Jonas Sterling and his nurse. She really was quite pretty, and I told her so. I don't think the words came out right.

"Mr. Carlson, try not to speak," said the good doctor, and I resented the fact that he felt he could talk but I shouldn't. This was a free country, wasn't it? I tried to make my position on that matter clear, but my words just didn't sound right, even to me. The doctor explained that I had lost quite a bit of blood, and should try to rest, which was thoughtful on his part. I tried to sit up, which seemed to panic everyone in the room. I didn't want everyone to get so worked up, so I let them hold me down. I was dimly aware of pressure on my side, and I looked down to see the doctor running a needle in and out of a long gash, sewing me up like he was mending a shirt. I found this to be ridiculous; after all, I'm not a shirt, and I explained this to him at length, rather impressed with my eloquence.

"Mr. Carlson, I've given you quite a dose of laudanum, which may make you feel a little out of sorts, so I'd appreciate it if you would quiet down and try not to exert yourself while I do my work." I did, but secretly I thought to myself that the doc was a little smarmy, and I'd have to think of a good response to that when I got a moment. Laudanum? I hadn't had it before, but I thought it was really good stuff. I felt fantastic, despite what they were telling me. I really wanted to go over to the saloon and sit down and have a glass of beer, maybe with the big fellow from last night and his friends. Just a bunch of lovable rapscallions having fun on a Friday night, that's all, right? I tried to be good and lie still, because the doc said that was important, and docs knew about these kinds of things, didn't they? Sure they did.

I lay there for quite a while, until my head started to clear and I could feel the sharp punctures of the needle going through the tender seams of the cuts all over my torso and arms. I drifted in and out of sleep, occasionally hearing phrases such as "Lucky to be alive ..." and "Said he was mauled by a grizzly ..." After some time I was fully awake, and the searing pain throughout my body sharpened my mind.

Dr. Sterling informed me that his nurse had seen me collapse from inside the diner, and went running to fetch him. Apparently I'd lapsed in and out of consciousness, raving about getting attacked by a grizzly, and had managed to relate most of the circumstances of that event. A little embarrassed, I wondered what else I'd said, and I hoped it was nothing too personal. The nurse gave me sly looks from time to time, and I gathered that they must have undressed me in order to stitch up my wounds. I was hoping to have cut an impressive figure, unconscious or not; it hadn't been a cold night, after all.

I was still feeling a little light-headed from the effects of the laudanum, but I was mostly stitched up now, and my wounds wouldn't tear open again unless I did something drastic. I wasn't planning on doing anything of the kind. All I wanted was to rest and heal, and wait for my money to come from Idaho.

William had kept watch with me through the night, and I finally got to see the pride on his face when he related the whole story of last night to me as if I hadn't been there.

I had to admit, it sounded a lot more impressive through his eyes. Not wanting him to get in trouble with his taskmaster and caretaker, I told him to leave me and look after his chores.

When Dr. Sterling had finished dressing my wounds and given me instructions to come back tomorrow for their changing, I paid the bill for his services and put on a clean set of clothes the hotel had brought over from my room. I was feeling quite tender at the moment, so I hobbled back to my room, and I hoped I could cross the street for once in this town without running into some kind of trouble.

I made it all the way to my room without incident, and the clerk was kind enough to send breakfast up for me. I stacked up some of the extra pillows thoughtfully provided and sat down to take my meal on the bed. I wasn't planning on getting up until tomorrow. I ate eggs and delicious sausages stacked on top of crusty toast and butter. The food here was delicious, and I sent back the empty plate with an accompanying dollar for the chef. It's good to show people your appreciation, especially when you're a stranger in town who's looking to be recovering for a while.

I checked my weapons and belongings, glad neither had been molested. I sat my two shotguns by the bed within easy reach and considered my situation.

I hoped the fight had settled whatever quarrels I had in this town, but from experience I knew that wasn't usually the case. The money I had coming to me would set me up for quite some time, and I would need a good week or so at least before riding on. I usually liked to keep moving, but for now I was happy to lie about for a while, rest, and heal. The good food here in Elk's Run didn't hurt none either.

I spent the next two days in my room, taking my breakfast there, and sending for my dinner from the diner. I'd had William go over to the general store and bring me back some books. I didn't know what they had for selection, so I told William to just bring back whatever he thought was good. Big mistake.

He brought back a book with a funny name, written by someone named Stoker, and a pair of shoot-'em-up dime novels printed out East, both of them full of ridiculous notions of life in the West. Tales of some outlaw named Wilder, and some farfetched shenanigans he'd gotten himself into. Awful though they were, it was still entertaining to read. William had brought me a piece of wood with the dimensions I asked for, and I set to carving him a wooden sword. Young'uns liked those kinda things.

My thoughts wandered, and I got the silver knife out of my saddlebag and turned it over and over in my hands as I thought about the mysterious skeleton and its origin. There was no accounting for it, a seven-foot-plus man with occidental features in the wilderness with metal tools. I took out the carved bone beads and looked them over again. Each bead was as thick as my thumb, and almost as long. They looked like they might have been teeth taken from some kind of animal, though it must have been huge. The Indians still told stories about gigantic elephants and other large mammals that inhabited this land and said there were a few still around, taking shelter from place to place in closed-off valleys in the mountains.

Despite the towns now dotting the West, I knew there was plenty of land that had been rarely traveled or explored, and I had no doubt there was still much to discover. If I was out East I could take the knife to a museum and there might be some educated man there who could tell me about it, or at least make better guesses than I could. The thought occurred to me that the Indians here might be able to tell me more than any professor, and I made a mental note to look some up, if they were friendly.

The beads had various markings on them, which I couldn't identify as any kind of written language I knew, but that meant little. A series of lines mostly, intersecting here and there. It was a mystery, and likely to remain so, no matter how much I turned them over and over and studied them. I liked holding them though, and I thumbed the beads as I sat and thought about what they might mean.

A faint smell was beginning to take over the room. Upon closer examination, I discovered that smell was my very own self. It had been a while since I'd had a bath and a shave, being on the trail and then being sliced up like a tomato, but I felt I could stand it. I dressed and walked over to the barber shop.

I decided to bathe first, and I read a month-old newspaper while a young man left to heat up the water.

There wasn't much news, but it was all news to me. A train robbery to the south, a band of Indians raiding off the reservation over the mountains, federal troops dispatched to restore order and punish those responsible, armed with the new lever actions in .45-70. I'd have to get myself one of those. My sharps had stood me good service for years, and I could reload it quickly, but if I could just carry one long gun that could reach out and touch someone like a .45-70, well, that was for me. I resolved to buy a pack-out mount for my extra horse; I'd need it if I was going to keep buying guns at this rate.

My bath was ready, and the steaming water stung at first but then felt good as I sank all the way in. Ahhh. I could stay here a while. I left my Colt on a stool next to the tub in case of unwanted interruptions, and I sank in the water up to my ears, letting the dirt and grime of the past week and a half wash away. It was quite soothing. No sooner had I fully relaxed than a knock sounded on the door. Irritated, and a bit suspicious, I picked up the Colt and thumbed the hammer back. "Enter," I called in a gruff voice, thinking seriously about shooting whoever entered, regardless of their intent. I had been enjoying my bath.

A tall man entered, dressed like a cattleman but with a bit of a paunch, and I expected it had been a while since he'd done much riding. He had a jowly, florid face, and he looked distressed.

"Are you Thorn Carlson?" If he mentioned anything about a brother, or a friend, I was prepared to shoot him out of turn.

"What if I am?" He seemed a bit nonplussed by that, as a man will when he's used to getting his way.

"Well, I ... well, me and some friends of mine ... I'm Richard Comstock ... well, I own a ranch, just south of here, and we've been having some problems ..."

He looked at me as if trying to gather his thoughts, and I could tell he was worked up about something. If it was the rows of stitches covering my body or the fact that I was naked in a bath, he didn't give any indication, but I thought it was something else.

"Well, like I said, we've been having some problems, and we're hoping a man with your ... talents could look into them for us." His voice trailed off. It sounded to me like he was offering me a job, and I was willing to hear about it, if he and his friends were willing to pay well enough.

"What's the job, and how much?" I thought that eloquently covered all the details I wished to know.

"It's like this," he began, and collapsed on a stool across the room. "We've been losing a lot of cattle lately, and some of it under, well, strange circumstances, I guess you'd call it."

Sounded like rustlers to me.

"Explain," I said.

"Well, there's been some attacks that look like an animal's done it, and even a few of the hands have fallen victim, though the one brought in a couple days ago was the first one that survived."

"And what does he say happened?" "That's the thing, he didn't. He died after the Bar K boys got him to the doctor, but all he could do when they found him was rant and rave about the beast that took him down. He was clawed up somethin' awful, and he died without describing it. I thought he said something to his brother, who found him, but the next day that fella lit a shuck to the south without even drawing his time."

I was interested at the least. Anything causing this much trouble and consternation was sure to earn me a bundle.

"What's more is that everyone's losing cattle, sometimes ten or twelve a night. At first it was just the northern spreads, but now it's reached all the way down to us. A griz or a lion might take one or two, and wolves go after the calves, but that's business as usual. This here's something different."

"Have you tried tracking whatever beast is responsible?" I thought they already had. I'd heard stories of rogue animals, and there were some predators that had been known to kill and kill again, just for the sheer fun of it. None of this surprised me, and I had no doubt it was just such a case. What I wanted was to get the man to admit his helplessness to me, and I'd use that to jack up the price even further.

"We've tried, but the tracks look different from anything I've ever seen, and no one's been able to follow them very far. It's like they just disappear into the trees. I don't know what to make of it."

Neither did I, but I'd pretend like I did. Part of being a good businessman is being a good salesman.

"I think I can help you. In fact, I've run into things like this before." I hadn't. I made an effort to appear knowing. I had to settle for sly.

"I'll find this thing, track it, and kill it, but it will cost you two thousand dollars." While he sat there with a dumbfounded look on his face, I continued before he could reply.

"I'll also charge fifty dollars a day in expenses, whether or not I catch the beast. I'll want two hundred of it now." His eyes were as wide as dinner plates, but I knew with the pooled resources of several ranchers in such cattle-rich country, this was a drop in the bucket. It was more than most would dare ask for such an easy job, but it's not enough to just do good work, you've got to have the skills to get paid for it. I was thinking toward the future. I could do this in a week.

"Well ... I don't ... my partners ..." He ran a hand over his big sweaty face. "Okay," he sighed. I wondered if I shouldn't have asked for more, but I know enough to quit when I'm ahead.

"One more thing," I said as he turned to go. "What's the sheriff doing about all this?" It seemed unwise to bring it up, since I'd rather get paid for the job, but it was an obvious question, and I didn't know why they'd come to me instead.

"The sheriff knows, but he hasn't had any more luck than the rest of us, though I dare say he's tried. Been trying for a year now."

I enjoyed the rest of my bath in silence, pleased with the prospect of money in the bank and easy money in front of me. The soap stung my cuts, so I didn't use much of it, but when I got out of the bath I felt fresh and clean. The cuts on my face had healed up enough to not require stitches, though they'd heal into ugly scars. I ran my hand over my face, glad to soon be rid of the itchy stubble.

The barber was a talkative man, and now that I had work to do here in Elk's Run, I found this to be an opportunity to learn more about the area. It seems everyone had heard of the trouble, strange maulings in the night of cattle and other livestock, unlike anything they've seen before.

I learned that Richard Comstock's ranch was called the Circle C, and the Bar K hand's name who died was Edward

Coker, and that there was an awfully pretty schoolmarm in town, from out East, the intended target of nearly every single man in Elk's Run who thought he had a shot.

The schoolmarm's name was Emilia Dawson, about twenty-five, which was old for an unmarried woman but five years younger than me. I wasn't planning on getting married anytime soon, but she sounded interesting from what the barber said. Knew Latin and Greek, taught all subjects, but learned history at some fancy college out East, no one knew which one.

As the barber shaved, I considered what would bring such a woman to country such as this. She was either running from something, or had been caught up with the desire to explore the vast, wild frontier. Either way, she was probably nothing but trouble.

I would start on the job as soon as I felt well enough, but for now I decided a nap was in order. I went to sleep clean and feeling good, and it was the next morning before I woke up again.

I was starting to feel a little stronger, and I wanted to leave my room and breathe the fresh mountain air. I had told William I would take him shooting, and so I would. I wasn't in much danger of doing anything strenuous, just walking out of town a ways and teaching the kid how to aim and work a rifle and if he picked it up well enough, I'd let him try my six-gun too.

When I went downstairs the clerk handed me a message. I opened the envelope and read a note from Sheriff Garrett informing me that my bounty was available for withdrawal from the Morgan and Rockwell bank as of noon today. I glanced at the clock. It was nearly two in the afternoon.

I strode over to the bank and confirmed that, indeed, the money was on hand as promised, and had them open an account for me. I made a draw of fifty dollars right away, feeling better now that matter was settled.

When a man has money, he feels the call of opportunity with it. With this amount I could easily open a business, here in Elk's Run or just about anywhere, and get away from the danger and constant travel of my current profession.

The desire was not great in me, though. I liked to travel, and I could not see settling down to serve meals or drinks to rowdy cowhands every Friday and Saturday night. I had to admit I liked my profession, as distasteful as it was to others, and I'd take whatever consequences came with that decision. Someday I would likely give it up, but not today.

I walked out of the bank, flush with cash, and more than a little generous. I was going to take William shooting. I knew he could read, but not much else, and I also knew there was a school in town, which he was prevented from going to by nature of running the stables single-handedly for his drunken uncle.

There wasn't much I could do about that, but I could give him an education in the one thing every man should know a sight about, and something I was eminently qualified to teach: shooting.

Making my way to the general store, I looked over the wares. There was a Colt lightning pistol in .32-20, which would have been a good fit for William's growing hands, but I thought first and foremost he needed to learn how to handle a long gun. There was a used Winchester in .44-40 that had been cut down to sixteen inches, just right for easy handling and a good length for the boy to be able to maneuver and control. I haggled with the shop keep for some moments and ended up getting a good price on it. It was well worn but well cared for, with all the scratches and nicks on the stock and receiver that showed it had done someone long and good service. I bought a few boxes of cartridges for it, and didn't regret for a moment the expense.

Full of smiles at my impending good deed, I limped my way over to the stables to find William. He wasn't there. I looked in on my horses; obviously they had been cleaned and groomed just that morning. My steel dust was in fine fettle, and happy to see me. I patted him for a moment, and rubbed his nose.

Just then I heard a sound from the loft above me. It sounded like a low cry of pain. Instantly alert, I climbed cautiously up the ladder and peered over the edge. Waiting a few seconds for my eyes to adjust to the darkness, I could see a small form huddled in the corner.

"William!" I whispered, "Is that you?"

I saw a nod, but he didn't speak.

"What's the matter?" He shook his head as if he didn't want to say. I finished climbing the ladder and made my way over to the staircase. He didn't move, just cringed a little as I crouched down next to him and struck a match. The light showed me more than I wanted to see. He had bruises all over his face, and one eye swollen shut. I thought his nose was likely broken. I had an idea of who had done this, but I wanted to hear it from him.

"William, did your ... uncle do this to you?"

"Yes, sir. He, I wouldn't do what he wanted, so he ..." His small voice broke off into sobbing, and I didn't want to ask further, but I had to know what happened.

"Will, what did your uncle want you to do?"

"He'd never done it before, mister, I swear! He came in drunk, and threw me out of bed, and told me to take off ..."

His sobbing broke out again, but he sucked it up and continued. "When I wouldn't let him, he beat me and then passed out drunk on the floor."

The rage started burning up from the pit of my stomach. I'm a reasonable man, and it takes a lot to get me going, but I was going now, and there would be hell to pay. This Bartlett hadn't actually committed the crime, but he'd tried to, and I didn't intend to let him try again.

Some men are just bent the wrong way, and Bartlett was one such. If he had managed to get done what he tried to do, I'd be using a different tool. As it was, I aimed to dole out some Old Testament-style justice on the man, and make him see the error of his ways, before I ran him out of the country.

Patting William on the shoulder, I slid down the ladder and grabbed a long leather whip off a hook near the door. You don't see many of these around anymore. It wasn't for horses, the kind that merely sting a little; it was a bullwhip, long and braided out of supple rawhide. With the whip coiled in my clenched fist I went to the bar. It was only eight in the morning, but I figured this would be the place to start looking. Sure enough, there he was, sitting at the bar, hunched over a half-empty bottle. I'd never seen him, but the slight resemblance to William was enough for me, and somehow I just knew him that instant for what he was.

"Bartlett!" I called, and he spun around, his eyes trying to focus. He'd been trying to drink away his hangover, but I had a better cure.

I ignored the other patrons as I crossed the bar room,

letting the long whip unfurl from my hand.

"What d'ya want?" he slurred and in answer I flicked the whip out and snapped it back, laying a bloody line across his face. I'd used one of these before in my youth, and with the years hadn't forgotten how.

As his hands flew up to protect his face, I lashed the whip around to let it coil about his neck, then yanked hard. The whip wrapped up on itself like I'd meant it to, and I jerked him off his seat onto the floor.

Ignoring the cries of surprise from the other patrons, I dragged him choking and gagging from the saloon out into the street. I snapped the whip free, noticing Sheriff Garrett and two deputies running down the street toward me. They weren't going to stop me. They'd have to shoot me first. I cracked the whip twice across Bartlett's back, and I heard screams of pain from somewhere far away as the rage boiled my brain.

Dimly, I was aware of William running from the stables to whisper in Sheriff Garrett's ear. The sheriff, God bless him, holstered his sidearm and leaned against a post, leaving me free to do my righteous work of cleansing this man's soul from all evil. I set to with a vengeance, stripping cloth then hide off the wailing man's back as he cringed and quivered in the dust.

The whole town gathered while I worked, and I don't think I left an inch of hide unscathed. His cries for mercy fell on deaf ears. No one in the town seemed to have any pity for him, not after they saw William's face in the condition it was. The West is a hard place, but folks have little tolerance for men such as Bartlett, who I gathered was generally disliked even before this morning.

My whip arm got tired eventually, so I crossed over to him and set to kicking him. I felt the ribs crack underneath my boots, and I think I broke his forearm when I stomped on it. I didn't strike him in the face though. I wanted him awake to feel every last blow.

I bent over, panting from my exertions, and grabbed him up by the hair. He squealed in pain, but I turned him loose and kicked him in the pants.

"Get going," I said, pointing toward the railroad tracks. "If I ever see or hear of you again, I'm going to finish what I started." He looked back at me in a mixture of pain and fear and started out of town as fast as his legs could carry him. He seemed sober now and made pretty good time for what I'd just done to him. I didn't expect him back in Elk's Run, not ever again.

So much for not exerting myself. As I hunched over with my hands on my thighs, William crossed over to me and put his arms around me. Sheriff Garrett tipped his hat and strode away with his deputies. Good man, that.

I put my arm protectively around William's shoulders and walked him over to Dr. Sterling, who'd just arrived, apparently having been warned that his services were sure to be needed by somebody. He gave me a disapproving look when he saw my panting, but when he noticed William's face he scooped him up in his arms and carried him toward his office.

I staggered back to the hotel, and left word at the desk to inform the doctor that any bill for William's care be delivered to me, and that I wanted to be kept informed of his condition. I went upstairs and drank some water out of the pitcher left in the room, then soaked a handkerchief and dabbed the sweat off my face.

A knock on my door came about an hour later. It was the clerk again, coming to tell me William had suffered a broken arm and nose, but should heal up just fine now that they'd been properly set. The doctor had been kind enough to send the bill along with it, as well as a reminder that I needed to come by to change my dressings when convenient. I paid the bill and lay back down on the bed, and didn't get up for the rest of the day.

CHAPTER 3

MORNING CAME, AND WITH IT AN INTENSE DESIRE
to recover my health and strength. I was sick of the slightest effort making me feel the need to lie down, and feeling sleepy by nine in the morning. While I was by no means old, I wasn't a boy either, and I resented it. Plenty of good solid food and clean mountain air was restoring me more rapidly than I could have hoped, despite my recent activities, and I resolved to be healed by the end of the week, for as much good as that would do me. I was a firm believer in the power of the mind, and I thought that maybe if I told myself to get better faster, perhaps I just would.

Still, it had been only about a week since the bear, and I was doing remarkably well, considering. After finishing breakfast I stopped by the doctor's to have my bandages changed. It would have been very pleasant to sit and watch the nurse as she redressed my wounds, except for the rank smell attending them. I managed to get through the process without wincing or crying out in pain, so I gave myself the appropriate honors and took a nice long swig of whiskey from my silver flask on the way out of town. I set my horse's head toward the south, and took out the makings of a cigarette, studying the countryside as I rode.

My Colt Lightning and the big bore Sharps made for good company, come hell or high water. If, by some chance, I got a shot at the animal, I wanted to be able to take it, no matter how far. I could hit reliably with the Colt to about two hundred yards, but the bullet already had considerable drop at that range, unlike the .45-70, a true long-range cartridge if ever there was one.

The ride was long, but eventually I started seeing cattle with the Circle C brand on their flanks. More than one had scars from being jumped by the wild animals about, though that was nothing new in this country. I kept a sharp eye out for any suspicious tracks as I rode, but didn't see anything that didn't obviously belong to a coyote or black bear. The ranch house was located just over the next rise, an attractive log cabin affair with double chimneys on each end, and a bunkhouse just beyond that looked equally comfortable.

A man standing by the porch ducked inside as soon as he saw me, and I could make out a little crowd of figures gathering near the front, rifles in hand. I rode easily, building another smoke, showing my hands were otherwise occupied and I meant no harm.

When I got in earshot, I called out "Comstock!" and waited to see his big frame step out from the doorway. It seemed to take a moment for him to recognize me, with my fresh set of clothes and clean shaven face. I took my black leather hat off to aid in the process.

"Howdy Carlson, glad you dropped by!" The big rancher waved and hitched his belt. He looked a little frayed around the edges. Worry takes a man apart as sure as shootin', just bit by bit instead of all at once.

"I'm here to get started."

"Glad to see it. We had another six cattle torn up just last night. Let me get my hat, and I'll take you there."

One of the hands, a short, burly man, spoke up. "Pa, I

already told you, I checked them tracks an' you just can't follow 'em any further! We don't need no stranger buttin' in."

His face was red, and he was practically fuming. "Junior, just shut your mouth, and let me take care of my business." Comstock's tone was warning.

The burly young hand, Comstock's son, as I gathered, wouldn't set loose of it. "I told you, Pa, me and the boys would take care of this!" Comstock whirled, not liking it one bit.

"You listen to me, boy, you ain't old enough yet that I can't tan your hide. Remember that, and keep your mouth shut. If you could take care of it, we woulda' found that thing already!"

"Junior "looked like he was fit to blow up like a stack of dynamite, but he just hunched his heavy shoulders and kept his mouth shut. The look he gave made me think it would be a good idea to just shoot him right then and there, but I didn't think Comstock would approve, and he was paying me after all.

Comstock rode past me without saying a word. I followed, figuring he'd talk when he was good and ready. It was a good half mile before he spoke.

"He's a good kid, that one, but he don't listen worth a damn."

"Seemed mighty upset." I wet the paper and finished rolling.

"He's just as mad as I am, maybe more so, cause he's been trying to track this thing down for over two months now."

Neither Comstock nor his hands had the look of a tenderfoot, but some predator had done given them the slip time and again. I carefully considered that as I struck a match and took my time lighting up.

"How long has this been going on, I mean, all over the valley?"

"A good year I reckon. Only lately has it reached my spread. Some of the spreads up north lost so many cattle, both torn up and disappeared, that they just sold out and moved on."

"Who'd they sell out to?"

"Jake Luna, over on the Crescent Ranch. He gave a fair price, I reckon, but I've never liked the man." I'd heard of a gunfighter by that name, years ago, down in Arizona, but there was no telling if this was the same man. That Jake Luna was supposed to be lightning fast with a gun, and he used it liberally enough to build up quite a reputation for himself as a man killer. It was something to keep in mind.

"Did all the ranchers sell out to Luna?"

"Well, no. Some of them sold out to me." He gave me a questioning look, as if following my line of thinking. I had no way of knowing the full truth behind Comstock's story, but it would be easy enough to check. Bigger ranchers running the smaller ones out was a tale as old as the West, and there were plenty of otherwise good men who'd built their first herd with a running iron and some injudicious roping.

"So when was the last attack?"

"Just last night. The boys were out riding this morning, and came across six of ours, torn to pieces and left lying by the stream. They tried to follow the tracks, but didn't get far. They end at a stream."

I followed tracks for a living. If they were there to follow, I had no doubt I'd be able to follow them.

We rode for half an hour, and Comstock pointed out the

boundaries of his land. It was quite sizable. There was plenty of grass for feed, and in several places streams ran down from the mountains. They were running high now; it was spring and the snow melt was keeping the levels up.

Before long we reached the scene of the carnage. I'd never seen cattle in this kind of shape. The entrails were slung all over the surrounding bushes, and hooves and heads lay scattered about. I couldn't think of an animal that would do this; such an act would require rage and exceptional power. Could be a grizzly, but if it was he was stone cold crazy.

When I saw the tracks Comstock pointed out I knew it was no grizzly. "Do they all look like this?" I asked.

"Sure, all the ones I've seen." "And how many times have you seen these tracks?"

"About ten or twelve times just this month, though usually I don't go out to look anymore. It's the boys that find 'em and tell me about it."

The tracks were canine in origin, but I didn't know what kind. If they were smaller I'd say it was a wolf, but these were spread wide and sunk in too much to be a wolf. I looked at my own print next to it. About the same size. A wolf with half my print would be around a hundred and fifty pounds, which was quite large, and I'd shot one once that must have weighed every bit of a hundred and seventy. Judging from how much deeper the print was sunk, this thing outweighed me by at least a hundred pounds. My mind wandered to the tales the Indians had told me, of strange animals no longer living. I looked back at the track again. Supposedly.

I told Comstock to leave me to my work. I took out my moccasins and put them on as I watched him ride away. I nearly always put on my leathers when I was out of town and doing anything other than riding. I didn't want Comstock to see what I was doing either. It helps when the person that pays you doesn't have tabs on the steps you took to get to the result. A thing can look easier than it is to an observer, and I'd rather produce my results and get paid by someone awed by what I had done than quibble over my methods.

I built a smoke and watched the old rancher disappear over the hills before scouting around. There were plenty of boot prints all over the place, but fortunately they hadn't stepped into the beast's tracks, so I was able to follow them all the way to the stream where they disappeared.

Now walking upstream to hide your tracks is the oldest trick in the book, so I was guessing the ranchers had followed them upstream for a while. If the tracks didn't come out on either side, I would just keep going until they did. A wet beast isn't coming out of a stream bank without leaving traces of his passing, and I might find hair or something along the way to give a clue as to what this thing was.

I kept to the side of the stream, not wanting to disturb the clear water. Sometime you could see the traces of a print still left in slow-running water, and this is what I was looking for. I kept my eyes on both banks, looking for the telltale signs of something exiting the stream. I came across deer tracks and coyote sign, even a place where a black bear had come to drink and then rest a while, but I didn't see the ones I was looking for. After a half mile I could see where the boots had stopped and turned back, giving up the chase.

I gave a soft chuckle and continued on. I felt sure it wouldn't be much farther now. The stream entered a copse of trees a quarter of a mile later, and I saw a few strands of fur dangling from a low hanging branch. Impossible. The hair was thick and greasy, black and gray, and the branch the creature must have rubbed up against was as high as my shoulder. Maybe it was some kind of bear after all. I kept my sharps rifle cocked and my eyes open as I moved through the woods like an Indian, ready to blast anything that moved.

The trees were dark, but I could see just fine. Some ways into the woods, a set of still-wet tracks came up out of the water and onto the muddy bank. They weren't the same ones I had seen earlier. These were human. An Indian maybe? Out hunting? These were bare feet, so I didn't know what to make of it. Someone coming down to the trees to hide something maybe? I looked around, but the rest of the ground didn't seem to be disturbed. An owl hooted in the woods behind me and I whirled around, then cursed myself for being so jumpy. I didn't know if it was the strange tracks or recently surviving a bear mauling that made me so nervous, but there it was. Taking a deep breath, I followed the footprints out of the stream as they wound through the trees. At the edge of a clearing, I could see hoof prints, and the footprints leading right up to them.

Someone had a horse here, and had left it for a while to go down to the river. I could see where they'd dismounted, and the route they took to the stream, and where they mounted again and rode off. I went back to my horse and caught up the trail again, following it for some miles while it weaved through trees and up and down hillsides. I never lost it once. I came out of the woods to see Elk's Run just ahead of me in the valley. I could see the tracks leading up to it.

I sat well back in the trees so I wouldn't be seen, and rolled a smoke. Lighting it, I considered for a while. First thing was to ride around to the south and make it look like I'd come from that direction. If there was something else going on in Elk's Run, whatever it was I didn't want to appear to be in on someone's secret. Even though I hadn't a clue what brought the rider to the stream in the first place, if they thought I did I might well find myself with a shot in the back from a dark alley.

The noon sun was high in the sky as I rode into town, and I had a lot on my mind. I wasn't feeling worn out for a change, and that brightened my mood. I might ride back this afternoon to look for where the tracks came out of the river, but first I wanted to figure out if the rider at the stream meant anything or not.

I decided to take care of a few things in town before investigating further. I stopped at the sign for Barnaby Slade, Attorney at Law. Stepping through the door, I was surprised to see actual tomes of law and court cases on the shelves. Many lawyers on the frontier were merely men who'd decided to hang a shingle somewhere, and much of the practice was predictably shoddy. When a short, frail-looking man with wire-rimmed spectacles entered the front office, a large book of some kind under his arm, I decided he at least looked like the real deal. He gazed up at me with squinty eyes, and introduced himself by the same name on the sign. Though a small man, his voice had the clear, resonant tones of the courtroom. Or at least what I thought a courtroom voice should sound like, since I hadn't been in many.

"How can I be of assistance, Mr. Carlson?" he said after I'd introduced myself.

"Simple. Young William, the boy who works at the stables, you know him?" The attorney nodded. "His uncle has left on a permanent basis, but neglected to file the proper paperwork transferring ownership of the property and business to his former charge. I want you to finish said paperwork, and in such a way so as to ensure this fine young man won't have any problems with it in the future, understood?"

The attorney knew what I was getting at, but hemmed and hawed a little, probably trying to find a lawyerly way to tell me that what I was describing was not quite legal. He stopped when I plunked down a few handfuls of crumpled bills on his desk, and without leaving time for him to answer, I left the office and walked down the street toward the saloon.

As I did so I took a glance toward the stables, and there was the boy, hard at work, his arm in a sling. I knew he'd make a go of it on his own; after all, he'd been doing the work already, he may as well collect the pay. The small, thrown-together shack he now lived in would be his as well, and as business was thriving, I'd no doubt he'd be able to make it. What I was worried about was his education. He wouldn't necessarily have time for much schoolin', but maybe I could see the local teacher and work something out in that regard.

I laughed at myself as I sat down on the barstool. Was I going for the local Good Samaritan award? I didn't think so. In fact, it had been a long time since I'd done anything for anybody besides myself, and doing such things was good for the soul, or so I'm told. Anyway, it just seemed right to me, and made me feel good besides.

I ordered a beer and sipped at it awhile, thinking over the problem in my mind. I needed to find this beast, whatever it was, and it seemed like it was visiting the Circle C often of late, if the stories told me today were true. When I was a young cowhand, years ago, I'd had to take out my share of predators and other varmints from time to time. I'd put down scraps of offal from the cattle we slaughtered for food, and laid up in a tree where I could keep an eye on it. Sooner or later the bear would smell it, and I'd tickle his ribs with a lead slug, and that would be that. Why try to track and follow the beast if I could get it to come to me, on my terms?

We'd just had the full moon, so there would be plenty of light out to see by. I could take a nap and give old methods a try. Something seemed wrong though. The animal that was slaughtering the cows didn't seem to have eaten them so much as tear them apart for the sheer joy of it. What I needed was live bait.

I borrowed a rope from William, who was more than happy to see me. I didn't tell him what I'd fixed up with the lawyer, just told him that legally he owned the stables now and it was up to him to make it work and to look after himself now. He nodded, seeming to grow an inch with the added responsibility of being his own man. I thought he'd likely find it easier than taking care of himself and Bartlett, but I didn't say so.

I went up to my room and stowed my lightning, bringing extra ammo for the Sharps and the double-barreled coach shotgun with me. If the light ended up being poor, or the critter was close in, I could be sure of blasting it with a double dose of buckshot, and there weren't many creatures on God's green earth that could survive that sort of treatment.

My steel dust had ridden far that day already, so I took the other horse, saddled him, and with the rope slung over the pommel, headed on my way. The sun would set soon, and I wanted to be on Circle C land before it went down. I didn't plan on informing Comstock of my activities, because

I didn't see a reason to. They hadn't seemed to have thought of this course of action before, but if they knew what I was doing, and it was successful, I'd like to not find the amount of my reward subject to contention. It would seem awfully simple, and ranchers are folks who like to think they can do for themselves. I planned to ride on in come morning, with the beast's head, and look awfully tired and hardly worked.

In reality I hoped to get this done before midnight and take a nice long snooze under the stars. I figured this to be a pretty good racket. With the amount of damage being done nightly to the different brand's cattle, I figured there must surely be more than one of these beasts, and I could make quite a pile of money taking care of this little problem. It was an added bonus that animals as a rule don't carry weapons, and so I wouldn't be in danger of getting shot at, for once.

I roped a calf and led it away bawling from its mother. She followed for a time then found something better to do, but the calf didn't shut up for a good long while. Cattle are cattle, and there's only one intended end for all of them, but I still felt a little bit bad for what I was about to do. Like I said, I have a soft spot for animals.

I tied it to a thin, weather-broken tree, not far from the stream where the tracks disappeared that morning. I led the horse well off into the woods beyond and ground hitched it in the middle of a small clearing. I thought it would be safe here, and the thick brush would hide his smell and keep the ever-present wind from carrying it toward the stream, where I expected the beast to come from. Animals tend to be creatures of habit, and when they find a situation that's convenient, they tend to stick to it. I was just adding to the attraction by throwing the wailing calf into the mix.

I wanted a smoke, but the scent carries far in the woods, and I didn't want the varmint smelling me before I'd sprung the trap. I frowned at the silver flask and stuffed it back in my pocket for just the same reason.

I waited, as the moon was high and it was full dark now, with a keen eye toward the stream and the calf I was using for bait. I tried not to shift around, but the branches of the tree I chose were hard and uncomfortable, particularly on my stitches. I was ready for this thing to appear, both out of natural curiosity and tiredness that washed over me. I fought sleep, but now and then my eyelids drooped and my head started to bob.

Something moved!

It came from the brush on the creek side, and I thought I could hear a faint splash. My eyes strained to pierce the darkness, but I knew I had to wait. A predator wouldn't have gone this long unnoticed if it was anything less than cautious. It seemed at odds with the rampant destruction of its prey, but somehow I knew it to be true. I waited so long as to think I'd merely imagined the movement and the sound, but just when I was ready to admit to myself I'd been dreaming, the calf started lowing and bawling afresh and struggling at the rope. I kept my eyes on where I'd last seen the brush move, but nothing appeared. I eased the hammer back on the Sharps as slowly as I could, glad for having oiled it recently.

Suddenly a rush of movement came from my left, the exact opposite direction I'd been watching. A huge black shape shot across the clearing, and I heard the snap of the rope at the same time the dark blue disappeared toward the creek. I didn't even have time to aim. I heard a strangled cry from the calf; it sounded like it was from beyond the water. Leaping down from my hiding place and instantly regretting it, I dashed for my horse. The sound of the calf being ripped to pieces let me know the animal would be busy for a moment, and I wanted to be well above the brush so I could get a clear shot. I leaped on my horse's back and dashed off toward the stream.

Just as I crossed it at a dead run, the moon disappeared behind a drifting cloud, and all I could make out was something black and large clawing and ripping at the remains of its prey. I waited, steady, for it hadn't seemed to notice me, caught up in the slaughter. The moon appeared again, and I could see the hunched form as it buried its muzzle in guts, black blood glistening off its fur in the moonlight.

I raised the Sharps and fired, being close enough now that I thought my shot would strike true. A quick yelp and the animal shot off into the brush so fast I could barely track it with my eye. I heard branches crackling and snapping as the beast tore through the woods with incredible speed.

I hadn't gotten much of a look at it, but I thought it safe to say it was no bear, or any other animal I knew of. It was large, almost as large as a bear, but it moved so fast I could scarcely believe it, even though I'd seen it with my own two eyes. There wasn't much left of the calf, and never had I seen an animal devoured so quickly. There wasn't much left but the hooves, the head, and empty hide.

I'd wounded it, at the very least, and even if I hadn't hit the vitals, the big 400-grain bullet was sure to have torn a nasty hole in the animal. It might be good at hiding its tracks, but now I had a blood trail to follow. Still, I have to admit that trailing it right then seemed like a powerful bad idea.

Most people think animals are dumb, but they can be

quite cagey, especially when they know something's on their back trail. Following that thing in the night, with it just lyin' in wait for me somewhere along the path ahead, gave me the shivers. As fast as it was I'd be lucky to get off a single shot before it rushed me, and that was if I was lucky. I knew that sometimes discretion is the better part of valor, and so with a mind to my own hide, I decided to withdraw until dawn. Sleeping out under the stars no longer seemed such a good idea, so I rode in open country all the way back to town.

I was hoping for a restful night locked safe and snug inside the warm hotel while I figured out what to do. It was not to be so.

Less than a mile from town I saw a riderless horse trotting about in circles on the side of the road. The horse was saddled, but it was lathered up and appeared to be bleeding from several places. A dark form lay sprawled nearby. It was a body. Dressed in homespun trousers, boots, and a plaid shirt, the man lay still with a six-gun clenched tightly in his hand. The body was still warm when I touched it, but there was no doubt about it, he was deader than a Thanksgiving turkey. There was a gaping hole in his throat, and thick blood coated his chest and the grass around him.

Squinting in the moonlight, I could see this was none other than the cowpoke I'd quarreled with my first night in town. His straw-colored hair and blunt features were still intact, though he had powder burns around the hole in his neck and on his face. I was at a loss for what to do. The best thing seemed to be telling the sheriff about it, and letting him take care of burying the body. It looked to me like the beast, or one of them, had gotten him. He was right by the road, and by all accounts it looked like he was just jumped by someone as he rode into town for a night at the saloon or to court one of the local girls.

Just to be thorough, I rifled through his pockets and saddlebags. I found a note in his breast pocket, smeared with blood. I wanted to strike a match to read it, but didn't dare attract attention. I could make out there was writing on it, of course, and the paper seemed fresh. This wasn't something he'd carried around for a while. Things like that tend to get soggy and wrinkled with sweat. The paper was crisp and clean, except for where the blood seeped through his clothes.

I folded the note up in a kerchief and stuffed it in my pocket. There wasn't anything else in his saddlebags except a bottle of whiskey, some cartridges, and a mess kit. I stowed it all away as I'd found it, buttoned his shirt pocket, and headed for town. When I got there my first stop was at the sheriff's office. I told the deputy about what I'd seen, the body, that is (I didn't say anything about my earlier activities), and bid him good night. As I led my horse back into the stables the sheriff rode past on his way out of town, flanked by his two deputies.

Once I was safe in my room, I unwrapped the bloody note and looked it over. The lantern in my room wasn't bright, but I could make out the words "midnight" and "alone" on the paper, with a symbol of some kind on the bottom.

Of course my first thought was that the note had summoned the cowboy to a midnight meeting alongside the rode into town, and there he had met his death. It could well have been something else, but I didn't have much to go on.

There was a lot of considering to do, but right now I didn't feel like doing any of it. I'd been getting better, but the day had taken quite a toll on me. My stitches itched, and I felt generally tired all over. Lying down on the bed and kicking my boots off, I rolled a smoke and took a few swigs of whiskey before falling asleep.

CHAPTER 4

I SAT A WHILE AFTER BREAKFAST, RELUCTANT TO
get on with the day. That there was a lot going on in this valley was certain, but I didn't know how much mattered to the
job I was trying to do, and that's all I was concerned with
at the moment. I decided the most obvious course of action
should be my first step. I had seen the beast, however briefly,
and that was what I was being paid to kill. I had a suspicion
there was more than one, but I'd worry about that later, after
I'd collected my reward for killing the first. I was planning on
being able to track it now, as a hole left by a Sharps lets a lot of
air in and a lot of blood out. In daylight, I'd be able to see the
thing if it crept up on me, and have a much better chance of
getting a solid shot at it, if I hadn't killed it already. No way of
knowing if I'd hit the vitals though, and an animal that size
can live a powerful long time with a bullet in its guts.

I wanted to take care of one thing before heading out,
and so I located the school and hoped to call on the teacher
before class started for the day. The school was little more
than a small wooden building with a sharply angled roof, and
I knocked politely at the door and waited. I smelled coffee
brewing from inside, and after a moment the door cracked
open.

A pair of big brown eyes looked up at me, though the
woman inside was tall. She was dressed in the eastern fashion,
lots of buttons, and I imagine a few petticoats under the long

purple dress with the high neck. Well, a woman of refinement. She had a light spattering of freckles across her nose, and her skin was the color of milk, unburned by the western sun. Long chestnut-colored hair was tied back, though a few strands hung loose, framing her face in a most flattering way.

I was at a loss for words, and I coughed into my hand to buy time. I certainly hadn't been expecting this. She waited politely for a moment, and I managed to stammer my name.

"Elizabeth Patterson," she said. "How do you do?"

I was glad she could speak, well, because at the moment I'd forgotten why I came.

"Oh, um, fine I guess. I'm here ... Well, I'm here to talk to you about William over at the stables."

"Yes?"

"Well, I wanted to see about getting him some schooling."

"You mean an education?" Sounded like the same thing to me, but I'd play it her way.

"Yes, that. He's running his own business now, so he'll need some kind of arrangement, perhaps in the evenings here and there."

"Are you his father?" "Well, no. His uncle ... had to leave town in a hurry and isn't expected back, and I suppose I've become his ... benefactor, if you will."

"I see." Her eyes were suspicious, though I didn't know if they were always that way or just for me. I've known many a pretty woman, mind you, but this seemed like a different class of creature altogether.

"He'll be needing it, as he lives alone and must cope with all the responsibilities a young man must, a businessman, and I'd like to see he has the ... education that requires."

"Very well, shall we set up a time for him to come to school, or should I talk with him to set up an arrangement?"

I figured William would know when he could get away from his duties, and he'd need to handle things like this himself anyway, so I chose the latter option. I didn't know how much you pay a schoolteacher, so I pulled out a wad of bills and thrust them at her. She looked offended by something, but I didn't pay that any mind. You never could tell what was going through a woman's head anyhow, even, perhaps especially, a college woman from out East.

"I'll be expecting young William, and good day to you, sir," she said and closed the door, rather abruptly, I might add. I stood there for some time like a damned fool, then turned and walked toward the stables. She was beautiful. Something about her snared me, and I knew I'd better be careful.

A woman like that has cost plenty a man his freedom, and I'd better stay well clear of this one. Just the same, I kept thinking of reasons to go back and see her again. Perhaps she'd be able to tell me more about the knife and the ancient beads I'd found in the cave. I'd taken to stowing the knife in my boot. It was a healthy chunk of silver, and I didn't want to leave it lying around. I could just go back and ask her, but I needed to get moving on that trail, and I didn't want to suffer another attack of speechlessness.

When I got to the stables I explained the arrangement to William. He promised to see her that morning once he got a free moment, and I saddled the gelding again. I figured to sell him to the Circle C when I brought in the beast. Remembering what happened to the rope, I gave him a few dollars for another, and headed out to pick up the blood trail.

I built a smoke as I rode, admiring the view of the mountains and cool, fresh air. The wind was light and the sky clear, which would aid me in tracking. I had brought my Sharps and the double barrel, with an extra pistol stuffed in my saddlebags.

It didn't take long to make the ride out to where I'd shot the varmint. When I located the spot beyond the creek, I saw the same mess. What surprised me, though, was the boot prints all around it, only one set from what I could tell. Curious, I trailed the boots first, and they led back to the tree where I'd laid up for the critter, then over to where I'd hidden my horse the night before.

This worried me. I hadn't told anyone at the Circle C of my plans, and the owner of the boots must have visited sometime in the night. It was still early morning, and if the Circle C boys had discovered the carnage, I was certain they'd have come out in force.

The boot prints looked the same as the ones I had followed from the creek yesterday afternoon. I didn't know quite what to make of it, but surely there was a third party involved. He'd been looking over what I'd done, though for what purpose I didn't know. There were no hoof prints other than the ones my own horse had made, so he must have been afoot or had stashed his mount somewhere in the trees well away from the stream.

I'd have to follow up on that later. I had a fresh blood trail to follow. There was a lot of it, and I could tell by the amount I'd hit a vital spot. The tracks were deep where the animal had been running, leaving blood on the ground and on branches and leaves as he'd passed. I was able to follow without dismounting, which made me a lot more comfortable. The scrub and brush was about waist high to a man, but

I had a pretty good field of vision mounted, and I would be able to see anything that size that might try and sneak up on me.

I followed the trail up a draw, and over the top to a finger with a steep slope on the side. More like a cliff. I dismounted and peered over the side.

Below was a sharp drop, maybe two hundred feet to the rocky bottom. The tracks seemed to lead right up to it.

I felt certain that if the creature had gone over the side he'd be still there on the bottom. I doubted anyone or anything would survive the fall. The blood had almost disappeared too. Usually, the more a creature travels, the more it bleeds, at least with as big a hole as a Sharps makes. It wasn't a wound that would just close up with time, at least not the time it would have taken for the critter to make it up to this spot. All told, I'd followed the trail less than a mile so far.

Studying the ground, I found the barest traces of his passing on the rock, leading away from the cliff's edge to the trees on the hillside below. It was then I realized my mistake. This was a sharp varmint: he'd made me follow his trail up so I'd be silhouetted against the sky if I followed, and could lay and wait in the trees below, setting up for an ambush. I wound the strap from the forend of the Sharps around my arm and cinched it tight, twining my elbow around it to hold my aim steady. My shotgun was cut short and the stock cut down, so I thrust it through my belt. I scanned the woods below just over the sights of the rifle, ready to make a shot if the thing attacked suddenly.

I studied the terrain and tried to think like it would, choosing the route I'd take to injun my way up to a spot where I could pounce. I followed the best way with my eyes and noted a large bush not twenty feet away. The slightest movement of the leaves is what saved my life. Something was breathing behind that bush. There wasn't enough wind to have caused it, just a few leaves at the bottom, rhythmically swaying back and forth. Such things, small as they seem, have saved my life many a time.

I took aim with the Sharps, and tried to guess just where its head was, my finger ready to break the shot as soon as I'd found it. There. A dull, yellow eye was just barely visible between the leaves. Just as I was about to pull the trigger, the thing must have sensed me tighten, because it launched itself up and over the bush, into the sky.

The furry black shape moved so fast it was like a blur, but I brought the rifle up and centered, squeezing the trigger. The buck of the rifle made me lose it for a second, but I heard a whine like the sound a coyote makes when it's hurt, and I threw myself to the side as the beast came crashing down where I had been.

Not having time to reload the Sharps, I ripped the double barrel from my belt and pointed it dead center on the creature. It was already turning for me, and I could see daylight through the hole in its stomach. It was a horrifying sight. It stood on two legs, covered in long black fur, with a muzzle and ears like a wolf and eyes of yellow. Its fangs were dripping with saliva, and its long arms covered with thick muscle under the fur. The claws were a few inches long, and I had no doubt it could eviscerate me with a single swipe. It looked like someone had put a wolf and a man together, made them larger than either, and added a dash of hellfire to boot.

I gave it both barrels, feeling the shock up my arm as the double load of buckshot discharged. The lead pellets sprayed across its chest and knocked it back, staggering. I leaped to my feet and dropped the shotgun, drawing my pistol and firing even as it charged back toward me. It was like a nightmare. I watched in slow motion as every one of my heavy bullets struck home in its chest, but it kept coming.

My six-shooter had fired that many shots and was empty. I dropped it and snatched out my derringer, putting two more into the thing before it reached me. With a howl it sprang, claws outstretched.

I brought the long, heavy barrel of the Sharps around as I sidestepped, and smashed it hard over the wolf-thing's skull.

It barely seemed to notice, just batted the rifle away and grabbed for me. My arm was tangled up in the rifle's strap, so I reached back and unsheathed my bowie knife, ready to make a final, desperate stand.

We circled each other for a moment, and I could swear the thing was laughing in the way that dogs laugh. I would have thought he was just panting if it weren't for the cruel gleam in his eyes.

When in a desperate situation, I've always thought it better to go on the offensive. It was better than waiting and trying to react to him, so I charged in slashing. I caught him across the forearm, and he snatched it back. I went in to stab the heavy blade for his heart, but he batted me aside like I was a kid. I stumbled, but when he leaped for me I slashed him across the muzzle, drawing blood. He gave a low whine and jumped back, but looked ready to charge again. I'd beat him to it. If I was going to die here, I was determined to take him with me. I lunged forward with the knife, trying to get under his arms. Something smacked me on the side of the head, and I went sprawling in the rocks.

I landed on my back with my head hanging over the cliff. One look down told me this was not a good place to be. My hands were empty; I had lost the knife. The creature's fangs were right above me, but he wasn't in any hurry now, taking deep sniffs, apparently savoring his coming meal. I'd be damned if I'd be it. I still had the rifle in hand, empty though it was, and I swung it like a sword across his skull. That got a reaction. His claws raked across my chest, tearing the shirt away and a lot of skin with it. I raised my foot and whipped the ancient knife out from my boot. It was small, but I wasn't done fighting yet.

One of his massive paws closed around my throat and started to lift me up to his waiting jaws. His long tongue reached out and ran over my cheek, as if getting a taste for me. Now! I slashed with the knife at the hand that held me again and again.

A high-pitched shriek split my ears, and the smell of burning flesh assaulted my nostrils, then a massive backhand sent me tumbling. I hit my head hard on a rock, and stars swam before my eyes. I felt myself slip over the edge, and just before I lost consciousness I knew I was going to die.

***

I CAME TO WITH A STRANGE FEELING OF WEIGHT-lessness and a pounding in my head. My arm felt like it was on fire. I was dangling from the strap of my Sharps over the drop below. The hopelessly bent barrel of the gun was lodged in between an outcropping and a dead tree growing from the side of the rock face. Below me there was a hundred and fifty feet or so of open space above the jagged rocks below.

I was in a bad spot. Out of the frying pan, into the fire, so they say. My arm above where the strap held it was numb.

There was a few feet between me and the actual side of the cliff, more than I could reach with my free hand. My boots had been jerked off by the sudden stop when the barrel had caught in the tree, but I figured this would only help me now. Gently as I could, I began to pump my legs back and forth, building up momentum and hoping the tree would hold. A shower of pebbles and dust rained down on me, and I knew I'd have to move fast. The dry wood creaked and groaned as I inched closer to the cliff face.

My shoulder shot streaks of hot pain up into my brain, until I thought it might just pop off. It was probably out of its socket. Finally, my fingers touched rock and I jammed my hand into a crack and held myself there. I wiggled my toes into shallow footholds, and began to climb. I didn't know which way to climb, up or down, but first I had to go up in order to free my arm. I managed to keep my hand in the crack while I climbed with my feet.

After a minute or two, I had shimmied my way up just enough to relieve tension on the arm bound by the strap. I couldn't let go to untie it, so I'd have to find another way. With the weight of my body no longer acting as a tourniquet, the numbness was soon replaced by icy hot pins and needles running up the length of my arm in time with the new blood flow.

It took some time before I could flex and move the muscles again. When I could, I grabbed hold of the strap and used my other hand to work the bonds loose from my upper arm. It hurt like hell, but I managed to rotate my shoulder this way and that until it popped into place. Knowing I couldn't hang on forever, I shook myself and began to climb. As I did, I considered what awaited me at the top.

It was my hope that the monster above had seen me go over the cliff and decided I was a goner. If he hadn't, he might well be waiting there for me when I got to the top. Only at the end did it seem like I had truly hurt him, and that with the small knife. My Sharps was hopelessly bent, and all the rest of my guns were empty and lying at the top of the cliff. I didn't feel like I had a lot of options though.

Grunting and straining, I climbed as best I could with sheer effort, digging in with my toes and hands to get to the top of the ledge. It took a good hour to get back that fifty feet I had fallen.

When I reached the surface, I tilted my head and stuck one eye up to have a look-see. I couldn't see any sign of the beast, but that didn't mean he wasn't lying in wait somewhere beyond in the bushes and trees. I'd have to chance it though.

Just as I was about to haul myself up and over, something strange caught my eye. There was a man's thumb severed and sitting right there in front of my face! The cut part was singed like it had been burned with fire, and I didn't know what to make of that. Like an idiot, I checked both of mine, but they were still there.

I rolled myself up over the ledge, staying low and quiet. Keeping my belly to the ground like a snake, I gathered my remaining weapons and reloaded my pistol and derringer. My saddle lay some distance away, and the horse it had been attached to was in pieces all around the place. I was glad for a moment I hadn't ridden my steel dust.

Finally I found my bowie, and the small silver knife, covered in blackened blood. It looked like someone had held it to the fire, charring the liquid into a tarry paste. I didn't know what to make of that. I recalled the smell of burning flesh when I had struck with the knife, but not with my bowie. Silver? Could that be it? I didn't know, but I slung the heavy saddle over my shoulder after taking shells from it to reload the shotgun, and started walking toward town. I wasn't going back the way I came. I felt sure the beast would try to waylay me there if he was still around, and if he wasn't right behind some bush or tree, waiting to pounce.

I moved quickly but quietly, ready to fight for my life again any minute. I held my shotgun in one hand and the knife in the other. It was some miles to town, and if this thing was still hunting me, I didn't have much chance, and I knew it. I was going to try, though, and God help that monster if I got even a small chance to kill him.

I was barefoot, but plenty of time in the woods had toughened my feet, so it didn't bother me much. I was given to wearing moccasins anyway, when I was out. I could have grabbed them from my saddlebag, but I didn't want to waste a moment getting as far from here as possible.

Carrying my weapons and the heavy saddle took a heavy toll on me, given my condition, but I had the strength born of fear, and a powerful desire to live. I tore strips from my shirt to soak up the blood from where he'd clawed my chest, as I didn't want to leave so much as a drop on the ground to aid his tracking me. The wind having picked up was probably enough to carry my scent, but I wanted every advantage.

I moved through the woods like an Indian, using every trick I knew to hide my trail and obscure my passing. I thought about doubling back, and laying for him, but I knew that was a bad tactic if my main goal was survival.

I stopped after a few miles, and cut a sapling with my bowie. Taking some leather cord from my pack, I lashed the silver knife to it like a spear. While I was at it, I put on my moccasins too. Taking up my saddle again, I trotted along, conserving my strength but making good time.

I was only a mile from town now, by my reckoning, though the trees were thick here, and I had to use the mountains in the distance to find my way. There was a small clearing up ahead, and a stream ran through it. I stayed back in the trees for a minute, studying the terrain for any hiding places where someone could watch from. Just ahead, the bushes were moving something fierce not twenty yards away. I almost fired, but I remembered how little the buckshot affected the creature, and so I crept up on cat feet, ready to jam the silver blade in between the wolf man's ribs at the first opportunity.

I figured the beast must be feeding on something, and it was making a terrible racket. So much the better to cover my approach. I was only yards away when I decided the time was right. I gathered my courage and my strength, and leaped out of the bushes with a shout, spear held high. The beast stood bolt upright and gave a little yelp of surprise and fear. It had long, curly chestnut hair and looked a lot like Miss Patterson. She had traded the proper purple dress for man's garb, a broad-brimmed hat and rough canvas pants. She was flushed and sweating. It made for an awkward moment.

I was standing there staring at her, no doubt looking like a wild-eyed savage, my hair all over the place, bare chested and bleeding. I was not at my best, but she didn't forget her manners. She gathered herself and glanced about, as if trying to determine which direction to flee.

"Um, Mr. Carlson, I believe."

I decided it would be a good time to lower my makeshift

spear.

"Yes, well, hello, Miss Patterson."

I shifted my stance, nervously, and once again, I was speechless, but for an entirely different reason. Maybe a more cultured man would know the proper etiquette for the situation, but I had no idea what to say after leaping out of the bushes at the woman with a spear. She must think me a savage, born and bred.

"Are you out ... hunting?" The nervous look was still in her eyes, though I'd thought I made it clear I wished her no harm; after all, I had lowered my spear.

"Oh, heavens! You've been hurt!" she exclaimed, pointing at my wounds. I thought it was a bit of an understatement, I'd almost been killed, but I didn't want to come across as whiny.

She sprang into action, all fear gone from her eyes now, replaced with an intense look of concern.

"Here," she said, holding out some sort of plant. "Crush this and press it against your wounds. It will help to stop the bleeding. I was out gathering plants for my studies when you came along. This one here is good for infection, you should add that too. Why, you're going to need stitches, certainly!"

As she gathered her plants, I noticed she had piles of them gathered and sorted; she'd been hard at work for some time. I had to admit she looked rather fetching in her long coat, hat, and boots, though it certainly wasn't any more revealing than her dress. I'd never seen a woman in man's clothing before, though it certainly was practical.

"Listen, Miss Patterson," I started, suddenly remembering the plight that had brought us together. "These woods aren't exactly ... safe right now. We'd better hurry back to town."

I tried to speak good, or well, to seem reasonable in light of my former conduct. I wasn't about to tell her a wolf man had been chasing me since I'd cut off his thumb, that was for sure. The look in her eyes gave me to understand that she thought the only dangerous thing out here was probably me.

"You don't understand," I continued as she went back to stacking her plants. "There's a rogue grizzly around here somewhere, and it's been chasing me. I shot it, but it got hold of me, and we need to get back to town. Now!"

She stood up from her work with her hands on her hips. Eastern she might be, but I recognized her stance as that of a woman who's about to deliver a piece of her mind. I didn't have time to wait, and though she might think me a brute, I had to get her, not to mention myself, out of the woods.

"Ow!" She struggled when I seized her by the arm. "Unhand me, you bastard!"

The kick she gave me and the language she used were quite unladylike in my estimation, but I bore it patiently and slung her over my shoulder next to my saddle. She kicked and struggled, but I started for town. If she kept it up she was going to get a good smack on the rump, no bones about it.

"What the hell is that?" I felt her head snap up and heard the fear in her voice. I'm afraid I dumped her to the ground when I whirled, but she sprang right back up again.

"Where?" I looked about, shrugging the saddle off my shoulders. The next moment, a black furry form exploded from the tree line, heading straight for us.

"That!" she screamed and pointed.

The beast looked mad, even from a distance. He wanted me, of that I had no doubt. I might die here, but I didn't plan on seeing the woman killed, even if she had called my lineage into question. I shoved her to the side, and she went sprawling in the mud next to the stream.

"Run!" I told her helpfully and turned my attention back to the ball of fangs and claws heading my way at incredible speed. I wished for a horse, or rather two, but I had a feeling I wouldn't be able to outrun it even then. But suddenly all fear was gone, and all I could see was the creature barreling toward me, with the grim certainty that I must either kill it or die in the attempt.

I chose the first option and unloaded the double barrel into its face as it reached me. I saw half the flesh of its face stripped away, and I dropped my shotgun even as the wolf tumbled end over end, dazed by the blast. When it came up again, I had my wheel gun out, but I stopped in sheer amazement as the flesh started to reform in front of my very eyes. It was healing, and fast. Whatever this thing was, it wasn't natural.

I began to walk toward it, thumbing back the hammer and pulling the trigger again and again, aiming for its face. It looked completely healed from the damage I had done it near the cliff, but I noticed its thumb was still missing, and so I had a plan.

The wolf whimpered a little and snarled as the heavy lead slugs impacted its face, but it didn't die like any normal creature would. I was close enough now to use the spear.

I could have thrown it I suppose, but I hadn't much experience in that sort of thing, so I braced my weight against it and charged, screaming my rage to heaven.

The point went in low, under the ribs, and I jerked it back out again to the sound of sizzling flesh and anguished wails from the wolf man.

I hacked downward with the blade, and it cut through his arm like a hot knife through butter. Not letting up for a moment, I followed the beast as it scrambled backward, sinking the silver blade deep, again and again. It tripped and fell back, a long, mournful howl escaping its throat.

I stabbed the blade deep and watched the blood sizzle and smoke around where it disappeared into his neck. I wrenched it this way and that, and his head seemed to melt off his body. I wasn't finished though, and I stabbed downward again, piercing the head and then flinging it far away from the quivering torso. I didn't know what this thing was capable of, but I wanted to be sure.

You know how burning flesh smells? Well, this was worse. The odor was enough to knock a buzzard off a gut truck. I suppose that when an unnatural thing dies, it smells worse than when a normal creature does.

Whatever the case, I wanted to vomit. Miss Patterson did.

Apparently, she lacked the sense to run, having instead picked up a heavy piece of wood to use as a club. Well, I have to admit I admired her sand. It was a foolish gesture, but I appreciated it, especially from a woman with a proper, peaceful upbringing.

Now she was leaning over the club, distributing the contents of her breakfast rather haphazardly over her precious plants. I waited like a gentleman while she finished. When she did, she looked up at me in amazement.

"You ... you killed it!" she stammered.

I reckoned I had, but I took another look back at it, just to be sure.

"I did." Honestly, I wanted nothing more than to collapse with relief, but for some reason it seemed important to make it appear as if this were the kind of thing I did every day. Before breakfast.

"Are there ..." She took a nervous glance at the smoking corpse. "Are there more of those ... things?"

"I don't know. I suspect there might be, but I've only seen the one. Just the same, I think we should head back to town now, don't you?"

She nodded her head vigorously, and I was glad she had finally come around to my way of thinking. I took a moment to search out the head, thinking it would be helpful to have it when I went to collect my reward. I found it, but it wasn't going to be that easy. Sightless blue eyes stared up at me, set in the lean, rawboned face of, not a creature, but of a man. I didn't recognize it, but it surely was the same head that I'd cut off the creature, burn marks on the neck and everything from the silver blade.

Just to make double sure, I touched the tip of my spear to it, and the flesh sizzled. Okay. I was clearly dealing with something out of the ordinary, but I'd figured that out already. I didn't think the townsfolk, or the sheriff, would react well to my parading the head into town on my spear and proclaiming their problems were over. I was probably out my bounty on the creature, since there didn't seem to be any creature to produce. Perhaps I could find a large bear, kill it, and let the ranchers see their midnight slaughtering had gone away. I would think that over when I got back to town. Miss Patterson seemed a bit unsteady on her feet, so I shouldered my saddle and helped her along. After a while, she spoke.

"Thorn, right? May I call you that?"

"If I may call you Elizabeth." See how I took the advantage there? I can be a smooth feller when I want to be, earlier encounters notwithstanding.

"Yes, of course. I hadn't met you before this morning, but I've heard talk of you. People in town say you're a bounty hunter."

"I am."

"And do you like your work?"

"I don't see anything wrong with it. Why?"

"Well, there's some who ... who find it distasteful."

I pondered that before answering. "It's like this, Elizabeth. Bad men often get away from the law, and there's no one to search for them and bring them back. Sure, a lawman could do it, but these critters can run far and fast, and a lawman is usually needed right where he's at. Someone offers a reward, and if a man's got the skills and the grit, he goes after the outlaw and brings him in. Dead or alive."

"And how do you usually bring them in?"

"Dead."

"That seems harsh, doesn't it?"

Not to me it didn't.

"Some might say that, but you've got to remember these men have, in most cases, been tried and convicted in a court of law. They're running for a reason. Think of me as a sort of freelance lawman if you want. Trouble is, most of these men don't want to be brought in. They're armed, and they know how to use their guns. If I tried to take everyone in alive, I wouldn't make it very long."

"Do you ever try?"

"Sometimes. If a man seems decent, and I can get him

dead to rights, I may wallop him over the head with something and take him back for trial and hanging. But most aren't willing to go quietly, or they wouldn't have run in the first place."

"Surely they must have some sort of rights?"

"They do, but they give them up when, like the last man I brought in, ended the lives of his wife and children, because his girlfriend, a whore, wanted him to."

"What happened to her?"

"She hung, the day before he did. Somehow, he got loose and ran quite a ways before I caught up with him."

"And then what did you do?" I could see the question in her eyes, and no matter how she felt about it, I wasn't going to hide it. "I shot him dead where he sat."

She looked away from me, then down. Neither of us spoke for quite a while. Finally, she broke the silence.

"Thorn, what are we going to do about this?"

I didn't know how to answer that at first. I noticed she had said "we," as if this were her problem now too. I was used to being in things by myself, and I didn't want to get her involved. This might not be over, and I saw no reason to put her in danger. Besides, what help could she be? I have to admit though, I liked the idea of someone being willing to share in my burdens, especially if that someone was a pretty girl with freckles on her nose.

"We do nothing." I finally said. "If we were to tell people about what happened today, what do you think they'd say?"

"They would say we were crazy, surely, and we'd find ourselves locked up for murder if they found the body."

"That's right, so we don't say anything to anybody. What we do is go on about our business, and leave the worrying to me. There's no reason for you to get involved."

When I got to the last sentence, she gave a perturbed little "humph!" but didn't say anything else. I could tell I'd hurt her feelings, but I couldn't imagine why. After all, I'd been looking out for her, hadn't I?

We were at the tree line just beyond the town now, and I decided to part company. It wouldn't do for a proper lady like her to be seen with a bare-chested man walking out of the woods, both muddy and disheveled.

It was near evening, so I watched from the trees as she hurried to her schoolhouse, and then worked my way along to the south end of town. There weren't a lot of people in the streets, but I noticed a strange group of men eying me hard on my way into town. I admit I must have cut an odd figure: filthy, covered in blood, shirtless and afoot, carrying my saddle.

I didn't recognize any of them, but I hadn't been in town long, and there were a score of ranches spread out around the town where the men could have come from. I walked through the main room at the hotel and headed up the stairs. The clerk began to open his mouth, but I cut him off.

"Don't ask," I said, and slammed the door to my room behind me. Bathing off the grime and blood, I decided I would, in fact, need stitches. Aside from the admonishment I'd no doubt get from the good doctor, I wasn't keen on anyone knowing I'd been in a tussle today. Whoever the wolf man had been, he was sure to be missed, and with the gossip of a small town, it wouldn't take long to put things together.

The long claw marks could just as easily have been knife wounds, and I wished I had the presence of mind at the time to dispose of the thumb on the cliff and bury the body. Well,

I'd just let things shake out how they would and deal with them later.

I finished bathing my wounds and tore strips from the bed sheets to make bandages. I put on some clean clothes, my last set, and headed across the street to the diner. The silver knife I'd put back in my boot, and I wore my six-gun on my hip and the other thrust through my belt for a cross draw. I tied a bit of leather to my left wrist and tucked the derringer up underneath it for quick access. I didn't expect any more trouble, but after the events of the day I felt more comfortable being well armed.

Heading across the street to Ma's Kitchen, I saw Richard Comstock pulling up in a wagon. His face was flush and sweaty, and he didn't look good. He waved me down, and I stopped in the street to talk to him. He seemed like he was thinking about what to say, so I took out the makings and rolled a smoke while he collected himself.

"Found a bit of rope and pieces of a calf out by my place this morning." He was eyeing me suspiciously. I didn't know exactly why.

"And?" I wasn't prepared to tell him anything he didn't need to know; the less I said the better.

"Looked like someone set a trap, even got a shot off, too." I had left an empty cartridge case there. I was hoping they hadn't followed the tracks.

"I laid up for the creature, and I shot him."

"You saw him! What was it? What did it look like?" He looked worried, and I couldn't guess why.

"I didn't get a good look. It was dark. Your boys find anything else?" I hoped not.

"No, I told them to leave it. After all, that's what I hired you for, right?"

"That's right. I think you're dealing with a rogue grizzly, but I can't be sure yet."

"Do you think ... you think you might have killed it?" He looked hopeful.

"No telling, lost the track, but I'll pick it back up again. I'm sure your troubles will be over soon."

"Well, hot damn! I'm impressed. Two days on the job and already you've managed to shoot the thing, which is more than anyone else has done so far. Tell you what, here's half the reward now. Just promise me you'll keep going until this thing, or things, are dead and gone, will you?" He was holding out on me, and I knew it. I didn't know what his angle was, but he sure knew more than he was saying.

He was offering me a thousand dollars, just for having shot the beast? It didn't add up. All I knew is he really, really, wanted me to stay on this job. I decided to play it cool. At least I had a good chunk of money now, without having to show any kind of proof.

"I'll stay on the job."

"Good." He smiled, too big. "Good, I'm glad. Be seeing you!"

With that he turned the wagon around and drove right back out of town, moving awful fast.

He was scared of something, and didn't want me to know what it was. If he had an idea what these wolf creatures were, that I could understand. Did he know? Or at least suspect?

I'd mull it over during dinner. I always think better with food in my stomach anyhow. Ma's Kitchen was serving up big platters full of thick steaks, with burned gravy and fresh, hot biscuits. I ate my fill and thought about what to do next.

Likely, I already had my reward in the bag. I just had to shoot a grizzly and drag it in to the Circle C to show off to get the other thousand.

Still, I admit I was hesitant to go out into the woods again, but I didn't imagine there were more of them. At least, that's what I wanted to believe. I'd have to talk to some of the other ranchers and see what they had to say, how many attacks they'd been having. Just the same, a wolf could travel miles and miles in one night, so why not a wolf man? There was no reason there had to be more than one.

I loosened my belt a little and sat a spell. There was a lot more going on in Elk's Run than I had first thought. The cowboy I'd shot had it in for me, no doubt, and if he was friends with Shamus McMasters, he'd probably ridden the hoot owl trail time and again. His death could well be for causes unrelated to my concerns. Someone had been following me though, as I went about hunting the wolfman, and I didn't think it was the fella that had turned into the wolf himself. I'd noticed the boot print I'd kept running across had a nick in the right sole, right where the outside edge met the ground.

The only way to know for sure would be to ride out in the morning and follow the wolf's back trail to see where he'd left his clothes, if he even bothered wearing them. I had a lot of questions on my mind right then, and so I decided to seek out educated advice from the one person I could talk to, Miss Elizabeth Patterson. I didn't suppose they taught about these kinds of subjects out East, but the fact that she was prettier than a summer sunset didn't enter into my calculations, not one bit. Honest.

As I headed out the door, I saw the glow of a cigarette

from the shadows across the street. A tall, lanky man stepped out of the darkness, wearing a tin star on his left breast pocket. I guess only the sheriff got the silver one. He motioned to me and turned to walk toward the sheriff's office. I followed him, like the right good and law-abiding citizen that I am.

Now and then he glanced back at me, but it didn't appear I was under arrest or anything like that. If I was, it was an awful funny way to go about it. I followed him inside to the sheriff's office, and the deputy left. Sheriff Garrett was tacking up wanted posters on the corkboard behind a broad oak desk.

He turned to me. "Have a seat, Carlson." He smiled at me, I suppose to put me at ease. He sure had a different way of doing business than other lawmen I had met. Maybe it was a mountain thing.

I sat, and he joined me behind his large, official-looking desk. While I was laid up, one of the characters in the dime-store novel William picked out had a horse pistol mounted under the desk, so the villain could shoot someone without their ever suspecting it. I sure hoped Sheriff Garrett didn't have the same setup. Seemed like a good way to ruin a desk.

"I went and checked out the body you reported last night." I guess this was the part where I was supposed to give away some clue that fingered me as the murderer. If that was his game, it seemed like an easy one to play. I kept my mouth shut.

"Problem was, I didn't find it." That threw me for a loop. The body was lying right there next to the road, with the horse standing right by it. I didn't figure he'd have missed it easily.

"I gave the directions to it, they seemed simple enough."

"They were, they were." Again with the grin. "I did find some blood, and the horse, but the body just must have disappeared."

"Well, I got a good look at him, and I don't figure he just got up and walked away."

"I don't either. Did you see anyone else out on the road last night? Anyone at all?" I didn't like where this was heading. In fact, I wished I had seen someone; that way the sheriff could go play games with someone else. I was a lot of things, but I wasn't the type to point the finger at someone who didn't deserve it ... unless I had good reason.

"No. I didn't see anyone. I came upon the body by the road, saw who it was, and then came and reported it straightaway." Thorn Carlson, citizen of the year.

"So you did know who it was."

"Like I said, I saw him. After the fact."

"You see my problem, Mr. Carlson? You'd quarreled with the gentleman, had you not?"

"We'd done more than that, and you know it."

"That's right. Look, I'm not saying I don't believe your statement, Carlson, but I've got to investigate all possible leads, you understand that, don't you?"

"Sure I do. Why don't you go investigate some then." That broke the toothy grin, finally. "I will. Rest assured of that. By the way, what were you doing that night? Coming back from somewhere, no doubt?"

"No doubt. If you must know, I'd been out to see Comstock at the Circle C that day. I've been considering staying here awhile. I liked the countryside and wanted to get a look at it."

"I see." I don't know what he saw, but I don't think he

bought my story. Not one bit. For a moment I considered telling him there was a half man, half wolf on the loose, eating people and cattle. Just to see the look on his face.

"What's so funny, Carlson?" His flinty eyes were glaring.

"Nothing, Sheriff, nothing at all." I elected against the wolf man option after all.

"Well, stay close to town, will you? In case I have any more ... questions?"

"Sure thing, Sheriff."

I didn't ask to go, because I didn't want to give him the satisfaction. He may have had suspicion, but nothing more. Still, men had been hanged for less evidence, and I wondered again if I should just get out while the getting was good. I left the office and drifted down toward the schoolhouse in a roundabout way. I walked as if I had no particular destination in mind, just harmless old Thorn Carlson, out for a stroll.

Once, I thought I saw movement in one of the dark alleyways, and I leaped back, afraid of a shot from the darkness. I didn't have any particular reason to think someone would try to shoot me at the moment, but it had happened before in other places, and I was feeling a mite jumpy besides.

When I peered around the corner, nothing was there. I made my way over to the schoolhouse without being noticed by anyone. I went around to the back and took a seat behind some bushes.

Now, a proper young lady such as Miss Patterson shouldn't be seen receiving male callers after a certain hour, and naturally as a gentleman I wanted to preserve her honor. So as to do things the classy way, I picked up a handful of pebbles and started chucking them at her window, one by one. After a moment the curtain was flung back, and a very exasperated yet pretty face appeared in the window. I smiled despite myself, and she must have seen my grin, because she returned it. Right away she covered her mouth, and I didn't know why. I thought she had an excellent set of choppers, white and straight.

Now, my smile was a little less than white or straight, but I still had all my teeth, even if some of them had been busted loose a time or two in saloons across the West. Ah, youth. She cracked the door and poked her head out like an owl. After looking about, she opened it wide and motioned for me. I darted out of the bushes and in through the door. She actually shut the door giggling. I was hoping it wasn't at the way I ran. I'm not a graceful man, but I don't think I look funny when I run either.

Maybe it was something else. Either way, she sure seemed tickled about something, all smiles and giggles, though I could tell she tried to look serious. When she wasn't look-ing I sniffed myself, but no, I didn't stink. I'd had a bath just three days ago, so that couldn't be it. She told me to take off my shirt, which I thought was a little forward, but then I re-membered my wounds and why I had come here in the first place, and I complied. She gasped when she saw the extent of the damage, but didn't shrink away. Lighting a few extra candles, she practically muscled me into an overstuffed chair and pulled up a stool next to me. She got out some kind of thin string of the same kind the doctor had used and then bent a sewing needle and held it over the flame for a moment. I was afraid it would burn, but I didn't want to show it, so I sat silently while she stuck the needle through me. It was cool when it touched my flesh, not that it helped the sensation any. Right then I wouldn't have minded some more of that laudanum.

"I see you've already got a few stitches, Thorn," she said as she sewed me up.

"Ran into a grizzly just before coming into town."

"Does that happen often?"

I shrugged. "Now and then. It happens."

That was the first griz I ever tangled with, but she didn't know that.

"How long have you been out here anyway, Liz?" She looked up at me sharply, but didn't correct the way I said her name. Elizabeth just seemed like a mouthful, that's all.

"Just a few months. I always liked the woods growing up, and I wanted to see some real wilderness. I studied history and botany in college, and I was hoping to do some new research, you know, make a name for myself."

"Why? They don't let womenfolk be scientists out East, do they?" The look she gave me was like the look a bull gives when he's about to charge. I decided to keep my mouth shut on that subject, and she didn't answer. *Women scientists? What's next? Letting them vote?*

She looked hurt, so I decided to pour a little honey on the wound. "I'm sure you'll make a fine scientist," I said, my voice sounding frank and honest.

"You don't have a problem with a woman being a professional?" She arched an eyebrow. She looked even prettier in the glow of the candlelight. I hoped I looked better too. I didn't know what she meant by professional. After all, I was a professional, wasn't I? I mean, I had a profession. Talking to this girl was a little confusing.

"Sure," I answered. "I see no reason why women can't be

professionals." I didn't have to mean it. Her eyes brightened some, and I knew I'd said the right thing.

She finished with the first one and drew out more thread for the next cut. I was really starting a collection. My wounds didn't seem to bother her, and I was glad she wasn't squeamish.

"You ever read about anything like what we saw today? In college?"

"Not in college, no. However, I have read about something similar, but it sounds silly."

"That thing in the woods today wasn't silly. Let's hear it." I'd take any scrap of information I could get at this point. I'm naturally curious, but not a lot of books came out West. When I had the time, I'd read whatever I could get my hands on. I'd never come across any books about animals that turned into people, or the other way around.

"There are legends," Liz began, "mostly medieval, about people that turn into wolves." I would have scoffed, except I had seen one that very afternoon and killed it.

"In folklore, they're called werewolves. On the full moon, they turn into wolves." We'd just had a full moon.

"What about at other times?"

"Well, it depends on who you read. Just the same, the wolf we saw, the one you killed, he turned during the day, didn't he? So yes."

"When I stabbed him with my silver knife, it seemed to burn him. How does that work?"

"There's nothing about silver in the old legends. Not as it relates to werewolves, anyway. Silver is thought to be a pure metal, and with other supernatural creatures, it was thought to be a deterrent, along with different kinds of herbs and even some religious items, like holy water."

This here was mostly Protestant country, so I didn't have a notion of how to get holy water, but right now I'd give anything a try.

"Tell me about the herbs."

"The only one I know of specifically, as it relates to werewolves, is wolfs bane. It grows in a few places, but I haven't found it here. Of course, that could just be more superstition. Just because the plant is called wolfs bane, doesn't mean it would actually do anything against werewolves. In fact, people used to think mandrake root could ... there, that's the last stitch, try not to open this up again."

"So we've got silver."

"Yes. You don't suspect there are more of them, do you?" I didn't know, but it didn't hurt to be prepared either. Once again, I wondered why I didn't just pack my saddlebags and ride on, as I'd been doing for the last ten years or so. I believed in keeping my promises, and I'd promised Comstock I wouldn't quit. But that wasn't it. Nor was it William and his situation; after all, I'd done my best to set him up, hadn't I? The food was good here, but that would never hold me to a place where I'd been mauled half to death twice, and once by some sort of supernatural creature. Didn't sound so super to my way of thinking. I thought it was the dumps.

Could it be her? Was I actually getting sweet on a gal I'd known only a few hours, and under less than pleasant circumstances? That was enough to make me want to get up and bolt right there. I felt a cold sweat break out on my forehead, and all of a sudden I felt like a trapped coyote.

I'd known my share of women, good and otherwise over the years, but never for any length of time. I'd valued my freedom, and I hadn't planned on being tied down for a long, long time. Maybe never. But when I looked at that sweet face in the dim light, I thought that might just change.

This was trouble I didn't need. A book I'd read once said the heart is a fickle thing, and I was feeling right now like my own was a rattlesnake that just up and bit me from somewhere unseen. My first instinct was to pretend it hadn't happened, but that wasn't likely to work much better than it would with the rattlesnake bite.

We sat, quiet for a while, and she finished stitching me up. Uneasy, I thanked her for the good job, and she blushed. "I've never actually done that before," she told me. "Well, it looks like you did at least as good a job as the doctor did." *And a damn sight more enjoyable too, despite the lack of laudanum.* She blushed again, and I can't say the sight wasn't pleasing.

"Thorn?" she began. "Yes?" I was buttoning my shirt. She frowned a little when I put it on, and I wondered if there was a certain way women preferred men to do it. I must have been doing it wrong. For all my experience in certain ... relations with womenfolk, I probably had a lot to learn. "Will you come back again? To talk more about this, I mean." Again with the blushing. I hoped I hadn't done anything too embarrassing. I made a note to take another bath in the next few days, whether I needed it or not. "Sure," I said, and I gave her a smile. She gave me one in return and shut the door gently. I sure did like it when she smiled.

***

MORNING FOUND ME DEVOURING A THICK SLAB OF bacon and fried eggs in the hotel, accompanied by coffee so strong the sugar just kind of settled down into it rather than sank. I was feeling good, and I ate enough breakfast for two men. The nice old lady what did the cooking, Mrs. Salsbury, had made flapjacks with the bacon grease, and there was fresh maple syrup to go on top.

William came running in, breathless. His face told me something terrible had happened. "Mr. Comstock was just brought in," he panted. "Someone found him out on the road, shot through the heart!" I cursed into my coffee. This was bad news. Guess I wouldn't be seeing that extra thousand dollars.

Well, that was the only thing really tying me to this town, and I supposed I should be glad. I could leave now with more than enough cash to take it easy for a while. I had no more reason to stay, right? I began to think of the trapped coyote again. Just then, the sheriff walked in.

"Carlson." He nodded toward the outside. His intent was clear. I saw he had his two deputies with him. The tall, lanky one (Judd Homer was his name, I had learned) gave me a big toothy grin, and I didn't think it was good natured. The other one, a husky fellow of average height, just glared at me. I guess they already had their ideas as to the suspect. I followed the sheriff outside, and he stepped out into the street a ways, away from the deputies.

"Where were you last night Carlson? I know you didn't ride in until after ten o'clock." I shot a glance back toward the door, to see the clerk shrink back behind the frame. I'd have words with him later. I didn't know what to say to the sheriff, as I certainly wasn't going to intimate how I'd spent the evening in the company of one of the most honorable ladies in town. It would cause a scandal, I was sure, and I couldn't do that to her. A good woman's reputation was worth far more than the little of my own that was left to me.

"I didn't leave town after I spoke with you, if that's what you're asking."

"That's not what I'm asking, Carlson. I want to know where you were, and if there's anyone who can corroborate your whereabouts."

"I didn't leave town, and that's all I'm saying."

"Not good enough." I sighed. He wasn't going to let me off the hook that easy. I needed to give him a story, and one that would check out. Preferably something corroborable, whatever that meant. Or at least believable. If I hadn't left town, I would have had to be somewhere I would have been seen. Unless, of course, I had been doing something ... embarrassing.

Gritting my teeth, I took that fork in the trail. "I'd really rather not say, Sheriff." I tried to look resigned and sheepish.

"Come on, Carlson, let's have it." I blew out a breath. I studied my toes for a while, though inside I was trying not to laugh. If I did, it would ruin the whole thing.

"Well, Sheriff ..." I stalled, making him force me to tell him.

"Damnitall, Carlson, let's have it!"

"All right then, if I must. You know, Sheriff, how it is for a man when he's without a woman for a long time, don't you?"

"Oh come on, Carlson, that's just sick! Really?"

I nodded, as if ashamed of my conduct. "I tiptoed out to the field behind the hotel after I left ..."

"Jesus, Carlson, don't say any more! You left at eight o'clock!" Again I nodded, looking bashful. "That's two hours, man! Why ... that's ... that's disgusting! Get out of my sight, Carlson!" he sputtered. I made it all the way around the corner before I cracked a smile.

I had just played the sheriff like a fiddle. I was convinced he was a good man, though a mite squeamish. I also knew he'd be too embarrassed to relate the story to anyone else, so the "secret" would stay just between us. I stayed in the alley between the hotel and the attorney's office next door, not trusting my ability to look the sheriff in the eye without busting up laughing. While I waited to regain my composure, I rolled a smoke and lit it, and considered the day ahead. The sky was growing cloudy, and it looked like a snowstorm was brewing over the mountains.

It was well into spring, but I'd heard this part of the country got brief patches of snow here and there, even in the summertime. I'd have to get a move on if I wanted to do any tracking today. I still wanted to look for the wolfman's, or werewolf's, clothing and see if his boots had a familiar nick in it.

A low, cold voice broke into my thoughts. "Think you're real smart, don't you, Carlson?" I looked up to see the lanky deputy, Judd Homer, staring at me with cold hate in his eyes.

"What's your problem, Deputy?" I asked, not in the least intimidated. I couldn't imagine what brought on this reaction, but something sure had this fella on the prod for me.

"You're my problem, Carlson. You think you've got things all figured out, don't you? Well, you're going to get a surprise, any day now. I'll get you, sooner or later."

I didn't think I had much at all figured out, but this fella sure seemed to think I was onto something. It would probably be awkward if I'd shot him out of hand, given my current status as some kind of suspect and he being a deputy and all, but I was tired of folks tryin' to ride herd on me, and

I'll be damned if I was going to take a second of it from this pipsqueak.

"Why don't you go ahead and drop that star and that gun, and you can have me right now?" I challenged, coming off the spot where I'd been leaning. I was feeling a mite stronger than I had when I fought the big man, and I'd take pleasure in administering such an easy beating.

This hombre had some lip on him, but I'd cut him down to size, in a hurry. He didn't respond, just gave a wide grin as he shucked his gun and flicked his star into the dust. We didn't have an audience, just him and me. I flexed my shoulders and cracked my knuckles, looking forward to the exercise. He walked toward me, and I met him, throwing a fast overhand right to knock him in the dust. It probably would have, if it'd landed. As it was, he moved like lightning, dodging out of the way and stabbing two fists into my belly. It hurt bad, but I pivoted and let go with a hard left, aiming at his face again. He sidestepped easily and walloped me across the jaw so hard I thought he had picked up an axe handle somewhere. I saw flashes of light and fell back against the building. I shook my head to clear it and went in fighting mad. This couldn't be happening. This guy was scrawny, but he moved like a rattlesnake and hit like a mule.

I faked with the left and caught him one hard on the chin. Finally! It was a hard punch, and I expected it to hurt him, but he just shrugged it off and grinned at me. I tried a different tack. I dove for his hips, tackling him against the brick wall. I could feel how strong he was, and it didn't seem right for that skinny body. I weighed more though, and I slammed him up against the wood. I drove my fists into his gut, one after the other, but he brought his knee up and I went flying back, unable to breathe. I charged him again, but he laid into me then, landing punches that seemed to come from every direction, impossibly fast and hard.

He grabbed me by the throat with an iron grip, and I thought my eyes were going to pop out of my skull. He held me up against the wall, and drove his other fist into my ribs, again and again. I couldn't breathe, so I kicked out with my boot and landed him one right in the pit of his stomach that knocked him back. He went down to a knee and I kicked him square in the jaw, then grabbed a hold of his vest so I could slam him face-first into the other building. He put out a hand against the wall, and as strong as I am, I couldn't budge him, not an inch. I was beginning to think I should have shot him after all when his elbow swung up and caught me under the chin.

The impact knocked me back against the wall again, and I hit the back of my head, hard. Dazed, I refocused my eyes just in time to see his fist shoot out toward my face. I thought I heard a ringing sound, and next thing I knew there were two Judds, and both of them were grinning, unhurt, as I felt my knees sink under me. I hit the dirt hard and rolled over, the world spinning above me. He gave me a vicious kick in the ribs and walked off, saying, "Soon enough, Carlson, I'll finish you." I took a deep breath and tried to clear my head. I'd just been licked by a skinny runt!

It hurt my pride almost as much as my body. He'd disposed of me easily, and appeared to be unhurt in the process, though I thought I'd landed a few good blows. I'd like to say I popped right up and carried on, but truth was I was out of sight, and just felt like lying there a while. My head hurt something terrible and my ears were ringing, and my guts felt like a buffalo had just danced a jig on them. Finally, I took a deep breath and rolled over in the dirt. What I saw surprised me. There was the footprint! The one that'd been following me the last few days. It had the same nick in the sole, there on the right side. No doubt about it. But what did it mean? I slumped up against the wall, sitting, and rolled another smoke, since my last one had been so unpleasantly interrupted.

Judd Homer was the one who'd been following my trail, and even before that had left his tracks at the stream where I'd been tracking the werewolf on the first day. I was a fool! Even after what happened yesterday, I hadn't considered the fact that the wolf that went into the stream might have come out as a man. And that man was Judd Homer, judging by the prints left. There was more than one!

The next night it had been a different werewolf, and that was the one I had shot and killed, and I'd seen Judd's tracks there as well. All that meant he was most likely aware I'd killed one of his brethren.

I lurched to my feet and ran out in the street. I looked all around, but I didn't see Homer anywhere. I wondered how many more of them there were. No way of knowing 'til they decided to show themselves. That they meant to kill me I had no doubt. Not only had I seen them, but I killed one of their number, and they were sure to want revenge. Judd himself told me as much.

I had a feeling that the beating I just received was only the beginning. I considered what to do. I was a man who'd always done his own lawing, but I figured if ever I needed help, it was now. I didn't think the sheriff was involved, or Judd would've just shot me dead right then and there. I took the silver flask out of my pocket and took a big gulp, fortifying myself for the task ahead. I would try to convince the sheriff of what I knew and hope for his help. It was a long shot, but worth trying.

***

THE SUN HAD BARELY BUDGED IN THE SKY BEFORE I had explained everything to the sheriff, starting from when Richard Comstock hired me for the job to my suspicions about Judd Homer (I left out the part where he'd whupped me within an inch of my life). The sheriff turned out to be a reasonable man, and so he listened patiently and intently to every word, a look of interest on his face.

He sat in deep thought for a while when I'd finished, then called his deputy in. Then he arrested me.

He'd whispered something in the deputy's ear, then they both turned and drew their guns. I might've been able to kill them both anyway, but they meant me no harm. They just thought what I would have thought a week or so ago ... that I was plum crazy. The deputy opened the cell door, and the sheriff locked me inside. I didn't have much to say. If they didn't believe me, they'd just have to see for themselves. I'd explained where the body of the werewolf I'd killed lay, and I'd done a good enough job apparently that the sheriff was going to ride out and find it. I knew what he'd find of course, not a wolf's, but a man's body. Then it was just a matter of time before my neck got stretched.

I wasn't too keen on that idea, and I had a few ideas of my own about how this was gonna shake out. Number one was to get out of jail. Then I'd ride down the sheriff and make sure he didn't get himself killed by one of those werewolves in the woods. It wasn't like we were partners or anything, but he was a fair man, even if he got on my nerves from time to time. Something about him dying while checking out my story, or more likely, looking for evidence to hang me, just didn't sit well.

Either way, it would be my fault. I acted resigned for a few moments, but I knew I had to act fast. The sheriff had sent for Judd Homer to accompany him, but Judd wasn't to be found. He'd left the other deputy, Harrell, to guard me. Harrell didn't look too bright to me. I tried to win him over with my charming personality, but he just told me to shut up or he'd shoot me.

I didn't figure it was likely, but just the same my approach wasn't working. So I taunted him. I began singing loudly, and off key (it comes natural) until he got, well, rather worked up about it. I made fun of the way he parted his hair, his boots, and finally, his horse. Harrell really liked his horse. I found that out when he crossed the office in two strides and grabbed me through the bars. This was what I'd been trying for. I snaked a hand through the bars and grabbed a handful of Harrell's greasy hair, slamming his face into the metal bars twice, hard. He dropped like a sack of flour and I grabbed the keys out of where he'd stowed them in his pocket.

Unlocking the gate, I didn't have time to go back to the hotel or even saddle my horse. I knew I needed to reach the sheriff in a hurry, and the absence of Judd Homer bothered me. The snow was blowing hard outside, and it accumulated quickly. I could see the hoof prints clearly where the sheriff had headed out of town. I knew where he was going, of course, and I hoped I could head him off before he got there. I leaped on what I assumed to be Harrell's buckskin gelding, gave it a slap on the rump, and tore up the dirt and snow in a fast gallop. The buckskin seemed a good horse, and I'd need every ounce of its speed now. I headed directly across town and out into the field behind the schoolhouse, riding hard. I picked up the sheriff's tracks, but I was almost at the scene of my battle with the werewolf. A shot rang out in the cold, crisp air, and I knew I was too late. I reigned up and waited for a spell behind some pines. All I had in my haste was my six-gun and derringer, grabbed off the sheriff's desk as I left. I had my knife in my boot as well, and that was the most formidable weapon I had to use against my enemy.

I'd sat my horse long enough to build and smoke two cigarettes, and I figured that would be enough time. I rode into the clearing at a canter, keeping a sharp eye on the woods. On the other end of the field a horse wandered, and I could see the sheriff's black overcoat in the snow, his hat some distance away. A bright splash of crimson shone like a beacon and told me all I needed to know about the lawman's fate. I sat my horse, cursing myself for a fool. I'd gotten a good man killed today. For all the good it had done me, I should have left him out of it. The distinctive click of a hammer being cocked made me stiffen in my saddle.

A soft chuckle came from right behind me. I glanced back to see Judd stepping out from behind a tree. He was good, I'll give him that. First he'd whupped me, and now he'd played me for a fool. I'd kill him for it, whether he got me or not. "Howdy, Judd." I did my best to appear at ease. Maybe he'd think I had something up my sleeve. The best time to let on that it's all part of the plan is when it ain't. At any rate, I needed some time.

"Why, howdy, Carlson. Funny meeting you here. Well, not so funny actually, I'd been expecting you. The sheriff was just a bonus. I'd been wanting to do that for a long time. You telling him how it is, which is why I expect he came here, is what gave me the excuse." His laughter sounded evil. Just then Harrell came riding up, horse in a lather. "Judd! You've got him! Take his guns, I'll show that bastard to ..." Harrell was cut short as Judd turned and fired, the heavy slug catching Harrell through the chest. He clutched at the wound, and stared at his bloody hands. He lifted questioning eyes to his fellow deputy before falling sidelong off his horse. Before I could move, Judd pointed the six-gun back at me. I had to keep talking if I was going to buy time.

"So you know what I did here yesterday?"

"Know it? Hell, I came right after. I'd followed your trail for a while, but I expected one of the pack to get to you first. It was Dawson you killed. He expected you to track him, and boy was he mad about getting shot. It took him a good hour to heal from that one. He showed me the hole it left. Could put your fist through it, no lie. Got to admit, it was impressive, having killed one of us. Almost a shame to lose you. You'd probably be good at this. I wouldn't actually offer though, 'less I thought you'd accept." I didn't know if this was an invitation or not. Of course I wouldn't accept, but I'd play it out if it'd buy me time.

"What conditions would there be?"

"Well, you'd have to obey the pack master for one. He's the big wolf. The leader. He'd bite you, or hell, I could do it, and you'd turn into one of us at the next full moon. It takes a while to get used to, I'll tell you that. And it takes some time to be able to change at will, but I think you'd pick it up soon enough."

"What's your game, Judd? What's the brass ring here?"

"Gosh, nothing that out of the ordinary I guess. Luna's gonna take over all the ranches in the valley, then we'll each of us get ours, that is, each of the pack. Once that's done with all we have to do is hold our territory, easy enough with powers like ours. Me, I like it when rustlers come around. Tasty ... almost as tasty as kids. You'll see, it's just like veal. Soft, so tender..."

Judd trailed off, you could practically feel him slavering. Chills ran down my spine and my trigger finger itched.

"Luna. He your pack leader?"

"The same. Though things can always change. You remember who offered you this chance, hear?"

"I will, I will. One thing gets me, though; how did Comstock enter into it?"

Judd spat, "He knew what we were, and made a deal not to tell in exchange for us leaving his ranch alone. We did mostly, but we had to take some of his cattle sooner or later, or it would look suspicious. That son of his came awful close sometimes, hunting us. We told him to reign him in, or we'd kill them all, his whole family! Of course, he probably figured out sooner or later we were going to drive him out too. He must've thought there was something he could do about it. When we found out he'd hired you, we decided he'd reached the limit of his usefulness."

That cleared a lot of things up, and the whole time he'd been talking, I'd been thinking. "Mind if I have a drink, and gnaw it over?"

"Go ahead. Don't try anything though, or I'll blast you out of your saddle." I had no doubt he could. I'm faster than greased lightning with the quick draw, from hours and hours of practice, but it was obvious that this skinny bastard had all kinds of ... "supernatural" powers, as Liz said. I saw how quick he'd moved when we fought, and besides, he could probably soak up my bullets all day long, unless ... I dug my flask out of my pocket and took a long drink. I wiped my mouth with my sleeve and asked, "Want a drink, Homer?" Before he had time to answer, I tossed the flask to him. He caught it automatically, and then jumped back screaming. The smell of burning flesh cut through the cold air and assaulted my nostrils.

Wasting no time, I drew and fired in one smooth motion. A gaping hole steamed up in the frosty air from between his eyes as he slumped to his knees, then over on his side. He might be able to heal up unnaturally fast, but I figured that should slow him down, at least for a minute. I was also willing to bet that a werewolf's powers were less while in human form, or else why make the change? I climbed down off my horse and walked over to where Judd lay in the snow. His forehead was already closing up, but slowly.

Clenching my jaw for the thought of what I would have to do, I drew my silver blade and went to work. It was a full five minutes before the skin on Judd's forehead closed up completely, not even leaving a scar. Must not be quite so quick to heal in human form. It was another minute before what was inside had knitted up enough for him to regain consciousness.

I'd had time to roll one and smoke half of it before the pale blue eyes blinked open. He sniffed the air, then turned to face me. He snarled like an animal and went for his gun. I'd left it in his holster; he was no longer a threat to me. He jerked his hand back up to his face, surprised. When he saw the charred stumps of his wrists, he screamed with rage and pain. I'd been expecting it to bother me, doin' that to him. It didn't.

"You son of a bitch, Carlson, I'll get you for this!"

"No you won't, Homer. That reminds me, I owe you something."

"What's that?" In answer, I bent down over him and delivered a wicked punch that sent teeth flying. It felt satisfying. He coughed and sputtered the remainder of his front teeth out onto the bloody snow. His eyes changed somewhat, and his features grew long and pinched, but he didn't seem to be able to make the change. Must be the effect of the silver. It wouldn't have mattered if he had been able to turn into a wolf though. I'd taken his feet too. One of the things my Pappy taught me was that if you have an enemy, respect him enough not to give him a chance.

Well, I figured Judd Homer should be feeling plenty respected right now, though he didn't show it. "The pack ... the pack will make you pay for this," he rasped. His voice sounded low and deep, unnaturally so. I could tell he was having problems forming words. His tongue had grown longer and his back teeth had lengthened considerably. "How many are there, Judd?"

"More ... than enough ... to kill ... you." He began to laugh, but it was more like a panting. His tongue lolled out from his mouth over the side of his cheek. I wasn't going to get anything out of him. Only one thing left. I seized him by the collar, and he batted at me with his stumps. He was weak now, and I suspected the silver sapped a lot of their strength. I could make use of that fact. I plunged the knife into his eye and held it there. His body quivered and shook so hard I thought for a moment he might explode, blood smoking and sizzling where it touched the silver. He went still after a time, and I pulled the blade out and wiped the blackened blood off on his shirt.

I crossed over the field to the sheriff, and saw he was past all the cares of this world. He'd brought a shovel, no doubt to uncover the body I'd told him about, and I made good use of it. I buried all four of them, having uncovered the remains of the other werewolf and assembled all the pieces. It was hard work, but the ground was not frozen as it would be in winter. The snow would melt within the next few days at most, and I didn't want to leave evidence out.

I didn't fear the law now, seein' as how I'd just buried it, just the other werewolves I now knew existed around Elk's Run. Comstock had told me of Luna, and the Crescent Ranch to the North, though I hadn't seen any of his men, unless they were the ones eyeing me hard when I came back into town yesterday. When I'd finished concealing the graves as best I could, I said a few words over the bodies.

I'd planted Sheriff Garrett and Deputy Harrell some distance from the others, and I let the werewolves lay as they were. I didn't figure they'd be having too comfortable a time of it right now, though I couldn't recall hearing a single scripture forbidding the turning of one's self into a wolf. I was going based on the whole eating children and drinking the blood of men affair as I discerned their spiritual condition.

In the end it didn't matter much to me. I was happy enough to send Judd on his way, the good Lord could sort them out all by his lonesome.

I mounted my horse and rolled a smoke, and it tasted good, the best I'd had in a while. I started all three of the other horses back to town before riding on. There was plenty of sign left, and I figured the pack would be able to sniff out the bodies, but they didn't have any reason to know anything had happened yet, or where it had. Sooner or later though, they were sure to notice two of their number missing, and they'd come looking. If they'd killed Comstock over hiring me, I knew they'd come looking for me first. I'd best be prepared when they did.

***

IT WAS ALMOST DARK WHEN I RODE TOWARD TOWN. I looped around and came in from the west, listening to the wolves howling in the distance. I used to like the sound before, but now it gave me the creeps, as I didn't know what kind of wolves were making the sound. I knew the full moon was an important part of this, and it was waning now; another week and a half, give or take, 'til it filled out again. I was tired from the exertions of the day. I had buried the bodies deep, which after the drubbing I'd taken, had turned out to be exhausting work.

I didn't dare go to bed yet, not without having some sort of plan in mind to deal with what was coming. I'd cheated death several times over the last few days and killed two werewolves. I'd also fought a grizzly with a knife, horsewhipped a reprobate, met a woman who turned my insides out in a good way, busted up a giant with my fists, and done a good turn for a child who surely needed it. I was sure there was a wildly exaggerated dime novel in my future if anyone ever took the time to chronicle my exploits. Well, at the least I'd be able to say I'd had an eventful life, even if it ended in the next few days.

I had no illusions about the odds that lay ahead of me. I'd come an inch from death each time I'd faced off with a single werewolf, and sooner or later I'd be facing a pack of them. A body needs to talk to someone when he's facing those kinds of odds, and it's even better if it's a beautiful woman. My stitches were itching something fierce, so I had a good excuse.

I tied my horse up in front of the hotel, and gathered my Colt lightning and double-barreled shotgun from my room. I darted in between the alleyways, turning up my collar against the cold wind as I made my roundabout way to the schoolhouse. It was full dark now, and I was sure I wouldn't be seen, so I simply knocked on the door. A peek through the curtain, and then it opened. I was never happier to see a pretty face in my life.

Liz ushered me in quickly, and when she shut the door behind me I all but collapsed into the nearest chair. I took out the pocket flask and guzzled the rest of its contents. She looked at me quietly, but with concern written plain on her face. I chalked that up to one of her virtues. A woman shouldn't bother a man when he was drinking. Impressed with her etiquette, I told her why I'd come. She knew there was something on my mind but kept quiet as she helped me off with my shirt, noting the fresh bruises all over my face and body.

She sat me down in the same overstuffed, comfortable chair and lit some candles for light. Then she went straight to work with a thin pair of scissors, cutting away the stitches and pulling the ends out with a pair of tweezers. To my credit, I only flinched a little. She pretended not to notice, God bless her.

I related the events of the day from start to finish, leaving out, of course, the part where I got my tail end handed to me by Judd. I didn't think it counted if the man you fought had supernatural powers, did it? She listened the whole time and even fetched me a glass while I spoke, and filled it full of whiskey so I could keep my whistle wet. This gal had new and endearing charms every time I saw her.

"Thorn?" she said when I had finished speaking.

"Yes?"

"Are you going to be leaving now?" This girl had me dead to rights, that was for sure. That was the big question now, wasn't it? Only a madman would stick around for the backlash that I knew was coming, and a week ago I would have hightailed it out of town without a second thought.

Some part of me felt I had to stay, had to set things right, though I couldn't tell you why. I suppose I felt somewhat responsible for what was coming, though that wasn't it either. By my way of thinking, folks had a duty to look after themselves. If anything, I had helped them out with a few of their problems, and the people of Elk's Run could see their own selves the rest of the way without my help. But then I'd run off after that sheriff, risking my own hide even further in a vain attempt to save his life, all while he'd been looking for cause to have a hemp party in my honor. Somethin' was happening to me.

What my head was thinking and what I was feeling inside were two very different things though. I was both cursing myself for a fool and feeling a stab of pride that I was considering sticking around for someone else's benefit. I took another drink of the liquor and looked down into those pleading, hopeful eyes, and pathetic as it sounds, my decision was made then and there. I couldn't justify it, even to myself, but I was definitely going to stay in Elk's Run, come what may, and die both bravely, and a fool.

CHAPTER 5

LIZ CAME TO ME IN THE NIGHT, WEARING A SMALL black petticoat. She straddled me and held my head roughly in her hands. Her lips were sweet, and her kisses tasted good, just like I'd imagined they would. She smelled of expensive eastern perfumes and her hair felt like silk. She nuzzled my ear, and it tickled a little, but I wasn't complaining. I felt my heartbeat rise and my breathing grow heavy. Hers was too. She gave me a coy smile and stepped off me and back.

I was about to protest when I saw what she meant to do. She lifted the petticoat in one motion and tossed it off to the side like it was a rag. I took a deep breath. She was just as I'd pictured. What held me though were her eyes, soft and warm. She gave me a soft smile, and then she spoke.

"Take me," she whispered with fierce intensity, and I sprang out of the chair and seized her like an animal, planting kisses all over her mouth, her face, her neck, her collarbone, until she grabbed me by my hair and forced my head up to look deep into her eyes. Her voice, when she spoke, was breathy and sensual.

"Two plus two equals four, two plus four equals six, two plus six equals ..." I awoke with a start. Looking about me, I saw I was still in the back room of the schoolhouse, where Liz lived. My head ached terribly, and I saw the bottle in front of me, empty. She must have let me drink myself to sleep in the chair, and thought the better of awakening me before her class started. I could hear the pupils droning on with their math formulas, and the sound was grating. The sun was peeking over the mountains out the window, and Liz had drawn the curtains and opened the windows to let in the fresh air.

I'd never had much schooling, having too much to do on the potato farm where I grew up, though I read everything I could get my hands on since that time. The sound of the students reciting their lectures was more than I could bear this early, and I was resolved to escape as soon as possible.

I couldn't simply walk out through the classroom, as amusing of a picture as that would make. I had to think of Liz's reputation, again, though I wasn't going to spend the day locked up here in the back; I had too much to do. The window was already open, so I took careful glances out it from every which way, staying well back for fear of being seen. Satisfied that my passage would go unobserved by whatever fine townsfolk would be wandering about industriously at this hour, I gathered myself and launched through the open window, rolling as I hit the ground. Okay, I tumbled more than rolled, but there was no one watching.

As soon as I came to the stop I injuned my way through the brush, trying to keep my clothes from getting too dirty. This was, after all, my last set. When I was far enough away, I rose from the brush and walked into the town proper, just good old Thorn Carlson, most recent addition to the fine, upstanding townsfolk of Elk's Run, out for his morning constitutional. I was hungry and had some serious thinking to do, which would have to wait until after breakfast.

I'd left my double-barreled shotgun at Liz's place, dimly remembering having explained to her how it worked, and a little more clearly remembering her showing me she could load, unload, and load it again in less than two seconds. She did it faster than I could've, and I'd practiced with it extensively. I remember being quite impressed, and for good reason. All of this reminded me of my promise to teach William how to shoot. I'd need to, and soon, before I got myself killed. I'd hate to die with unfulfilled promises on my soul, regardless of whatever other dirt was already there.

Breakfast at the hotel consisted of two silver dollar-sized flapjacks on either side of a mess of fried eggs and bacon, sprinkled liberally with syrup, a combination I found delectable. I could hold it in one hand and my coffee in another, which was most convenient. I'd have to ask Mrs. Salsbury to make them again, if I lived long enough.

I kept glancing toward the door, half expecting to see a pack of huge wolves come barreling down the street, devouring all in their wake. I very much doubted they'd appear that way, or that they would come so soon, but I held the silver knife in my boot and my guns ready, just in case.

It was problematic that I could not shoot them and expect to do much damage. My best hope lay in getting them one by one and incapacitating them long enough to stab them. I could feel an idea right there, lurking about in the shadows of my brain, but I needed more coffee to dislodge it from its hiding place.

Two cups later I'd found it. I would make silver bullets. I still had to figure out where I would get the silver and how I would then make it into bullets, yet I was nevertheless impressed with my own genius.

I had a long day ahead of me and some figuring to do before I started working, so I decided to think it over while I took William shooting. My day's plans laid out in front of me, I rose from breakfast happy and alert, ready to tackle the challenges in front of me head-on.

As if fate herself had heard my thoughts and decided to punish me for my hubris, I stepped outside to see the dour countenance of a giant staring at me. It was the big man I'd beaten days ago, and he was sitting on the bench outside of the hotel, waiting for me. If he'd come for another fight, he'd get worse than the last time. I was fit now and almost healed, the beating I got yesterday notwithstanding.

"Thorn Carlson?" he asked with respect.

"Yes?" I was still waiting for him to take a swing at me with one of those massive fists.

"I've been to see my brother. Told him what happened. He told me you were a fair man, and he don't hold no grudges." The big man looked down at his boots and grinned.

"He also told me if he wasn't locked up he'd take me by the ear, beat the tar out of me, and make me apologize." That sounded about like Shamus. He was a few inches shorter and a few pounds lighter than the man standing in front of me, and I still remembered our fight. The reward was bigger for taking him in alive, and so I'd challenged him to a fistfight in a saloon down south, and it took a good hour of the worst punching, kicking, and biting I'd ever experienced before I'd pounded him into unconsciousness and nearly died in the process.

"What I'm tryin' to say is ... I come to apologize." The big man looked sincere, staring down into his beard and worrying the brim of his Stetson in both hands. I didn't think this was a trap.

"No need. I would have done the same for my brother."

The giant looked up suddenly, no longer embarrassed.

"Really?" he asked under raised eyebrows.

"Really," I confirmed.

"I say, will you shake?" I was still wary, more out of habit than honestly doubting his intentions.

If he was setting me up, as soon as he took hold my hand he'd make his move. If he did, I was prepared to draw with my left and blow his brains out of the back of his skull. I was in no mood to soak up another beating.

I stuck out my hand to meet his. "Warren McMasters," he said by way of introduction. My hand hurt a little, but I could tell he hadn't tried to crush me out of malice; he was just a bear of a man.

"How is your brother?"

"Good, they only gave him five years. He expects to escape before winter."

I laughed. "That's Shamus all right!"

He put on his hat, tipped it to me, and made his way across the street over to the saloon. I continued to the stables, where I found William hard at work. My steel dust was happy to see me. I could tell from his eyes he wanted to get out and tear up the countryside, but that wasn't going to happen. I was just glad I hadn't brought him with me over the last few days. We'd been together so long it was like we were partners, and I would hate myself if I'd gotten him killed at the hands of some beast. I'd wait 'til I really needed him to use him.

William was busy hauling bales of hay up into the loft, already preparing for winter, even though it was far off. I'd brought the Winchester with me, and I held it out to him. He dropped the hay bale and gave me a big grin, which was worth more than the price I paid for the rifle, ages ago it seemed.

"Ready to learn how?" I asked. His shining eyes told me yes. We marched off toward the woods, but stopped well within sight off the town. For obvious reasons, I didn't want to get too far out. I'd brought a few tin cans, and these I placed about fifty yards away on a stump.

William learned how to load the gun quickly, and I let him take a few shots to find out how well he could aim. On his fifth try, he nicked one of the cans, sending it spinning off into the grass. He would have to do better.

Taking a stick, I drew in the dirt a picture of how the sights should look when lined up. He nodded, and commenced to hit the other two, though it took a full seven rounds to get there.

We spent a good hour there, me teaching him how to breathe correctly and the best way to relax and use his own bones for support. He picked it up well enough, and by the time we were out of ammo he was able to hit three for three, though none of them were dead center. I had given him the basics though, and he would be able to practice on his own from now on.

During that time I'd been thinking some but hadn't figured out a good way to put the silver into the bullet itself. I hated to ask Liz for help, even though she was an educated woman who might just have an idea or two in that regard. I don't suppose they taught much about bullets in those eastern schools, but she might just have an idea based on something she knew. Perhaps that was why I didn't want to ask.

I left William with the rifle and walked over to the general store. I made a show of looking at a new set of clothes, which I needed, but I was really wracking my brain for something that would make a bullet into silver, quick like.

The store keep must've thought I was really fussy about my duds, but an hour later I walked out with two pairs of trousers, three shirts, a string tie with a silver snake set into it, and a pair of long beeswax candles.

A short trip to the saloon, where I weaved in and out between groups of cowhands having fistfights, and I had a bottle of very questionable-looking whiskey to fortify me for the evening's work.

It seemed the place was rowdier than usual, being the sheriff wasn't around. A pair of women in long dresses and frumpy hats walked by, gossiping about the lawmen's absence. I was just glad no one had seen fit to point the finger at me yet.

All in all, Sheriff Garrett and his deputies had only been missing for a day, and though his absence was noted, there was no cause for anyone to be overly suspicious. A few days would bring that, I was sure.

In the meantime, the cat was away and the mice were already playing. One brawl was already spilling out into the street by the time I reached the hotel. Being a man who likes entertainment, I set my goods down on a bench and watched.

Two cowhands were rolling in the dust, throwing punches and butting heads like a pair of rams. Some of the less reputable women in town followed them out of the bar, watching and even offering advice. Before long a crowd was forming, and people brought their drinks outside, hollering and whooping while the battle raged. One of the cowboys, a long, lean fellow, had gotten a hold on the other's shirttails and ripped it up and over his opponent's face, covering his vision. The other cowboy was shorter but stouter and continued to throw wild punches. He wasn't connecting much and was taking quite a beating in the process. Guess that's what happens when you can't see who you're trying to hit.

After some moments, the blinded cowhand managed to free himself, and the tables were turned. They went to the ground again, but the shorter man was on top now and beating the other's face to a pulp. They rolled some and came up separate, circling each other and breathing like a blown horse.

They continued to shout at each other, and some very unpleasant things were said, ancestries called into question, lineages besmirched. The two men were too out of breath to keep fighting, but they managed to spout insults instead.

One decided he had enough and went for his gun. They fired at each other, and fortunately the crowd either ducked behind cover or dove to the ground. Bullets ricocheted off walls and windows crashed. It was over awful quick, but the air was still, and so I rolled a cigarette and lit it, waiting for the thick smoke to clear.

When it did, the two cowboys were rising, and I looked them over some. One had been nicked across the inside of his shirt, and the other had two creases bleeding on his right thigh. Nothing serious.

They went for each other, guns empty, and just when I thought they were goin' to start slugging, they fell all over each other, suddenly best friends. Apparently the exercise hadn't sobered them any, and I watched as they went inside and blew a month's pay buying drinks for the whole bar. I could have stayed in the saloon. But I had work to do.

A minute later I had my things laid out on the bed, and I took a long pull off the whiskey and set to. I hated to do it, but I drained the flask and took out my knife, shaving small chunks off the finely engraved surface. A few minutes later I had a nice little pile of silver flakes, and I set to work on the bullets. The soft lead bored out well enough, though it was a careful job, working my knife into the points to hollow them out some. I slipped once in a while, cutting my fingers and cursing.

Two hours later I had thirty of the bullets laid out on the dresser, each with a hollowed-out tip. I pinched a bit of the small silver shards into each hole, then poured wax from the candle over the top to seal it in.

While that dried, I went to work on the shotgun shells. I carefully opened them up with my knife and removed the lead pellets. Going to work on the flask again, the blade hacked larger pieces of silver until the vessel was a ragged, chipped mess. I had a few handfuls of the chips, most about the size of buckshot, though it would be lighter by far. Any shots I made with the scattergun would have to be close, or the lighter metal would lose its power quickly, and with the ragged pieces I was loading into the paper shells, would probably fly all over the place. It was a start though.

I closed up the shells once I had them full of silver, and poured a little bit of wax over the top of each. This I smeared around with my finger, and they looked good as new. The flask was mostly gone, but I stowed it in my saddlebags, figuring I'd make some more when I got the chance.

That task accomplished, I finished the rest of the bottle, and before I knew it, I was asleep.

I woke with a start. There was gunfire outside, though from the cheering and laughter I knew it wasn't serious. Probably just a few hands in town, deciding to have some more fun. It was early evening, and I'd fallen asleep around two in the afternoon. My stomach growled suddenly, reminding me I'd been neglecting it.

A meal at Ma's Kitchen sounded like just the thing. Pulling on my boots, it was mere moments before I was crossing the street to the diner. A group of cowboys were racing along the main street, their friends at the end taking bets and exchanging money. A few of them drew and fired into the air as the contestants crossed the finish line drawn in the dirt. This sure was a lively town, come an evening.

Maybe too lively. A pair of women were trying to walk past the saloon but were stopped by three men. The ladies tried to walk around them, but they found their way blocked by wide shoulders under broad-brimmed hats. My anger burned in me. I didn't get involved much in others' affairs as a rule, but no western man likes to see decent women mistreated. The men circled around the pair of frightened women, laughing and making crude remarks. They were obviously well into their bottles, but it was no excuse in my book.

There were some who would have called out and told them to stop. Not me. In my mind, they'd already crossed a line, and it was time for action, for punishment. There was a wagon parked out in front of the hotel, filled with goods from the general store. A few axe handles, made of solid hickory, caught my eye.

I snatched one of them up and crossed over to the damsels in distress.

"Hey!" I called, and all three of the men turned to look at me. I caught the first one across the forehead, and was glad I did. I surely would've killed him if I'd struck anywhere else. I was only looking to teach a lesson, after all. The other two were caught by surprise, eyes wide at my sudden assault. I jabbed the next in the stomach before bringing the handle up with both hands, catching him under the jaw with the middle of it. He went down in a heap. The third leaped at me, and I cracked the handle across his thigh as he came. He staggered, and I rapped him lightly across the cheek with the wood just to make sure I had his attention. Seizing him by the shirt, I hauled him up close and snarled at him through gritted teeth.

"Why, you no-good snake!" I bellowed.

"We didn't mean nothing fella! We was just funning, that's all!"

"Well, you can find somewhere else to do your 'funning' then!"

I slugged him hard across the jaw, then heaved him up over my shoulder into the trough outside the saloon. He went in headfirst, making a tremendous splash. I stood with my fists clenched, seething between my teeth as I waited for any of them to make a move.

The one I threw in the trough came up sputtering, and the other two were sitting up, hands on their heads, trying to focus.

"Where you boys from?" I demanded, still raging.

"We ride for the crescent!" The first one I'd hit was the one that spoke.

He glared up at me, but didn't try to rise. If he had, I'd have knocked him into next week. After a moment, I was sure they weren't going to do anything, and I turned and started walking back to the hotel. I had forgotten all about my meal in my rage, and besides, I was in no mood to eat now.

A sudden scream rang out, high and shrill. I whirled around and saw the cowhand still in the trough, clutching his hand and splashing around in the water. A mountain of a man stood next to him, thumbs in his belt, grinning.

"Evenin', Thorn. This'un decided to draw on you, soon's your back was turned. I don't think anyone would blame you right now if you shot him dead."

If I was mad before, I was livid now. Red swarmed before my eyes as I crossed over to the trough. I kicked the other two cowboys back to the ground, and seized the last one out of the water by his hair. He was howling and gripping his hand, but I had no pity in me.

Using all my might, I slammed his face up against one of the posts holding up the walkway, again and again. This little cur tried to backshoot me, and just for a little beating, which he deserved.

I didn't stop for a good while, and when I let him go, he fell limp in a puddle of his own blood. Warren walked up to me, slowly.

"Reckon we oughta stash these ones somewhere for the night. Sheriff's gone, but the cell there should do just fine."

"Fine," I answered, my voice cold. We picked them up, me carrying the one closest to me and Warren shouldering the other two like they were children. We stowed them in the cell and locked it. I tossed him the keys.

"Do me a favor and let them out in the morning, will you? I don't think they'll be very happy to see me, and I don't feel like having to kill anyone. Not before breakfast anyway."

Warren smiled at my joke. I considered for a moment. A man had tried to kill me tonight, take a shot at me while my back was turned, and Warren's stomping on his hand might've been the only thing between me and an early grave. He'd saved my life.

"Thanks, Warren, for what you did back there."

He looked surprised, then nodded at me, grinning shyly. Big man and all, I don't think he'd gotten much praise or thanks for anything in his life, the way he reacted. Given what I already knew of his family, I wasn't surprised. I left the big man at the jail blushing, and walked back over to the diner. Now that I'd had time to settle down some, I was twice as hungry as before. I could see through the windows that the diner was full to bursting, and a chalkboard outside said fried catfish was being served. Well, that sounded mighty good, both to me and my stomach, cause it rumbled in approval. I walked in and looked around for a place to sit.

I nearly jumped out of my skin and back out the door when I heard the sudden noise. For a moment I'd thought someone had started shooting. Instead, it was a round of thundering applause. Everyone was looking at me. I saw the two ladies I'd aided some minutes before standing in one corner, and I guessed they'd told the story. I'd never had anybody clap for me before.

Suddenly I felt a mite sheepish, just standing there, not knowing what to do. I hoped I looked presentable. Liz was taking her meal in the corner, but I saw her beaming at me with what looked like pride.

My face got real hot then, and I wanted to back out quietly and head straight for the saloon. I stood there awkwardly as the applause died down, and looked about for a seat. A few fellows I didn't know stood up and clapped me on the back or the shoulder as I squeezed between the packed tables, which I found irritating, but it seemed impolite to object. In fact, I just plain didn't know what to do about the whole situation. It felt kind of good, but I was unused to such attention.

I didn't know if I should sit down by Liz or not. She sat

by herself, but I didn't know what people would think if I just moseyed on over and plopped down next to her, so I grabbed a chair on the other end of the room. She looked down suddenly, and then set to picking at her food. She'd been looking awful approving just a moment ago, and I wondered what I'd done wrong. Women.

The catfish was good, and I had double portions, but when I went to pay they wouldn't accept my money. Well, that was something I could get used to. I looked around, but Liz was gone. I felt a sudden urge to drop by her place for a visit, but didn't know if I should. She looked mighty disappointed the last I saw of her, though I didn't know what had caused it.

Once again I was reminded of how little I understood the ways of women. Good women at least. I could track an outlaw across bare rock, and read the woods and men of the West like a book, but I had to confess I was out of my depth with this sort of creature. I desperately wanted to see her, just to see those big brown eyes and that pretty smile she had for me, but I also wanted to treat her right, and I worried that our association would reflect poorly upon her. I figured most folks wouldn't want the woman who taught their children their readin' and arithmetic to be seen consortin' with the likes of me, least ways, not going to the schoolhouse after dark. Perhaps I should call on her tomorrow, like a proper gentleman would.

Turns out I'm no gentleman. Ten minutes later, after casting a much wider trail than I probably needed too, I was waiting in the dark beyond her back door. She had the curtains drawn, and she was painting something. I couldn't make out what was on the canvas, but she was moving the brush with light, elegant strokes, and I thought she looked very striking in the candlelight.

I watched her for a while, and then for some reason the watching made me feel kind of guilty and uncomfortable, like some kind of coyote out in the darkness. I kept watching through the window though as I walked up and reached out a hand to knock softly on the door. She looked up in surprise, then started blowing softly, almost frantically, on the paint before throwing a cloth over top of it.

What was she hiding? She gathered her brushes and paints and shoved them in a drawer, then ran in a frenzy throughout the room, picking up odd things here and there and straightening them where they lay. She rushed over to a mirror, and then started fluffing her hair, scowled, and tied it back quickly with a ribbon. She made a few faces in the glass, bared her teeth and peered closely, then finally took a deep breath, put on an easy smile, and came for the door. I didn't know what to make of it all.

I leaped back and stood casually before she opened the door. She gave me a bright smile then looked around outside before ushering me in. I was a little tense, having seen her a minute earlier.

"I'm glad you came," she said finally.

"Well, I guess we're both glad." I suddenly realized I hadn't thought of an excuse for needing to see her. This was going to be awkward.

"So what brings you around at this hour?"

Damn. I was hoping for at least a moment or two to come up with something believable. Instead, I said the first thing that came to mind. "Uh, I wanted to ask you about bullets."

"About ... bullets?" She looked down quickly, and there was a moment, just a moment, of frustration in her eyes. I guess it was the wrong thing to say, but I didn't know what she was looking for, that's for sure.

"Sure," she said evenly, "I can't say I know much about ballistics, but what's your question?"

I didn't know what she meant by "ballistics," as I'd never heard the term before. I'd picked up more than a few twenty-dollar words just by reading though, and I figured it must have something to do with bullets.

"Uh, well, I tried to make some out of silver today, and I was wondering if you thought it would work on the were-wolves." My voice sounded lame, and she didn't really seem to be focused on what I was saying. She was looking me over, and I was hoping I still looked neat and clean, after the fight I'd been in. Maybe it was time for another bath.

"Well, I don't see why they wouldn't. Who knows? Why don't you have a seat. Would you like a drink?" I sure did.

"I do," I said, and she disappeared for a moment while she fetched me one. I took the opportunity to do something I knew I shouldn't. I couldn't help it. The painting was right by me, and it would only take a second to have a peek. It felt wrong, but I just couldn't help myself. I threw the black cloth back in a flash.

My mouth dropped open. The painting showed a tall, wide-shouldered man in high boots and a black hat. He wore a white shirt, torn in several places, and open at the front, displaying a well-muscled chest and flat stomach. The man's eyes seemed to dance with dangerous laughter, and he held a smoking six-gun at his side. Mountains stretched out behind him, tinted blue.

His pose suggested some kind of triumph, as if he'd just won a fierce battle. The face was mine. There was no doubt about it. I'd had more than one woman tell me I was a handsome man, but when I looked in the mirror come a morning, I didn't see anything like this fellow. He looked ... heroic.

That the face was supposed to be mine, I had no doubt, but I couldn't credit the way Liz obviously saw me. I was speechless. Footsteps, coming back in the room, I flung the cloth back over the painting, but it landed all wrong. There was not time to adjust it, as she was stepping back into the room. I hoped she didn't notice.

No such luck. The first thing her eyes went to was the painting, covered haphazardly now by the black cloth. She seemed to miss a step, but didn't say anything. She wouldn't meet my eyes, even when she handed me my drink. Her cheeks turned a shade of red normally reserved for sunsets, and I think I was blushing a little too, for the second time this evening.

We sat, awkwardly, and studied our feet. I took a long drink for fortification. I was sure she was going to lay into me good for spying on her artwork. She didn't. I was trying to think of something to say when she spoke.

"People ... they liked what you did tonight."

"Wasn't anything special, I'm sure plenty of others would have stepped in. I just happened to be the one that was there at the time."

"Not with those three they wouldn't. Do you know who they were?"

I shrugged. "Said they rode for the Crescent Ranch."

"That was Tom Macklin, Freddy Bolan, and Dake Peters you beat up tonight."

The names didn't mean anything to me. All I thought of was that they rode for the Crescent Ranch, Luna's ranch, and I figured I had trouble coming with them anyway. Liz looked worried.

"Those three, they cause trouble every time they come to town. A month ago they killed some of the Bar T hands, over a saloon rat named Peggy Summers. Macklin's the worst. He's the one that tried to take a shot at you. Bolan and Peters follow him, do whatever he says. I saw it happen. Macklin shot two of the hands down, even though they drew first. Two others tried to step in for the other Bar T men, but Freddy and Dake gunned them down where they stood."

"Well, I'll be sure to keep on my guard then, all right?"

"Please do that, Thorn. I ... I don't want anything to happen to you." She looked off into the distance when she spoke, then suddenly her gaze met mine. Her lips looked moist and a fire burned in her eyes.

"Thorn?" she spoke, softly.

"Yes, Liz?"

"Are you going to kiss me, or what?"

I did.

CHAPTER 6

I'D JUST FINISHED MY BREAKFAST WHEN I HEARD the news. The town was all abuzz, everyone talking about the bodies found on the road just past town: the sheriff, his two deputies, and another man, apparently known as Trevor Dawson. Homer had referred to him as the first werewolf I'd killed. This was bad news. I figured they'd find the bodies sooner or later, and figure out who to blame.

I mulled the recent developments over in my mind as I rolled and lit a cigarette on the bench outside the hotel. Everyone was walking around talking about it to whoever would listen, so I had no need to see them for myself. After thinking it over for a while, it seemed to me the news wasn't as bad as I'd first thought.

One, it seemed to me this was a message, though a vague one. If I had to guess, and I did, I'd say it was intended to show that someone knew what had happened. The other important fact was that someone probably didn't know who to blame, as of yet. Having the sense of smell of a wolf, I'd figured they'd trail me back to town and find me easily. Now, I held out hope they wouldn't be able to identify my scent after so long, and I'd been there when it snowed. That snow had long melted, and it was unlikely they'd be able to identify me specifically.

Still, they must either know or suspect someone in town had done the deed, and that meant sooner or later there'd be hell to pay. Once again I damned myself for a fool for having decided to stay here in town. My thoughts were broken when a wiry, bespectacled man sat down on the bench next to me. "Mr. Thorn Carlson? I'm Harry Rainwater. I own the general store, and the people of Elk's Run have voted me mayor for the last five years running. Pleased to make your acquaintance."

I hadn't seen him before, but I immediately decided I didn't like his put-on smile or his greasy, smooth tone. Elk's Run might be a small, one-horse town, but I guess politicians are the same everywhere you go. When he saw I didn't reply, he shrugged his thin shoulders and went on.

"As you might have heard, there's been a tragedy in town. It might seem callous, but part of my job is to see the good people of this town are provided for, and that means we will need a new sheriff ..." He trailed off, studying my face. The look he must have seen there was likely less than pleasant. I thought I knew where this was headed, and I didn't like it, not one bit.

"Thorn, if I may call you that? Folks in town seem impressed with you, and even though you're new here, I think you've got the sand to make a fine officer of the law. What do you say?"

I didn't say anything, just thought it over a bit. Even though I supposed it wasn't too far off from my current profession, I'd never wanted to be a peace officer, wear a star, or spend my nights corralling rowdy drunks in town, though when I thought about it, I'd been doing exactly that, but without getting paid for it. I'd decided to stay and see things out, and the good people of Elk's Run could at least pay me for my time and trouble. Still, the idea rankled me. Lawmen had never really cottoned to me, or I to them. I decided to sit on it, maybe sleep on it – a few times. Maybe the idea would grow on me.

"Well, we'd all appreciate it if you'd think it over and let me know when you're ready."

The mayor walked away after giving me that big fake smile of his, and I was glad to see him go. I decided my mind could use some lubrication if I was going to think about something like this, and I crossed over to the saloon.

A nice, tall glass of beer or two later, and things were working pretty well, or so I thought. The people inside gave me a wide berth and left me to drink in peace. I'd made up my mind, and that was that. I had no business being a sheriff, at least, not any more than I did being a preacher. I was no lawman, just a drifting bounty hunter. I didn't want to get tied down, and there truly was no reason for me to. I'd talk to Liz tonight, and tell her she could either come with me or stay, but I was leaving. Had I lost my mind, telling her I'd stick around for a fight I had nothing to gain from? It seemed likely I had, but a woman pretty as that can do things to a man's reason, and mine was clearly impaired. In fact, perhaps it would be best to just jump on my steel dust and head out of town at a gallop.

First I would take a look at those new wanted posters in the sheriff's office, and see who my next ... but my thoughts were interrupted as I was crossing the street by the sound of hoof beats. Looking up, I saw seven lathered horses trotting into town. On those seven horses were seven hard-looking men, dressed in long rider's jackets and wide-brimmed hats. I didn't need to study them to know they hunted trouble; it was in the air all around them.

They all carried rifles in their saddle scabbards, and wore guns like they knew how to use them. They stopped several yards away from me, right in the middle of the town.

"People of Elk's Run!" The man in the middle shouted the words like a threat. He was obviously tall, broad shouldered, and heavy handed. He had a deep-lined face, and it looked like he shaved his head to the scalp. His icy green eyes seemed almost to glimmer as he looked around. I thought I knew who he might be.

"The other day my brother came up missing, and I come into town to see he's been murdered and laid in the street like some kind of animal! I don't know who's responsible, but I'll find you, sooner or later, whichever one of you it is. In fact, I've a good mind to burn this place to the ground, right now! If anyone knows who did it, now would be a good time to come forward, before things get ugly!"

Great. This must be Luna, owner of the Crescent brand, and the man (or wolf) I'd killed had been his brother. That I didn't know. The townsfolk all had their faces pressed up against whatever glass they could find, but no one dared step out into the street. Just so happened that I was the only one visible, standing out in front of the seven angry men with murder on their minds.

It was not where I wanted to be. The speaker turned his gaze to me, standing there all by my lonesome in the street. I'm no shrinking violet, but he looked at me as if I were a little lost lamb and he was the big, bad wolf. Being that he was, as far as I knew, actually a big, bad wolf made the picture all the more vivid in my mind. We stood there for a moment, staring at each other. I didn't just glare – I took the time to make what calculations and mental preparations I could if things got nasty.

I was wearing only my six-gun along with my ever-present derringer. That left me with eight shots. One for each, give or take one. I knew enough to know that it's a lot harder to make hits count when someone's shooting back at you, I don't care who you are. The other part of that is the men in front of me might all have a good dose of that wolf magic, or whatever it was, and that would make them a lot harder to kill.

I was glad I had my silver bullets, but doubted I'd even get to fire more than one or two of them before they shot me down. Seven against one is not good odds for a close-range gunfight, that's for sure. The man looked me over with his brutal eyes for another moment, then sniffed the air. He closed his eyes and inhaled slowly, and I noticed, to my consternation, that the wind was at my back, giving him a good whiff of me.

I wished it had been a long time since I showered and that I'd just eaten a plate of beans. His eyes snapped open, and I swear he almost went for his gun right then. A moment of blazing intensity writ large across his face, then he seemed to relax and gave me a toothy grin.

"New around here, aren't you?"

It wasn't really a question. I nodded.

"I don't know, but for some reason, you just seem …" He paused and gave the air a pointed sniff. "Familiar."

His face grew serious as he spat the last word. I knew what he was doing, of course. He was letting me know he'd pegged me for the one that killed his brother. He'd know for sure if I gave any sign I understood what he was saying. Regular killers don't worry about other regular folk catching their scent of course. I admit I felt a cold thrill of fear crawling up my spine. This made me mad though, and when I do get mad, really mad, I tend not to think of the consequences. Besides, he knew I was the one, and there was nothing I could do to avoid that now. I'd just have to play the cards as dealt and hope I had an ace somewhere I'd forgotten about.

A couple of them unconsciously flexed their gun hands, and I figured I didn't have more than a moment before this got settled by gunplay. Knowing the probable results of that, I tried a different tack. It wasn't a card I wanted to play, but if I didn't play it now I might not live to get the chance.

"You must be Luna, right?" I tried to give my most disarming smile. The trick here was not to seem afraid. I had to make them think there was something they didn't know in the mix and put them off balance.

"I heard of you. The Crescent Ranch, right?" I smiled and stepped closer.

A few of the men with him glanced at each other, probably trying to decide if I was just an idiot who didn't have enough sense to know he was about to be gunned down in the street, or if somehow, I didn't have to be afraid. I was leaning toward the idiot explanation, myself. As I stepped closer, I could see a familiar pair of eyes looking at me out the general store window. *Liz. Damn.*

The only way I can explain what happened next is that when a man has feelings for a woman, her presence can give him a boost of courage, or perhaps, give him a little too much. It made me angry before, standing in the street by a gang of threatening men, but that was gone now. I felt no more fear, just indignation, and a little mischief thrown in to boot. I lowered my tone as I approached, and went with my gamble.

"You bunch look like men accustomed to handling things with bullets ..." I grinned, standing just in front of

Luna's horse.

"True. But there's other ways ... ," Luna whispered menacingly. I thought I saw his eyes flash a tiny glint of red, and standing so close to him, the only way I can describe it is he looked ... predatory.

"Well, did you ever see a silver bullet?" I let the question hang in the air and gave him a smile to match his. These men had most likely come to think of themselves as invincible, as I might if I had the power to turn into a bear-size wolf, heal almost instantly, and soak up lead like it was rain. But as hard as these men might be, they wouldn't cotton to the fact that someone might have a bullet that could end them as easily as a lead one used to, and I was counting on that to throw them off.

None of them looked like cowards, but when you get used to the idea you can't be killed, the idea of it happening becomes more than you're willing to deal with, or so I'd hoped. Luna's head shot back as if I'd struck him. The others had heard what I said, even though I'd whispered, and they were glancing at each other again, but nervously now.

"Bullshit," Luna spat when he'd recovered, but I saw the fear in his eyes. He might have been dead to rights, with his six riders to gun me down, but he'd know I could kill him first, and he wouldn't heal up.

"Care to try me? See if I'm being honest?" I said it easily, as if daring him to go for his gun. Luna and the others started looking about, and I could tell they didn't know what to make of it. Here they'd been expecting to tree the town, and when they'd seen me, they figured to have a little fun before shooting me dead in the street.

Now here I was, practically taunting them, and they wondered what I had up my sleeve. A few of them started

145

studying the windows and rooftops, as if I might have rifle-men stashed around town, ready to open fire. I thought it was a great idea and really wished I had some right then. Just then Luna sneezed, then started rubbing his nose.

The rest of them broke out a second later, sneezing, hacking and coughing. I didn't know what to make of it. It wasn't pollen or anything I knew of. The dry mountain air didn't tend to irritate most people that way. They looked confused and miserable suddenly, both at my revelation of having silver bullets and with whatever was afflicting them.

I could tell the surprise would wear off in a moment, and they might go for it anyway. I didn't plan on giving them the time. Taking one of the bullets off my belt, I tossed it up and told Luna, "Catch!" He dodged away instead of toward it, which let me know he believed me, and it was a good thing too, since I'd just thrown a regular old lead bullet. The rest were loaded into my guns.

In the moment he flinched, I threw my best right hook into his horse's jaw, and then backhanded the one to my right in the same spot.

A horse is a big, strong animal, but most people don't know they can be knocked out even more easily than a man. If you hit a horse right there on the side of the jaw, he'll drop like a rock, right there. I'd done it before, more than once in similar situations, though I always feel bad afterward. I like horses.

Luna's mount keeled over to the left, bumping and jostling the other horses, and they went down in a tangle. The same thing happened on the other side of the line, and so with two fast blows I had knocked all of them off their feet. If I'd had my lightning with me I might have gone for it then and tried to take them all, but I knew my chances were slim, lightly armed as I was.

I turned and walked away, doing my best to appear unconcerned while the men behind me cursed and tried to sort themselves out. Three of them were stuck under their animals, and it sounded like they'd broken one or the other of their legs. They were distracted enough not to notice me again 'til I was some distance down the street.

"This isn't over, you son of a bitch!" I ignored the voice and kept walking, cool as an October evening.

The sound of them galloping off reached my ears a moment later, then I let out a long breath. I hadn't realized I'd been holding it. They might have come after me, but I was ready to dash into the hotel and up the stairs so as to at least be able to meet them with my long gun and shotgun in hand, and then I could give them a fight. They'd been embarrassed and confused, so they'd left for now, but I knew they wouldn't be far.

I knew them for what they were, and I'd killed their leader's brother, apparently. Not much chance we'd be able to come to an understanding. I was sure they'd try for me tonight. I turned then and watched them ride away. I was hoping to see where they'd veered off into the woods to wait, but they left a cloud behind them, and I figured they'd move around some anyway.

Sitting on a bench outside the barbershop, I rolled a smoke and tried to look calmer than I felt. There were still people watching, and I wanted to at least be able to look like this was all no big deal. I wanted to vomit a little. Everyone was leaving their stores and places they'd holed up in, and now they crowded down the street in my direction. Leading them was the scrawny mayor, and they stopped when they reached me.

"Well folk, looks like we've got ourselves a new sheriff!" His arms spread wide, and he looked more like a circus ring-master than a mayor. I saw a circus once, down in Missouri. I was about to tell him what he could do with that job, since I certainly hadn't told him I'd take it, nor had I intended to. Liz was standing off to the side, and something in the way she looked at me then made all kinds of noble emotions leap and dance in my chest. I stood still while the mayor produced a silver star and pinned it to my shirt. The people actually cheered. Liz just beamed at me with her big brown eyes.

Aw, hell!

CHAPTER 7

MY FIRST ACT AS SHERIFF OF ELK'S RUN WAS TO go straight to the saloon and order two shots of whiskey. Liz had just given me a look that (I reckoned) meant to come by and see her later, then sauntered off. As much as I wanted to follow her home like a lost puppy dog, I had bigger issues on my mind. They were coming back, and soon. I figured they'd wait until evening, and I probably had until then to come up with a brilliant plan to save my hide.

They'd threatened and frightened the townsfolk before, but now they were entirely centered on me. I didn't know how many men Luna had all together, but the other six I took to be wolf men just like him. He'd most likely strike with what he had; the rest of his hands, fighting men or otherwise, would be unaware of his condition. It's probably hard to keep cowpokes on the payroll if they know you're an evil monster who changes into an animal and devours people and cattle whole.

The way I saw it I had three options. When you know someone means to kill you, the worst thing you can do is try to hole up and prepare for any eventuality. I needed to either seek them out and attack first, escape, or set up the time and place where they would attack me and have a trap laid when they did.

The first option didn't sound so great, as searching them out meant going scouting about in the woods, and they'd have me there. I was able to move and track through the forest like an Injun, but I figured they had the advantage with their senses, and I wouldn't get far. Escape was unlikely, even though I could draw them away from the town, but they'd find me pretty quick, and then they would just come back.

My last option was the best. I'd present a target and make them come just where I wanted them. But where? And how? That's where my brilliant plan would come in, as soon as I had it. William came running in moments later with a small brown paper parcel, tied up with twine.

"Mr. Thorn, it's for you!" he said, and he looked up at the star on my chest with wonder and something like awe.

"What is it? Who sent it?"

"You'll see when you open it. In private," he added.

"Okay. Thanks, William."

"No problem, see you later!" he called back as he ran out the door, back to work. I finished my drink and went back to the room. There weren't many angles where someone from outside of town could take a shot at me, but I was watchful nonetheless, and I checked each of them before I walked outside. Inside the room, I practically tore the paper off the package. Inside, there was a small leather pouch with a strong herbal odor, and a note. It read:

Thorn, Keep this with you, it's wolfs bane. I found some yesterday when I went out into the woods. Please don't be angry with me, but I thought it would help. I sprinkled some into the air today while you were talking to those men, and I don't think they liked it much. I think the star looks good on you. Please be careful. For my sake as well as yours.

Your Liz

Well, I'll be damned. I didn't know how I'd use it yet, but I was sure there would be a way. Liz hadn't listened and had gone back into the woods, which did make me mad. Still, the girl had grit and had found me something more I could use, and I needed every advantage. I liked that she had courage, but I didn't want her taking any foolish risks like that again. I'd have to visit her later, and have her draw me a picture of the plant. I'd harvest it myself if I needed to. First I let them pin a star on my chest, now I'd be picking flowers. Awful things can befall a man if he doesn't take care.

I put some of the crushed plant in my shirt pocket. If they got near me tonight without my knowing, maybe they'd sneeze or cough and buy me a precious second or two. The thought had occurred to me that I might need some help, but I didn't think for a minute anyone would believe me, or even if they did, do anything other than pack up and leave. Except for Liz, who I wanted involved as little as possible, I was on my own in this. It had always been my way, and so I'd play the hand as dealt and hope I could slip a few more aces into the deck.

The first problem was surviving the night. I couldn't sit back and hole up somewhere, with my guns loaded and ready. Sooner or later they'd find a way to come at me, and I'd be at a disadvantage. I'd have to take the fight to them and find some way to gain the upper hand. A plan began to form – risky – but perhaps it would work.

Not being one to waste time, I set about it immediately. I changed into a new set of clothes and carried the old ones under my arm as I went out to William's stable. I told him to have my steel dust saddled and ready to go at dusk. He didn't ask questions, just nodded and went about his business, grooming and feeding the horses. He had his hands full, and I was glad things were going well for him. There was some straw and hay behind the stable, and I stuffed the clothes full and buttoned them up. Before long I had a crude scarecrow. I stuffed a stick into the neck of the shirt, and hung my beloved black leather hat on it. I would need all the scent I could get on the dummy I'd made.

Now all I had to do was set back and wait for dusk. The waiting was a chore in itself, knowing I would be putting my life on the line tonight, and yet not being able to do anything more about it irked me. I lay down on my bunk for a nap, hoping to be well rested, but sleep didn't come easy. A few pulls of a bottle did the trick though, and I awoke just in time for a hearty meal. I was hoping it wouldn't be my last.

Dusk was settling over the valley now, and I didn't think I had long to set things in motion. They'd be itchin' to take a shot at me, and I'd give it to them, but on my terms. After a cup of strong black coffee and a smoke, I headed over to the stable where, sure enough, my steel dust was saddled and ready. He'd be at some risk tonight, but if any horse could handle himself, this was the one.

I threw William a dollar and walked the horse out back. I had the Colt lightning, my lever shotgun, and the extra pistol, all loaded full with my silver-tipped bullets. I was ready for action, come what may. I'd stowed the packet of wolfs bane in my shirt, and I sprinkled some out now and rubbed the horse down with it. I hoped it would keep the things from actually touching him, but I didn't know. He'd come straight for me if I whistled, and that was part of my plan tonight.

It was full dark now, but a bright moon was shining in the sky. It looked awful close up here in the mountains, and gave me as much light as I could ask for. It was a guess, but I'd figured if these men could smell like wolves, they could see like them too. I set my dummy on top of the horse as life-like as possible, loosely tying the reigns to the cuffs of the jacket sleeves. I had to hand it to myself, it looked pretty damn convincing.

I picked a few handfuls of grass and scrubbed my face and hands. My clothes were fresh, and I'd done all I could to obscure my scent. I checked my guns and took a deep breath. It was time. Giving the horse a slap on the haunches to send him walking, I stayed low and cat-footed it some distance back behind him, careful to keep my silhouette below the level of tall grass surrounding the town.

The trees were some distance off, and I figured they'd be in them. My guess was they'd be on the opposite side of town from where they'd left. If they figured I might run for it, it would make sense for me to leave in the opposite direction from their ranch and the way they'd last been seen going. I had hazarded a lot on guesses, but I'd taken action on less in the past, and I had no choice but to go with the best plan I could come up with.

A lot of men become paralyzed, not from fear but desire to have all the facts, and a sure advantage before they act. Sometimes it's best to risk boldly and trust yourself to roll with the circumstances, such as they are. I was awful nervous, out there in the night, with who knows how many enemies waiting somewhere in the dark. I tried to keep my breathing even and shallow, watching my horse's ears for any sign of danger.

A man learns to trust to his horse when in the wilderness, as he'll surely notice anything of consequence long before you do. The wind was blowing straight at us as we traveled

– me, my horse, and the silent straw man, hunched over the saddle. I saw his ears perk up when we were only fifty yards from the woods, and knew the moment was near. I dropped all the way to the ground and set down my rifle.

I would use the shotgun first, as aiming would be impossible. The rifle I would save for when things got close enough for me to just point and shoot. I was hoping things wouldn't get that close. I'd just gotten into position when the attack came.

Two long, loping figures materialized out of the woods, running fast. They were on four legs, big furry beasts that moved like dark water through the tall grass.

Before I could raise my gun and fire they were almost to the horse. They'd have expected any normal horse to just turn and try to run, but mine was no normal horse, no sir. I think he'd been bred in the stables of hell and just wandered off for me to find him, because as I've said before he was the meanest, most cantankerous and bad-natured animal I've rode. His eyes rolled and he snorted and turned, not away, but toward the beasts.

Lashing out with his hooves, he caught the first one in the head, sending him down with a whimper. The next one he charged straight on, riding him down. As fierce as he was, I knew he'd only had the element of surprise on his side, because the beasts were almost as large as he was, had fangs and teeth, or else I'd have happily set back and watched him do my dirty work. The steel dust pranced and tossed his head, then charged again. The angle was such that I could not fire without fear of hitting him. Damn!

The wolf he'd trampled had already risen, and the other looked like he was about to, shaking his head as if to clear it while the dent in his skull popped itself back into place and healed up. The one that was up dodged the charge and circled, while my horse wheeled to meet him, stabbing his hooves in the air and snorting threats. The next instant the other wolf leaped in a flash, taking the straw man off his back and to the ground in a flurry of claws and teeth. Bits of straw flew into the air, and I was glad it wasn't me.

I'd run up now, and I leveled the shotgun and let go a load of buckshot into the one that was still savaging the scarecrow. He whimpered, and I shot him again and then another time. I had to turn then, because the other was coming straight for me. I had large red fire bursts still in my vision from the muzzle blast, and I could barely make him out. I pulled the trigger, but he kept coming.

My horse saved me then, slamming into the charging wolf from the side, sending him sprawling end over end. I levered another shell into the chamber and whistled. While the horse ran to me, I fired off my last two shells, and from the sounds I knew each had struck home. Shoving it in the saddle scabbard, I leaped onto the horse and rode to retrieve my rifle. I swung from the saddle, barely managing to catch hold of it as we passed. Whirling now, I rode as close as I dared, and the two wolves were gaining their feet. They circled, one to each side, and I hoped they were wary enough of my horse now to keep their distance for a moment. Divide and conquer.

I leaped the steel dust at the one to my left, and fired, pumped, and fired again and again. I was shooting so fast it sounded almost like one continuous blast, watching the great beast jerk and twitch with every shot. My rifle clicked empty and he dropped, hopefully for good.

I turned just in time to throw myself from the saddle as the next one jumped at me, and watched him sail overhead as I hit the ground on my back. My horse was gone, and I spotted him knocked over on his side and struggling to get up at the same time I was. I made my feet just in time to see the dark blur shooting straight at me. I jumped to my left, but we still collided, and I was thrown hard to the ground. My vision doubled, and I knew I hit my head, hard. I'd been doing that a lot the last few days.

Suddenly the wolf loomed over me, blocking out the moon and starry sky. He huffed then, a sort of dog's laugh, and lunged in, his teeth bared. I shot out my arm, and it was the only thing that kept him from ripping out my throat. His teeth closed on it next to the elbow, and I felt the tremendous force of his jaws but no pain. With the sort of desperate strength a man gets when his life depends upon it, I held him back. He growled in anger and frustration, raising a clawed hand to the sky to tear me apart.

My free hand shot down then, and I worked one of my six-guns free. Slamming the barrel into his neck, I pulled the trigger six times before the teeth let go. He rolled off to the ground, shaking. I dropped the pistol and grabbed the other. Aiming carefully, I put two of the heavy slugs in his head. Let him try and heal that. The wounds were smoking slightly, but nothing like when I had stabbed the other with the silver knife.

I found the other one, lying in the grass some yards away. He was curled up and his wounds hadn't healed, but he wasn't dead yet. I gave him the same treatment as the other, and his brains leaked out onto the grass, sizzling. They were dead. The fight seemed like it had gone on for some time, and yet no others had shown up to join in. Surely if there were more, they would have heard the shots and come running. These creatures were fast, and would have been here by now to finish me off. I was alone.

A quick search of the woods beyond found me what I was looking for. Two horses were tied to a tree set well back, out of sight. I whispered softly to them and led them back to the scene of battle. They didn't like the smell of blood, but I managed to keep them calm.

One of them was a mare, and apparently she was in heat, a fact that was not lost on my stallion. Predictable events ensued, and so I was forced to stand, slowly watching the bodies of the wolves transform into two men I recognized from earlier. The steel dust had his dander up now, and there would be no stopping him. Besides, he'd earned it, and so I waited some moments for him to finish his business before completing mine.

It was awkward, to say the least, but my horse was not shy, and gave my presence no mind. I kept my gaze averted and gave him the courtesy of waiting til he was good and finished. It took a while.

When he was done I took the bodies and heaved them up onto their saddles. They must have left their clothes and weapons in the woods too, but I'd no mind to search about for them. I was ready to be gone from here as it was. I fished a length of cord from my saddlebags and tied their hands to their feet. Now that they had changed back, the many still-unhealed bullet holes in each man made for an awful sight. They were bloody and naked, and that suited my purposes just fine. I would send a message.

Slapping each horse on the rump, I knew they would

instinctively head for home, and that meant back at the Crescent Ranch. When they arrived, I was hoping it let Luna and his men know I was no easy prey. I didn't expect it would end the matter, not for a minute, but I wanted to make him stop and think a while, and buy me the time I needed to regroup and rearm. I only had four rounds left now, including my derringer, and I was mindful that this was not a good place to linger.

Had there been more I surely would have fallen, but it seemed their overconfidence had worked in my favor. They'd gotten used to the idea that man killing was easy. Tonight would change things some, and I was still alive. Mounting my horse, I gathered my dropped weapons and headed back to town at a gallop. My arm was bleeding something fierce, so I tied a handkerchief over the bite tightly. It only took moments before I was within the safety of the buildings. I didn't figure they'd try anything here, at least not in their wolfish form. William was still at the stables when I arrived. He didn't say anything about my bandaged arm, but I knew he saw it. I rubbed my horse down myself and spent some time patting him and talking softly in his ear.

"William, do you have any sugar?"

"I do, sir. Be right back." The steel dust liked sugar above all things, exceptin' of course the female of his species. I gave him a few handfuls after what he'd done for me tonight and thanked my lucky stars I had such an animal to ride the river with.

Before I went to my room, I walked a slow circle outside the hotel and sprinkled liberal amounts of the wolfs bane all around. I was hoping if they tried to sneak up on me in the night they'd cough or sneeze, and I'd hear them coming. I laid my weapons out on my bunk and checked them over, after moving the dresser up against the door. I still had six silver rounds left, on top of the four still loaded.

I would need more, much more. Unwrapping my wound, I poured whiskey over it to clean it and managed not to scream with the pain. The wounds were deep, but not long, and so I didn't think I needed stitches. I managed to make fourteen more of the bullets before the remainder of the flask was gone, and my arm had stiffened up enough by that point so as to make using it nearly impossible. The edgy feeling I had from the battle had long since worn off, and I felt my eyes grow heavy. I would sleep, but I made sure my guns were loaded up and pointed toward the door in easy reach.

Dawn found me in fine spirits, despite my troubles. I ate two plates of bacon and would have had more if old Mrs. Salsbury hadn't shooed me from the table like you would a hungry varmint. Ma's Kitchen was serving breakfast, so I crossed the street and settled into a chair. I'd had my fill of bacon, so they cooked me a steak to match the size of my appetite, and I polished the whole thing off, everything but the bone.

Fortified by a few cups of strong coffee, I figured I ought to visit my new office and see to this sheriff business. It felt strange to wear a star, but people nodded and tipped their hats to me as I passed, which was more than I'd gotten before I'd been roped into becoming the town's lone peace officer. It occurred to me that I didn't even know what my salary was, but if I lived long enough, I'd get around to seeing the mayor and making him agree to my terms.

The chair behind the solid oak desk was comfortable, though it creaked a little. I leaned back in it and went through the desk. A few old wanted posters, some receipts in illegible handwriting, and a few tin stars for deputizing the local citizenry, I guessed. A rack of Winchesters lined the wall, and there were boxes of ammunition piled under it.

I looked under the desk, but there was no horse pistol on a swivel underneath, as I'd earlier suspected. I'd have to rig one up myself. A cabinet behind me was stuffed with stacks of paperwork, arrest reports, sworn statements, and the like. I was hoping I wouldn't have to do any of that nonsense.

The bottom drawer held a set of reloading tools, bullet molds, and such. One of them was in .44-40, and I got excited. This was just what I needed. I could cast my own silver bullets, as many as I needed! Now all I needed was more silver. My badge would work, but I wouldn't get more than a few bullets out of it. I needed more. The problem was figuring out where to get it.

There were mines all over the territory, but I couldn't exactly go riding around the countryside, what with a pack of revenge-bent werewolves thirsty for my blood, and all. A long, low whistle echoed through the town just then. A train. Only one or two had stopped during my entire stay in Elk's Run, and so I went out to look. The big machine rolled to a squealing stop, belching smoke and steam into the air.

It was magnificent. William was tearing down the street to have a look, and I decided to join him. I've always loved trains. It blew my mind to think of how much work it took to lay the track and build such big locomotives. You could cross the country in mere weeks instead of months. Truly, there was no faster way to travel, though I'd never been on one. I found William sitting on a bench, watching the men bustle about, doing some sort of train work, though I didn't know what they were about.

Given my needs, I was naturally curious as to what they were carrying. Rolling a smoke, I casually walked over to where two men crouched, doing something with wrenches to one of the wheels.

"Howdy, Sheriff," one of them said, glancing up at me. He was short and fat, wiping his sweaty brow with the sleeve of his greasy coveralls. He had a friendly face, brow wrinkled up while he tried to figure out some kind of mechanical problem well beyond my understanding.

"How are you, fellas? Fine morning, isn't it?" I put on a smile that probably looked a lot like Mayor Rainwater's.

"Say, what are you carrying on this thing anyway? Looks like you've got about twenty cars attached."

The other one, a tall, lean man in the same coveralls, said, "Mostly ore from the mines northeast. We haul that south, where it goes east to the big cities out there. Bring back all kinds of stuff."

"You fellas hauling silver or gold?"

They looked at me quickly, but answered, "Sure, mostly silver though. Keep it well locked up in that car right there, behind the engine. Engineer's the only one's got the keys."

Well, it turns out being a lawman has all kinds of advantages. If I'd just been some drifter, they probably would have told me to get lost. But no one suspects the good and noble sheriff to be up to anything, now do they? Still, I'd try to do this the honest way.

"Who does one need to talk to for buying some of that silver?"

"No can do, Sheriff, this order's already bought and paid for. Going down to Denver."

Well, so much for the honest way. I bid them good day and went on about my business. That business just so happened to be figuring out how to rob a few bars of silver from a locked car on a soon-to-be-moving train. Hey, I'd tried to buy it outright, hadn't I? It wasn't something I'd have done if I didn't desperately need it, and it certainly didn't seem very sheriff-like of me, but I was going to do it nonetheless ... just as soon as I figured out how.

***

THE NICE THING ABOUT TRAINS IS YOU KNOW where they'll be going. I happened to know where the silver was, in the locked box just behind the car. I didn't want to hurt anybody, just get a bar or two of precious metal to make bullets with. I sure wasn't going to rob it here in broad daylight in the middle of town, so I'd have to find a way to stop it or get on board when it left. Thinking hard enough to furrow my brow permanently, I grabbed a change of clothes and went to the stables. I would have to figure this one out as I went.

When I rode out I headed south, then doubled back once I was out of sight. I rode carefully through the woods, alert to any sound or sign of another presence there. I was vulnerable here, but it was a risk I'd have to take. I'd loaded the ten gauge up with slugs and my rifle with the silver-tipped bullets I had left, just in case. I figured the heavy ten-gauge chunk of lead would destroy the lock well enough, so I just had to take care of getting into the box while the locomotive was moving. My steel dust was a fast horse, thank God, and so I would try to ride alongside the train and climb aboard.

Train robberies were not at all uncommon, and so I figured there'd be an armed guard somewhere, though I hadn't actually seen one. I picked a spot a good two miles out of town and dismounted. The tracks felt warm, but most likely just from the sun; I didn't think the train had passed by yet. From my vantage point well back in the woods, I would be able to see the train some time before it passed, and as soon as the engine went by, I would go for it.

I changed into my other set of clothes while I waited and tied a bandana around my face so just my eyes were visible. If things went to plan, the engineer wouldn't see me or even know anyone was there until they arrived at their destination to find their lock blown off and a few bars of silver missing. The chug-chug-chug sound reached my ears long before I could see the train. My nerve endings tingled with anticipation.

I stayed put until the train got just passed me, then jabbed my heels in and sent the horse off at a dead sprint. The train was moving fast now, well away from town and picking up speed. As fast as my horse ran, it wasn't enough. The train was flying by us. Desperately I looked for a handhold.

The train was jostling about on the tracks, and at a dead sprint, my horse was not a steady platform to say the least. I took my feet out of the stirrups and reached out for the end of one of the cars. My hand missed, and it was a narrow thing just to stay on my horse. Two more cars passed, and the caboose on the rear was coming up fast. It was now or never. I'd seen it done before at shows, but it seemed like a stupid thing to do.

I gathered my courage and put my feet on the saddle. I was on top of the horse in a crouch, and it felt like I'd be thrown clear any second. I would have to leap for the end of the caboose as it went by, and heaven help me if I made the slightest misstep. Suddenly, just as my target came by, I felt my steel dust stumble on a loose rock. Instinctively I leaped out into the open air. Everything seemed to move real slowly, and I could hear a high-pitched sound like someone screaming, which I guessed was me.

My hand shot out and grasped the rail on the end, and I thought my shoulder would be wrenched from its socket. I swung wildly and slammed into the railing. I'd tied a cord to my shotgun and had it slung over my back. The next moment I was up and over the railing, staring into a rear window full of passengers. They all looked at me blankly, and I suppose I did the same. Howdy, folks. Then a woman screamed, and I decided it was time to get a move on. There was a ladder leading from the rear platform up to the roof of the car, and I climbed it like a polecat. I was on the roof and walking forward, slowly, while the car swayed under me, bucking slightly every time we passed a joint in the tracks.

This was tricky, and it took a second to get the hang of just walking on this thing. I had twenty or so cars to cross, and I'd better do it in a hurry. Running now, I leaped over the edge onto the next car and fell flat on my face. I thrust myself back up and continued on. It was not pretty or graceful, but I managed to reach the front without falling to my death beneath the wheels of the train. There was a bit of space on the side of the car I wanted, where a man could stand and unlock the doors. I just had to get down there. There was just enough room for my feet, and I didn't want to simply drop down. If the car swayed even slightly, or the wind caught me, I was a goner.

I dug my fingers into the edge of the roof and stretched down, but there was a few feet left between me and the thin platform below. The car swayed back and forth, threatening to tear my grip free and send me hurtling out into space.

I tried to time it so I'd drop at just the right moment to land directly on the platform. Cold sweat stung my eyes, and I think my heart was trying to beat its way out of my chest, no doubt trying to escape my untimely demise. I took a deep breath and dropped. As soon as my fingers let go, the car bucked hard, and only the edge of my toe landed on the ledge below. My arms windmilled, but it was no use. I was falling back. My hands shot out to clutch for something, anything to get hold of, and my left caught in a death grip on something. The lock!

I seized it in both hands and pulled myself in toward the train with effort. I was in a bad spot. The lock was the very thing I had to remove, but without it to grab hold of I had no way to secure myself to the train. The movement was wild and irregular enough to throw me from my perch easily if I didn't keep a tight hold on something. I had to think, and fast. This train robbery thing was a lot harder than I thought it would be. I was sure if I'd had more time I could have come up with a better plan than this, but I was operating on the fly, and I'd have to make do where I was. That's when I saw it. A tunnel was coming up, leading straight into the side of a small mountain in our path. I had to move, and fast. I was worried about the sound of the shot, not so much because I'd be discovered as I thought they might throw the brakes on the train and send me flying head over heels to a certain death. I figured the noise in the engine compartment would get pretty loud when they entered the close quarters of the tunnel, and if I shot just after they entered, it might go un-heard.

Gritting my teeth, I shuffled sideways to the forward end of the car and locked my fingers tight around the edge there. I unslung the shotgun and raised it one handed. The lock was only feet away, but the car and myself were moving all over the place. Holding tight to the lever, I snapped the barrel downward, then back up to jack a shell in the chamber. I tried to calm myself for the shot, but it wasn't happening, so I tightened up as rigid as I could and squeezed the trigger. The lock blew away, and the force of the wind made the right-hand side door slide open to the rear. Right then my car entered the tunnel, and the sudden rush of wind combined with a violent jolt made me lose my grip.

I stumbled forward on the thin platform and managed to throw myself just inside the door. Everything went dark as we entered the tunnel, and I felt all around. Wooden crates were piled high. I struck a match, but it guttered out immediately. I worked one of the boxes open and felt smooth bars of metal, wrapped in individual cloths. Grabbing a pair, I stuffed them into the pockets of my rider's jacket and felt my way back to the door.

Peeking out, I could see a light at the end of the tunnel, not far off now. I had another problem. I hadn't done much figuring about what to do after I got hold of the silver. No doubt about it, I was a terrible train robber. I had no way off the train. We came out of the tunnel, and my problems got worse. The ground was moving by awfully fast now, except it was a good forty feet below the train.

We were on the side of a cliff leading downhill to a stream, and picking up speed as we went. I'd have to jump for it, and I might as well do it now, before we went even faster. I was hoping the mud under the shallow water was soft and not filled with hard rocks. With all my will, I forced myself to leap out into the air above the stream. Fear rose in my throat, and my arms and legs moved on their own as if I was running in the air. It didn't do much good. I hit the water with a tremendous splash and sunk deep into the mud below. I picked myself up, spitting water and mud, and stumbled my way over to the bank. The train was gone.

It was a good hour before I made my way back to my horse, and I swear he looked at me like I was a fool. I looked it too, covered in mud and bruises everywhere. The two heavy silver bars I stuffed in my saddlebags made me feel a little better though. The soft chuckle I heard behind me didn't. I whirled around and grabbed the rifle from its scabbard. There was no one there. I scanned the woods, but I couldn't see anything, anything at all. I waited, tense, with my finger on the trigger. The woods was quiet, dead quiet. The hairs on the back of my neck were up, but I couldn't see anything. Had I imagined it? No, the steel dust's ears were perked, rotating back and forth, and he sniffed at the air, apparently not liking what he scented. I mounted then, and my horse needed no prodding to make off with speed. That someone had been in the woods, watching me, I'd no doubt. If it was Luna or one of his men, why hadn't they attacked? Surely it would have been an easy thing to shoot me where I stood. If it was someone else, had they noticed what I'd just done? The thought made me uneasy.

I was well east of town now, further than I'd traveled that way, and the land was unfamiliar. I took a different route back in case someone had discovered my trail and was lying for me along the way. I felt like I was being watched the whole time, but saw nothing. Now and then the wind would shift and my horse would increase his pace, so I knew something was out there, but not what. I was of a mind to double back and set up for an ambush, but I admit I was plumb spooked and wanted nothing more than to be back in town at the saloon, beer in hand. I made it the rest of the way without incident, and came in from the same direction I'd left – that is, the exact opposite from where I'd robbed the train.

I was sincerely hoping the laughter I'd heard was just my imagination, brought on by nerves, and I wouldn't be seeing a wanted poster sent up from Denver with my description on it. That would be a change, for sure. I rubbed down the steel dust myself and left him at the stable. Liz was walking through town, parasol in hand, and she looked a sight for sore eyes. She winked as I walked past, and I suddenly felt the urge to see her, to talk to her and confess what I'd just done, my fears for the future, and all that was in my mind to do. No doubt, women were nothing but trouble.

Making a mental note to see her later and discuss the merits of wolfs bane (really), I ordered a beer at the saloon and sat over it, planning and plotting. The horses would have borne their deceased owners to Luna's ranch by now, and if he was going to ride in and shoot it out he would be here by now. I was hoping the message I'd sent would give him a caution and prevent him from acting until I could figure out what to do.

There was a blacksmith in town, but I daren't go and ask him to melt down the freshly minted bars of silver I just happened to come across. I'd have to do it myself, inexperienced though I was. The main problem I saw was that the silver would be quite a bit lighter than lead, and though it would make the bullets go faster as a result, I didn't know what other effects the change would have. Silver was also a good deal harder than lead, and that would mean the bullets wouldn't mushroom and flatten as much and might damage the rifling inside the barrel, which would change my point of aim as well as ruin my weapons. I'd carried my Colt lightning for as long as I could remember, and it had sentimental value to me as well. There were two ways to go about it, to my understanding. The bullet could be formed with lead around a silver core, which seemed difficult, or the silver mixed with lead before molding. The latter option seemed best, and simplest. It would also stretch my supply of silver further.

In an hour I was all set up, with a brand new thick steel pot over a fire of the driest, hottest burning wood I could find. I set up well back behind the stables, but not too close to the trees, and I kept my rifle ready. Taking a pliers I pulled the lead bullets out of the cartridges and set the casings aside, well away from the fire. I had a bar of silver melting in the pot, and I added the lead to it. It took a long time, but with the help of a billows I borrowed from William, I managed to get the fire hot enough. With a few rags wrapped around my hand, I poured the silver and lead mixture into the mold and pressed it into bullets. I kept it to one-third lead to two parts silver and hoped it would be enough. It was all guesswork. It was a time-consuming process, to say the least, and hot work. The sun was beating down at the same time I stood next to a roaring hot fire, and before long I was soaked in sweat and the sun was well on its downward arc behind the mountains. I managed to replace the cooled bullets back into their casings and crimp them tight before the light faded. I threw dirt on the fire until it was out, and then returned to town.

I had a hundred and twenty .44-40 rounds, and I'd

chipped off enough silver to make a full twenty shell's worth of rough buckshot. I was just stowing the molds and pliers when the mayor came storming breathlessly into my office.

"Sheriff! Come quick! Everyone in the saloon is fighting! There's a bunch of Bar T and Circle C boys in there, and they're tearing the place apart!"

Well, it just sounded like good clean fun to me, but I was the sheriff now, and it seemed the townsfolk expected me to stop this kind of thing. From my experience, men prevented from settling their differences with fists usually turn to shooting one another, and that's just more fuss and trouble for all concerned.

"All right, I'll be along presently," I said, and the little man nodded and disappeared, most likely as far from physical combat as he could get. I shut the drawer and noticed my palms were awful red, and a bit tender. Must have been the heat, but I hadn't recalled burning myself none. Perhaps they coated the bars with some kind of chemical after they made them, and this was irritating my skin. I washed them good, and it seemed to help a little. Finally I made my way around the corner and across the street to the saloon.

Sure enough, the two brands were going at it, and just as I arrived two fellows went crashing through the window out into the street. I wanted to sit down on the bench outside for a smoke and watch the fun, but I remembered I had been called upon to stop it. I had started many a brawl in my younger days but never actually tried to break one up. Inside there must have been twenty cowpokes, biting and kicking and smashing the odd piece of furniture over one another.

Well, I'd figure it out as I went. I waded into the room and began to shout for order. It seemed like the right thing to say, but the next thing I knew something wooden smashed across my back, and I was in the middle of it. Well, I was feeling good and full of vinegar, so I grabbed the nearest man and slugged him across the jaw, sending him over a table and onto the floor. I didn't have time to admire my handiwork, 'cause there were two more coming at me, one from each side. Rather than wait for them to get me at once, I charged the smaller one on the left and, driving my shoulder into his gut, slammed him against an overturned table before lifting him up and dropping him over my shoulder. My hand found a bottle, and I shattered it over the other's head just as he reached me. This was fun!

A big meaty fist from somewhere cracked me hard just then, and the next thing I knew I was bowled over a chair by a rush of bodies. I went down hard and tried to get back to my feet while I was trampled by the fighting cowboys above. A boot landed on my fingers, and that made me mad. I slugged its owner in the knee as hard as I could and leaped to my feet. I grabbed the nearest man by the collar and threw him, much farther than I would have thought possible.

He slammed into the wall opposite the bar room, and everyone stopped and just stared, including me. I'd just thrown a grown man twenty feet! I was strong, and I knew it, but I wasn't that strong. I straightened then, since I had everyone's attention, and told them they'd best knock it off or they'd get more of what he (the cowhand lying unconscious on the other end of the bar) got. Everyone stood still, and I sent word over to Ma's Kitchen to bring over hot coffee and raw meat for those whose eyes had already swollen shut.

The sweat and smoke and liquor in the saloon suddenly seemed an overwhelming stench. I walked out into the fresh air, and it got better. I could smell something delicious cooking over at Ma's, and I followed my nose, settling into a chair to order steak, cooked extra rare, and two of them. I'd worked up a powerful appetite, and in a few moments two large, bloody hunks of meat sat on a platter in front of me. They smelled delicious. I tore into them with a vengeance, cutting off big chunks with a knife and wolfing them down, barely chewing. What was wrong with me? I usually liked my steak well done, and I just threw a cowboy across the bar like he was a horseshoe. Maybe the fresh mountain air just agreed with me, but I didn't think so.

Back at the room that night, I noticed the bite had all but healed, and that in just a day! I was feeling healthy and well rested, despite the exertions of the day, and I remembered I'd planned on seeing Liz. I changed clothes again, and made my way carefully over to her place; no one saw me.

"Well, you look like you're in a good mood," she exclaimed when she let me in. I was. I handed her a bouquet of wildflowers I'd run out and picked in the moonlight, even though I felt a little sheepish doing that sort of thing.

I'd heard women liked that stuff, but I'd never done it before, not once. Liz's eyes lit up when I gave her the flowers. She really made a big deal out of it, cutting the stems a certain way and putting them in a vase with some water and a handful of sugar. She said the sugar would keep them alive longer.

It seemed to me that if she wanted them alive, maybe I'd be better off just finding some in the future and then telling her where to go so she could look at them whenever she pleased. I sat down in her comfortable chair and instantly felt relaxed and at ease, despite my worries. Liz seemed to have that effect on me, I'd learned. She was a good hostess too, and brought me a glass of neat whiskey without my so much as asking.

I could get used to this. She sat across from me and instantly launched into an explanation of wolfs bane, which she'd found on a hillside not far from town. I scowled then, thinking of her putting herself in danger for my benefit. She picked up on my displeasure immediately, not that I'd tried to hide it. "Don't look so concerned, Thorn! That's actually very sweet of you though. You needn't worry. I was very careful. I even brought the shotgun you lent me, as well as this." I wasn't concerned, I was mad, but I didn't correct her. I'd never had anyone call me "sweet" before, but from Liz it seemed a good thing.

What drew my attention now was the horse pistol she held out to show me. It was a Colt dragoon, an old cap and ball job that must have weighed around five pounds! During the Civil War, soldiers had carried them in a holster strapped to the saddle as they weighed so much. I almost laughed to imagine her aiming and firing the thing.

"Have you ever shot this?" I asked.

"No, but my father taught me how to load it before he … never mind. Why don't you teach me how to do so tomorrow? Say, at noon? I'll bring food and we'll have a picnic."

I had the feeling I was being roped into something, though I didn't know what. I liked spending time with Liz though, and I wasn't planning on robbing any trains tomorrow or fighting werewolves, so I nodded. She gave me another one of her bright smiles. I told her about my battle with the two werewolves the other night, and she hung on every word. Now it was her turn to look angry, or concerned, if that's what it was, and I took a page from her book and assured her I had been very careful, though that wasn't exactly gospel truth.

"Thorn, what are you going to do about this? From what I hear in town, Luna's a hard man, and he's got a rough bunch with him. They've tried to kill you a few times now, and I for one don't think they'll be letting up. I don't know why you're staying, but as much as I like having you around, I don't want to see you get killed. You're not just staying around for me, are you?"

Women are curious creatures. I knew Liz was sincere in not wanting me dead (and probably in rare company at that) and her words said she didn't want to be at fault for me staying around, but I thought I detected a glimmer of hope in her eyes. *What was she about anyway?*

"No, I'm not here for you at all! Hand on the book! I'm staying, because ... um, well, I've got a good job here now, and I kind of like it here, despite the werewolves, I mean."

It was a lame horse of an excuse, even to me, but she asked me not to say she was keeping me here, didn't she? She looked down, and her smile was gone suddenly. I swear I'll never figure women out. I'd just said exactly what she told me she wanted me to say, and here she was, looking crestfallen.

Suddenly remembering, I dug a box of the silver shotgun shells I'd made and handed them to her. "There's silver inside. Keep them in the shotgun, just in case." She thanked me, but looked irritated rather than pleased. Perhaps it was time to go. I'd said something that bothered her but I couldn't put my finger on it, and I didn't think it likely I'd be getting any more kisses, not tonight.

I took my leave, but waited a while in the bushes outside, watching her through the window. She got up after I left and stood in front of the flowers I'd brought, looking down. I thought I saw a single tear run down her cheek, glistening in the candlelight.

**

THE NEXT DAY I DECIDED I WAS AS PREPARED AS I was likely to get, and had best be ready for the full moon coming up. From what Liz told me these creatures had a special relationship with it, and the legends said they were most active during the period when the moon was at its peak. One never knows how much of legends is true, but if there really were werewolves, then I believed the legends to be mostly credible. I'd been busy the last few days, and I had silver bullets and a packet of wolfs bane, so I purchased a book at the general store and sat down to read. I loved reading, but seldom found the time for it. Today I had a copy of the book Beowulf. It was in Old English, but I could puzzle it out nonetheless and found it a welcome distraction. I was just at the good part, when the hero fights a terrible beast called Grendel, when I noticed someone standing by me. It was William, waiting patiently to be noticed. I closed the book, and seeing something was the matter, patted the bench next to me. He sat down silently, and I could see by the way his brow was working that he was trying to figure out what to say. It was some moments before he spoke.

"I've come to make a complaint, Sheriff." The way he said it was very dignified and adult, and I could tell he wanted to be taken as such. He addressed me in my official capacity, and so a sheriff I would be.

"And what would be the trouble, Mr. Johnson?" I'd learned his last name just that morning, when I was haggling with the mayor as to the terms of my office. I'd talked him up to three hundred a month, and he'd agreed to allow me to hire deputies as I saw fit, to include one full time, if I so chose. I didn't intend to spend all of my nights at the saloon, waiting for trouble to break out.

"I have a customer, Sheriff, who refused to pay me."

"Did he give a reason?" "Yes, he said the service wasn't up to his standards, and his horse looked poorly. I groomed the horse thoroughly, Sheriff, and fed it extra barley and oats, and that without him asking, nor did I charge him for it."

"Well, let's see the horse then."

I followed William to the stables, and I noticed he stood more erect than usual. I thought this was an important event in his coming adulthood, seeing the local lawman about a problem, and I was determined to treat him as a grown man, and he was trying very hard to play the part. He pointed out the horse, and it only took me a moment to see what was the matter. As one knowing about horseflesh, I could tell in a moment that this particular one had been ridden to the limit, and beyond some. I'd ridden a horse that hard a time or two, but only times of direst need. It was a fool who would ruin a fine horse such as this had been, and a bigger fool not to know what he'd done. I already disliked this man, whoever he was.

"And who was your customer, William?"

"Mr. Brownbeck, sir, I mean, Sheriff. He's over in the saloon, last I saw."

"Very well, Mr. Johnson, I'll investigate the matter carefully, and take the appropriate action."

He nodded solemnly. I knew how this would turn out of course. I didn't doubt William's honesty for a moment, and I saw the condition of the horse with my own eyes. There was another thing though. I didn't plan on being sheriff forever, and William would indeed be a grown man soon. He might not always be able to call upon the law for help, and I wanted to show him how a man collects on his debts. There was only one way to deal with a rascal like this.

This Brownbeck fellow tried to take advantage of a child, whether knowingly or not, and I knew there was only one way to deal with such a rascal. It would be a good time for William to learn. I told him to follow me and watch carefully. William pointed him out to me. At the table with a bunch of cowhands was a grossly fat man, dressed like a dandy, in a suit of fine cloth and a dapper little bowler. He had a fake rose stuck in his lapel, and his hair carefully greased back. There was a trim little mustache and he wore a diamond pinky ring that was both gaudy and effeminate. They were playing cards. I know a professional gambler when I see one, and he was the genuine article. The cowboys he was playing with obviously hadn't figured that out, judging by their stacks of rapidly dwindling chips.

The fat man, Brownbeck, had already just about cleaned them out, and the rest apparently hadn't the sense to quit playing. I had an idea or two about that. I crossed the room in a few long strides, and the players looked up from their cards. By way of introduction, I slapped the rotund gambler twice, then grabbed him by his greasy hair and slammed his face into his pile of chips. He started spluttering something, trying to speak, but I have to confess I wasn't all that interested in what he had to say. I had a piece of my mind I wanted to deliver to him, so I slammed his head into the chips again to get him to shut up. He did. To accentuate my point, I drew my six-gun and pressed it behind his ear.

"Now, listen hard, Brownbeck. You just tried to cheat an honest man out of his fee, and that doesn't cut it in my town. You want to ruin your own horse, that's fine by me, but you'll pay what you owe. Now let's have it."

I didn't let him go, but held one hand out. He dug in his pockets and produced William's money, plus a few dollars. I wasn't done with him yet.

"One more thing. If you plan on playing cards in this town, you'd better start playing honest." It was a hunch, but I picked him up to his feet, still by the hair, and ripped his suit coat off before he could move. Sure enough, there were little bands around his wrists, with kings, queens, and aces stuck in them, along with a small derringer. I snatched the derringer away and dropped it on the table.

"Looks like you get your money back, boys," I said to the cowhands, and they smiled in thanks before returning their glares to the gambler. Scum he might be, but if I left him there in the saloon, he'd be gunned down in a heartbeat.

"Come on, Brownbeck, it looks like you'll be moving on," I snarled, and still keeping hold of his greasy hair, I rushed him out into the street and tossed him in the dust.

"William, get his horse." The gambler lay where he was, wiping a thin trickle of blood from his pulped lips. I tossed his suit coat in the dust next to him. William was back in a flash with the horse, and the gambler wasted no time getting on it and riding off at full speed. I felt sorry for the animal, but there's only so much one can do. William was staring at me like I was some kind of lesser god out of a Greek myth. I admit I felt a touch of pride then, and I was glad I could show him the proper way to take care of his responsibilities.

I thought then that someday, I would make a pretty good

father. Suddenly, I turned to see Liz, frozen in her tracks and staring at me wide eyed. She'd seen the whole thing. I gave her a grin, and I thought she must look that way because she was proud of me. Her mouth hung open, undoubtedly impressed with what a fine lesson I had taught the young man. I turned to William and I suppose I crowed a little.

"That's how you collect your money when someone tries to cheat you, William. Anyone else does that, you come see me straight away."

He nodded carefully, then turned and ran back to the stables. Liz fluttered her eyes suddenly and then said, "We really must have a talk later." She looked flabbergasted then, but she had a hint of a smile in her eyes. Somehow, I wasn't sure what she thinking. Women.

I spent the rest of the morning and afternoon checking and cleaning my guns. I knew I needed to be ready for whatever was coming. I just didn't know it would be so soon, or take this form. Going down to my office, I heated some coffee and was just enjoying the cool night air wafting in through the door when a scared-looking man walked in. He had a welt over one eye and looked nervous.

"Mister, I was sent to deliver a message. A feller that says he's Lee Martin came into the saloon an hour ago, braggin' 'bout how he was going to kill you. He went on to call yuh a bunch a names not worth repeatin' and when you didn't show, he walloped me over the head and sent me to come find you."

I couldn't blame the cowhand for not tying in with this character. If it was Lee Martin, well, there weren't many who would. Lee had a reputation as quite a gunman. Rumor had it he'd killed his first man when he was twelve, and accounts after that varied from eight to fourteen men. Folks would say he'd been in this town or that, and he must have drifted some, but I was no fool not to realize what this was. Lee Martin needed no reason to cause trouble, nor did he have one. I doubt he ever had heard of me, and even if he had, I'd no reason to quarrel with him.

This was a setup, plain and simple. Luna must have shied some after I'd taken out two more of his pack and decided it would be easier to send in one of the worst gunfighters anybody ever heard tell of. I was plenty fast with a six-gun, but I had no intention of going that route. Martin had his intentions, and I had mine. There was no reason to leave anything to chance that I could help.

I grabbed a Winchester from the rack on the wall, checked it over, loaded it, and walked out. It was only a short distance to the saloon, but I walked the opposite direction, around behind some buildings, and then crossed to the saloon from the opposite direction. There was no way I was going to walk into a trap and get gunned down along the way. What Lee Martin wanted was obvious: for me to walk into the bar, ready for a confrontation, some kind of words, a challenge, whatever. He probably counted on the fact that most men would talk some before working up the nerve to draw. As soon as I walked in, he'd draw and fire. Sheriff I might be, but I wasn't going to tell him to drop his guns either. The man had clearly expressed his intention to end my life, and I had no qualms about ending his first. You could see him clearly, even from outside the saloon.

He had a girl on one arm, and a neat glass of whiskey in the other hand. He was on the short side, squat, and with a poorly grown-in mustache. Not very impressive in appearance, but I knew better than to judge by that standard. I watched for a moment. I would act, and soon, but it never hurt to know more about the man you're going to kill before you went and tried it. His attitude was relaxed, careless even, but under that veneer there was the air of a man on the hunt. Every sense was tuned, and his eyes kept up a regular motion, always returning to the doorway. No doubt he was expecting me any second. He was looking often toward the front door, and I saw he'd placed himself at such an angle where I'd have to enter then turn to the right to face him. He wore two guns, one on his left and the other on his right hip, butt inward for a cross draw. The handles looked well worn, and I was sure, despite his slovenly appearance, he spent much time every day practicing.

The blonde giggling away on his arm was also placed between Martin and the batwing doors. The presence of the woman would keep him from being shot at suddenly. He was also near enough to the window where he'd be able to see from an angle just before anyone came into the bar. He couldn't see me of course – I was standing just out of the light across the street.

I had to hand it to him, he was good. The one thing he hadn't counted on was that I was just as much, if not more, of a cold-blooded snake as he was. I'd killed at least as many men, if under different circumstances. I lived by the gun, as did he, and only one of us would continue to live tonight. You can guess where my sympathies lay.

He had me right on a few things, at least. I had no intention of shooting with the girl so close to him. I had a better plan. Keeping an eye in every direction, I stuck to the shadows and crossed over behind the saloon. Softly, I opened the back door and went inside. It was dark there, and the noise from the front room drifted lazily back along with cigar smoke. I walked slowly, softly forward. There was an opening in front of me, and I peeked from well back in the shadows. The entrance to the front room would put me on the same side as Martin; when I came through the door, he'd be dead ahead. The girl with him got up and crossed over to the bar, and that's when I decided to make my move. Rifle raised, I stepped into the harsh light. "Martin," I called, and fired. Not wasting time to see how the first shot landed, I worked the lever from the shoulder and fired again. As I pulled the trigger, I felt a white-hot streak sear my left side.

I stepped to the right, firing as I went. Martin had braced himself against the table after my first two shots had hit him in the chest, but wasn't done yet. I fired again quickly, at the same time he got another shot off, and the bullet caught him in the shoulder and spun him half around. He slumped against the table, but I shot twice more, and he finally rolled off and hit the ground with a thud. I swept the rest of the room, but didn't see anyone that looked like they wanted to make a move. Guess he didn't bring any help, didn't think he'd need it. If I wasn't sneakier than a coyote, he wouldn't have, either.

The man was fast, I'll give him that – and hard to kill. A rifle beats a handgun any day of the week, 'specially since you're already holding the rifle. The bullets hit harder, and it's easier to be sure of your aim. As much time as I spent practicing, I'd missed plenty with my pistols at the moment of truth, even when the distance was very short. It's one thing to shoot at tin cans and bull's-eyes, and quite another when it's another man shooting back at you. Folks flinch, or try and shoot too fast, and if any man tells you his rear hatch isn't buttoned up tighter than a snare drum in such a situation, well, he's a damned liar. I would live, at least for the night, and he was gone to meet his maker. I didn't think he'd be having a real good time with that and made a note to try and cuss less. No point in making things worse for myself, bad as they were already.

My shirt was ruined, a long tear taken out near the hip where the bullet had scathed me. It was bleeding some, but wasn't much more than a scratch. I was glad I'd landed the first shot, or his aim might well have been true. Giving a man like that a chance was pure suicide. A couple of helpful citizens dragged Martin's body out of the bar and into the street. Now what was I supposed to do? As far as I was concerned he could lie there and rot, but I supposed it was part of my job to finish cleaning up the mess I'd made.

Some minutes later, I roused the undertaker, and after guaranteeing payment from the city (for the cheapest pine box available) the surly old man got to work. That problem solved, I took a bottle of liquor up to bed with me and drank myself to sleep.

***

I DREAMED OF RUNNING THROUGH THE WOODS, NAked but not cold. A huge moon loomed overhead, and I called to it, delighting in its silvery light. I could smell a delicious variety of odors, and they all smelled like food. I followed my nose and sprang into a clearing where I startled a herd of deer. Ignoring the scattering does, I targeted a big buck and ran him down. I sunk my teeth into his throat, and held him and shook until he stopped moving. The blood tasted delicious, warm and salty on my tongue. Lifting my blood-stained lips to the sky, I howled a long, triumphant howl to the moon, directly above.

I awoke to see daylight streaming in through the open window above my head. Sitting up, I could see I was covered in dark, crusted blood. What in tarnation? The dreams had been strange, and if I'd been gnashing about, I could have bitten my tongue and made quite a mess of things. As it was I had blood all over my mouth and chin when I looked in the mirror.

Something didn't quite add up. I bathed in front of the dresser and went downstairs. It was past breakfast, but I wasn't hungry, not in the least. Perhaps the dream had turned my stomach, and waking up covered in your own blood can make a man lose his appetite, for sure, so I didn't pay it no mind. I settled for coffee. My sleep hadn't been restful, to say the least, but I wasn't exactly tired. I just didn't feel like doing much at all. The day was hot, so I took a seat in the shade outside the hotel and rolled a smoke. After one or two puffs, I had to put it out. It smelled awful and tasted worse. Tobacco must have gone bad. I'd pick up more later. I was feeling awful hot and sweating, so I rolled up my sleeves. Curiously, the wounds on my arm where I'd been bit were healed, there wasn't even a scar. Suddenly, I lifted my shirt to see there was no mark where the bulled had creased me either. Strange, very strange. I went back up to the room and stripped off my shirt. To my amazement, my scars from the battles with the grizzly and the werewolves were gone! I mean, not a trace!

My skin was as smooth and flawless as the day I was born. The many other scars I'd collected in the last thirty-odd years were gone too, and I checked them, every one. I'm no fool, and I knew then something was afoot. But what?

I would see Liz. She would know what this meant. Even if she didn't, I wanted to see somebody then, and Liz always had a way of making me feel at ease. As I stood and began to cross the street, I realized the town was awfully noisy, even though no one else was outside. The sounds of pots and pans banging and clattering, people talking and laughing pounded in my ears. Why was everyone making such a darn racket?

As I covered my ears and started toward the schoolhouse, I knew I couldn't see Liz. The children were reciting some sort of lesson, very loudly, and she'd be tied up with teachin' 'til sometime in the afternoon.

Wait a minute! The schoolhouse was still over a hundred yards away! There's no way I should be able to hear the children here, particularly with all the ruckus and noise around me. A glass broke somewhere, and I cried out with the pain. It was a terrible high-pitched tone, and it felt like I ruptured an eardrum. Something was wrong, awful wrong, but the din grew in my ears 'til it got so bad I staggered across the street to the hotel.

All I wanted to do was go up to my room, pull a pillow over my head, and try to shut out the noise. Suddenly, a wave of dizziness overtook me and I fell to my knees. My stomach lurched, and a pile of raw meat splattered on the dust. I hadn't eaten dinner last night, unless ... To confirm my suspicions, a lone eyeball lay staring up at me from the pile of half-digested meat on the ground. Covering my mouth, I stumbled and lurched my way up the stairs. The clerk started to say something to me, but I waved him off and slammed the door to my room. Throwing myself on the bed, I lay curled up into a ball, the pillow pulled tight over my ears. The room started spinning then, and I felt myself descend into darkness.

Ugh. Whether my head was pounding or it was just the sounds of dinner being put on downstairs, I couldn't tell. It took a moment for things to come back to me, and when they did I felt panic welling up in my throat. Strange things were happening to me, things that just didn't seem humanly possible. Humanly possible? That might just be the explanation. I could hear things far away, and small, quiet noises sounded like a racket to my ears. Even now I could smell the leather from my saddle in the corner as if it were pressed to my face. The whole place smelled of gun oil, sweat, and wood.

I needed a drink. Digging in my saddlebag, I found a half-drunk bottle of whiskey and immediately doubled over, sneezing in fits. My eyes burned and watered. Covering my face with a bandana, I located the source of my troubles. I still had a bit of the wolfs bane left in its pouch, right next to the whiskey. It stunk like the smoke of hell, and I grabbed the bag between two fingers and tossed it out the window, couching and hacking all the way. I waved my arms about, trying to move the air around and dissipate the smell that was giving me such a reaction. OK, so now I couldn't stand to be around wolfs bane either. I didn't want to consider it, not even for a moment, but it seemed I was turning into one of the same kinds of things Luna and his men were.

A werewolf.

I shuddered at the thought. Out the window, somewhere in the darkness, a coyote yipped and howled in the evening light. It would be dark soon, and if my guess was right, I was about to have another dream – except the dream was real. I had changed into a wolf, run through the woods, slain and eaten a deer. I wanted nothing more than to see Liz, hope she could tell me something, find some way to stop this, but I knew I couldn't risk going near her now. I had an odd feeling, like every nerve ending in my body was on fire. The air felt electric, and something deep inside the pit of my stomach stirred and seemed to growl. I had no idea what to do, how this worked, but the sudden, ravenous hunger I felt when the smell of cooking wafted up to me gave me no choice. A crazy, insane urge threatened to drive me downstairs and tear into whatever was there. My skin felt all aquiver and mighty strange. I couldn't risk being around people right now. No telling what might happen.

Buckling on my guns, I threw open the window and dropped out of it. It was some distance to the ground, but I landed catlike, crouched and alert. I sniffed the air, feeling a mite silly as I did so. Smells of juniper, sage, and all manner of flora and fauna flooded my nostrils.

There was a hare not twenty yards off, hiding in the brush. I could smell him there, and if I was still, hear the quiet rustle he made as he shifted in the long grass. Somewhere beyond in the woods, a herd of elk was bedding down for the night, making satisfied little noises even as the grass crunched underneath their shaggy bodies. The smells were intoxicating.

What's more, they served to intensify the hunger to a painful level. I wanted to kill with my teeth, and feast in hot, salty blood. I was a wild man. I ran into the woods, knowing from the sounds and smells that nothing there was a threat to me. I'd never been a fast sprinter, but now I flew in long leaps and bounds over the grass and into the woods. I was scared, but there was another feeling: exhilaration, a desire to run, to hunt, to feed. It was overpowering. I still had no idea how this worked, but as I entered the woods, I figured I needed to get my clothes off, before ... Too late. One glance up at the bright, fat moon above and my skin seemed to burst with thick, black hair. My bones seemed to shift and re-form, my mouth became a long muzzle bristling with fangs. My ears lengthened, and even my fingernails turned into sharp claws. I ran. Fully conscious this time, I was nevertheless not myself. My senses were far sharper than before, my strength greater, and the hunger with it. I was driven toward one thing. To hunt. I could not have stopped if I wanted to. I didn't want to. I could see the forest floor, every twig and fallen branch as if it were broad daylight, though it looked much different than that.

Every now and then I lifted my head to let out a long howl; it sounded just like a wolf's, only deeper and stronger. I'd always thought the sound was mournful, but now I realized it was one of purest rapture. I looked up at the moon as I ran and felt drawn to it. There was a deep connection there, a longing, something hard to explain in the words we have. I'd never felt anything like it before. I paid tribute with wailing song and seemed to grow stronger somehow. The scent of the elk distracted me, and I was on the chase. Much larger and heavier than I'd been before, I still ran swiftly and silently. It was as easy to run on two legs as four, though I preferred the latter. Bursting into the herd, I saw them breaking and running before me. I could have taken one of them then, easily, but I wasn't ready to end this glorious hunt yet.

I zeroed in on a fleeing cow and kept pace easily some hundred yards back, trailing by scent and sound as much as sight. I'd always enjoyed hunting, but this took things to a whole new level. The elk's fear rolled off in waves of delicious perfume, and I basked in it. The heady feeling it gave me was too much to bear, and I closed the distance, eating up ground in long loping strides. A sudden crackling in the brush ahead, and the elk crashed to the ground, wailing pitiably. I reached the spot in an instant, where I was confronted by a large black bear. He must have weighed eight hundred pounds, covered in glossy black fur. I was a good deal lighter, but not to be denied. This was my prey, my kill. The bear growled a warning, but I circled, instinctively trying to get behind him. He charged, and I easily dodged to the side, thrilling to the combat.

Darting in, I slashed at him with my sharp claws, and then away. He lunged after me, but I leaped over his back, sinking my teeth in as I went. He shook himself free, and then turned on me, and we collided in a flurry of teeth and claws. He was larger than I and incredibly strong, but I was faster, and the wounds he inflicted healed up moments later. We fought for a while, but I clearly had the better of him, and he turned and ran. I let him go. Triumphant, and my hunger sharpened even further by the battle, I sank my muzzle into the throat of my still-live prey, and worked at the soft flesh, tearing out its windpipe in a spray of hot blood. Delicious.

My teeth opened up the thick hide easily, and I gorged myself on everything inside. It tasted better than any steak I've ever had, raw and still warm. Sated, I lay down in the woods some distance off. I felt drowsy and bloated. I lay down on the cold ground, but it didn't bother me none. I was warm and snug in my long black coat, and before long I curled up into a ball and slept. You ever see how a canine always turns around a few times before laying down to sleep? That night, I found out why.

CHAPTER 8

I BLINKED MY EYES, TRYING TO GET THEM TO FO-
cus in the harsh morning light. I was not alone. I smelled
smoke, strange herbs, and another smell I couldn't place.
Sitting up with a start, I realized I was still naked and sought
to cover myself. There was a man sitting in front of a smoking
fire, his back to me. He had a leather bag suspended over the
flame, and something boiled and bubbled in the leather pot.

The smell was terrible. A heavy buffalo robe lay next
to me, and I shrugged into it, rising. The man didn't turn
around, but I saw by the way his ears cocked he was aware
of my movements. He had long black hair, like an Injun, and
wore a robe much like the one he had left for me. I didn't
think he meant me any harm. After all, he could have easily
killed me in my sleep, couldn't he? I walked over to the fire
and sat down across from him, still wary.

He looked up then, and gave me a smile. His face was
striking. Wide and thickly featured, he was probably the
largest Injun I had ever seen. Many of them were well built,
but this man was colossal. I was guessing he stood a full foot
taller than me, and weighed perhaps twice as much. I'd never
seen someone so large in my life. With thick fingers he picked
up a stick and stirred the foul brew.

"What be your name?" he said, after thinking a while.
He creased his brow before he spoke, as if trying to remember the words. He spoke English like he hadn't done it in a

while, and when he did, there was something odd about it. Not the way an Injun speaks, but more like an Englishman.

"Thorn Carlson. Uh, pleased to make your acquaintance, I guess." I was a little dumbfounded, but I'd been raised to remember my manners, and it seemed a good thing to do when talking to someone who looks like they could rip you in half without breaking a sweat.

"Long time since I talk to anyone. Longer time still since talk to white man." He took up a bag and pinched some sort of dried plant out of it and dropped it in the boiling liquid.

"Who are you? What's your name, I mean ..."

"Name not important. I have no use for name. Not for long time. What important is you learn, quick. You new to this ... change, yes?"

I wasn't sure exactly what he meant, but the knowing look in his eyes told me it had something to do with the fact that I'd transformed into a giant wolf and had been out gallivanting around the countryside. There didn't seem to be much point in lying.

"Yeah, I guess this is the second time. How do you know?"

"I can smell. You are new. The moon, she brings the change. First time anyway. Can't help. There is much to know. Much to learn. I teach you, maybe keep you alive, little while anyway."

"What do you mean?"

In answer, he swept a hand toward the east.

"The others, they come for you last night. They followed. Five of them. They stop when they get to my ... territory. Know better than to come here."

He smiled then, but I can't say it was a pleasant one. He

looked to be about twenty, maybe twenty-five, but his eyes were much older, as if he'd seen the ages. Huge he might be, but I saw he carried no weapons, and I couldn't figure why the werewolves would be wary of him.

"You need be more careful, if enemies like that you have. Not know why they want you, but they do. They know you change too, and you not able to ... control it yet, so you are ..." He ran a thick finger in circles next to his head, the universal sign for crazy. "for hunt. You must learn to control your totem. If you not control animal, it control you."

"And how do you know all this?"

"I know, 'cause I same. Same but ... different. I have totem too, but not puny wolf. I strong. I bear."

He leaned back a little and actually pounded his fist once against his chest as he said it. A bear? No wonder he was huge.

"Is that why you're so large?"

"I always big, but not this big. You grow some too, since last time I saw."

When had he seen me before? Suddenly, I remembered the feeling of being watched after my brief tenure as a train robber. Off in the distance, I could see the tracks spiraling away to the west. This must be his "territory."

I looked down at myself. Indeed, I seemed a little larger, though I hadn't felt so next to the big Injun. I didn't have any frame of reference then, but my limbs seemed thicker, and more muscular.

"You talked about controlling this ... change. How do you do that? Where does all this come from? How do I stop it?"

"You ask many questions, white man. Slow, and I will try

to answer." He sat silent for a moment, stirring the pot and thinking hard. It was some time before he spoke.

"Many year ago, a white man come. He not like you, he different white man. First my people saw. He tall, tall as me, and his hair color of sun. His eyes color of sky. We never seen man like him before. He say he came from far lands, away over big water. I never seen big water, but he say is there. I ask him once if big water like lake, and he tell me big water would make many ... thousand lakes. Then, I not say anything, but to myself I think, "he seemed to search for the words, "he full of ... shit."

The big man laughed a loud booming laugh, and took his time before continuing, "Anyway, he was Akbaalia, or you would say shaman, medicine man. Ver' powerful, ver' strong. He could change his shape, change into animal, whatever he want. Tribe listen to him, and he teach many things. He teach others to be like him, to change into animal, to totem. Others could only do one, he could do all. Ver' strong medicine. We grew powerful and won many battles. Some warriors want more power, try to take over tribe. Much fight, much die. Tall man kill off all others, only one or two escape. He fight with knife, made of silver. Against man he would fight with very long knife he bring with him from big water. Finally, when almost all changers dead, he come for strongest, Andiciopec. Strongest kill tall man, hide him in cave. He was good fighter, but Andiciopec better. Andiciopec alone then, wander mountains many year. Not part of tribe anymore, but he not need anyway. More year, then another tribe come to land. Crow, they call. Andiciopec lonely, he go in to them, live with from time to time. White man come, this time with different kind of medicine. Guns, we learn.

They shoot many, but Andiciopec help fight. Andiciopec mean 'not hurt by bullets.'

That what they say now, but it was just name, many year before anyone know of bullets. Name not true anyway. Bullets hurt ver' much, just not die. Andiciopec great warrior, but even he cannot stop many white men. He live alone in mountains then, for many year. Not talk to men much, just few time, when lonely."

"What happened to Andiciopec?"

"I am Andiciopec." He looked fiercely proud then, sitting tall with his big jaw rigid. Had the skeleton I'd found been that of the strange man from years ago? Could be. And this man in front of me, who looked to be no older than his twenties, had seen the arrival of the white man and been around for some time before, maybe hundreds of years before. How was that possible?

A few weeks ago I'd have called it stuff and nonsense, but I'd seen plenty since then to broaden my mind.

"So how do you stop it? The change, I mean."

"That what I make now. This help, keep under control. Tall man, he teach us how to make. Been long time, but think it right. Here, you drink."

It had been exhilarating, the night before, and the hunt. But I did not want to be this, this animal, hadn't asked for it, and had no intention of running through the woods every night like some kind of monster. He held out a crude wooden cup, filled with the foul-smelling liquid. I recoiled at the odor, but pinched my nose shut and took a gulp. It smelled worse than it tasted, thank God, and I handed the cup back to him, empty. Not so bad.

"How you feel?" he asked, looking a little worried.

"Well, fine I guess. That stuff smells worse than it …"

Ugh. Oh stars. A shooting pain ricocheted around in my gut something fierce, and I doubled over. I began huffing and puffing and rolled onto my side, curled up like a baby. I was gasping for air, but I couldn't breathe. I swear I thought I was going to turn inside out. I could feel my heart pounding like an Injun war drum, and the blood rushed in my ears. Everything got real dim for a second, and then, just as suddenly, it went away.

"What the hell was that?!" I asked, rising to my feet. He could at least have given me a warning.

"Glad you OK. The medicine, when I make, not sure if have it right."

"And what would've happened if it wasn't?"

"Then you die. But all okay, is right. You take this when sun come up, and when sun go down. You not change. Just swallow though, no more."

"Okay, so drink it twice a day, and I don't turn into a wolf at night?"

"That right. But only need drink during full-moon time. Just take care not get mad, and you be fine."

"What happens if I get mad?"

"Then you change. You plenty mad right now. See hair on hands?" I looked down at my knuckles, and sure enough there was thick black hair sprouting on them. That could be awkward, in a different setting. I closed my eyes and took a deep breath and conjured up Liz's face in my mind. It helped. When I looked down again, the hair was gone, though I didn't know how.

"If not drink stew, you be wolf right now, and we fight. Is good for you we not fight." Looking at the big Injun, and imagining him as a super powerful bear, I didn't doubt that for a moment.

"So what's in that stew, anyway?"

"Some things wolf, he not like. Those things go in, but not too much, or wolf die. I make more for you later, take skin with you now and go back to white man town. Come again when need more, and I show you how to make. It nice to talk to someone, even ugly white man like you."

He grinned at me, much like a bear might've, I guessed.

"So each animal, they have different weaknesses? How about bears?" I said it casually, hoping he'd answer. He seemed friendly enough, but I wanted to know if there was something else I should make some bullets out of, just in case.

"My only weakness honey."

"Honey? I thought bears liked honey. How does that hurt you?" I didn't think I'd be able to find a way to make bullets out of honey.

"It not hurt. I not able to ... resist though. Get many stings. Paws, nose, everything hurt. Ver' bad. Sometime, go far to find honey. Never enough. Always gone too soon." I didn't know if he was being serious or just teasing me, but I sensed that was all I'd get out of him. I needed to get back, and get seriously working on a plan to take out my enemies before they got me. I didn't know how they were aware of my condition, but if they knew I couldn't afford to be running around in the woods at night, half out of my mind.

The "medicine" would prevent me from changing during the full moon, and I now knew to avoid getting angry. Easy enough, I guess. Right. Andici-whatever went back to staring into the fire, and I got the sense he wasn't inclined to further conversation. Taking the hint, I took the skin full of disgusting brew and staggered off through the woods. I'd return the robe another time.

I knew I could make better time if I ran, as fast as I was now, but I didn't feel much like running. It only took an hour or so to get back to my clothes and guns. The gun belt was undamaged, I'd gotten that off in time, but the rest was in shreds. I'd literally burst out of it. At the rate I was going, people would think I was some kind of dandy. Seemed I had to get a new set of duds just about every day. And that had been my last.

Buckling on the gun belt to keep the robe in place, I crept as silently as I could into town and tried to stay out of sight. I made it back behind the hotel without being seen. It was a good fifteen feet or more to the window of my room, but I leaped up and caught on the sill easily. A moment later, I was inside. I didn't fancy walking around barefoot in the robe, and it dawned on me that even if I had clothes, they wouldn't have fit me anyway. Looking into the mirror, I saw I was now a good four or five inches taller, and I had muscles like a draft horse. I'm not a vain man, but I was pleased with my new appearance, hard as it would be to explain.

Maybe I could say I'd been doing one of those "Physical Culture" courses from out East that they advertised in the newspapers. I leaned back out the window, looking out toward the stables. I had to wait awhile, but William eventually came out back to gather some more hay for the horses.

"William!" I hissed. He looked up, and then all around, searching for the source of the noise.

"Over here!" I called, and he saw me and came running over. "Where'd you get that crazy robe, Mr. Thorn?"

"Never mind that. I need you to go over to the general

store for me, get two sets of the largest pants and shirts they have, and a set of the biggest boots they carry, OK? Here, take this."

I dropped some money down to him. He went running off, and twenty minutes later I had a knock on the door. It was the clerk, with a thick parcel.

"The young man asked this be delivered to you, Mr. Carlson."

The clerk stank so bad I wrinkled my nose. He looked at me curiously through his thick glasses while I tried to place the scent. For a second I thought ... no, he wasn't a werewolf. It was a smell I didn't like but it wasn't that of a wolf. Hell, the man probably just needed a bath. For that matter, I did too. I took the package from him and shut the door. The shirt and pants fit well, but the boots were a little tight. They'd stretch some. I took a look in the mirror and realized I shouldn't have given William those dime novels.

The shirt and pants were raven black, and the boots, which I fancied, were hand-tooled black leather jobs. The shirt, was that ... silk? If it was, it explained why there'd been no change. There was something else wrapped up in the paper, and when I took them out I saw it was a pair of neat kid leather gloves, died black.

My black leather hat was the only thing surviving from my previous wardrobe, and when I put it on it completed the picture. I'd thought it would make me look like an undertaker, but when I looked in the mirror again it wasn't half bad. In fact, I thought I looked rather dashing. I made a note to present myself to Liz tonight, so she could see me in all my finery before I inevitably ruined it. I also reminded myself to buy more clothes at the earliest opportunity. After a late breakfast of as much bacon as I could stomach, I loosened my belt and headed for my office to do some plotting and planning. It was not to be. Richard Comstock, Jr. was there in my office, waiting. "Sheriff." He was curt. I nodded.

"I've had some more cattle slaughtered last two nights running. It stopped for a while, but then started back up again. More and more cattle are missing every day. I was also hoping you'd made some progress on the matter of my father's murder." I had indeed, but didn't quite know how to break it to the young man. Before, he'd come across as young, pigheaded, and insolent.

He looked like he'd matured some in the last week or so, since he'd inherited the Comstock brand. Responsibility can do that to a man.

"As a matter of fact, Mr. Comstock, I have made some progress, but it's not the sort of thing I'm going to talk about now. In a few days I hope to have the situation well in hand."

It was sort of a lie, but sounded like the thing a sheriff was supposed to say, and I was still learning that part of the job. I figured I could be forgiven.

"I'll ride by your ranch this afternoon and take a look. With any luck, I'll be able to trail it again and dispatch the critter."

"You mean you've seen it?! What was it, a grizzly?" His eyes were wide, and I realized I'd made a mistake.

"Um, well, yes, it was a grizzly. I'd wounded it and trailed it back into the mountains, but lost it. I figured he died, or at least wouldn't be coming back. I'm sure I can do it again, just promise me you'll leave it to me and not go chasing after it, will you?"

"If it's just a griz, I'm sure me and the boys can take care of it. Thank you, Sheriff. Good day."

He turned and walked off. I'd just screwed up again. "Richard, wait."

He turned. I spoke quickly, "You haven't seen this thing. It's no ordinary grizzly."

"Is that so, Sheriff?" He looked doubtful. I'd have to try harder.

"That's so. It's maybe twice the size of an ordinary grizzly and three times as ornery. Its teeth are stained red from all the blood it's consumed, and I saw a leather boot hanging from one of its back teeth. Looked like it'd been there awhile."

His eyes were wide, clearly impressed. "I don't know, Sheriff, sounds like ..."

"Trust me. It's bigger than you'd believe. He's got bullet scars all over his body. It doesn't appear as if they can hurt him."

That seemed to make him stop and think, so I pressed on. "His jaws are big enough to bite a man, or a horse, in two, and his paws would cover your torso. His claws alone are at least as long as your hand." In for a penny, in for a pound.

"Well." He swallowed hard. "You are the lawman hereabouts, Sheriff, and if you say you have it handled, I'll leave you to your business." He tipped his hat and walked away, looking a little unsteady. I hooked my thumbs into my belt, proud of my yarn spinning. I wanted to keep him away from the wolves. There was no sense in him dying trying to hunt an enemy he couldn't kill. That was my job. As I looked down at the star on my chest, I realized it really was.

CHAPTER 9

I FIGURED TO PAY A VISIT TO THE CIRCLE C, NOT only to show my face and that I was on the job, but in hopes of getting the drop on a werewolf or two and further reducing their numbers. This problem was not going away, not 'til one or the other of us was dead. It was Luna or me. I was going to go on the offensive, but I didn't think an all-out assault on the Crescent Ranch would do me much good, not with their present strength anyway. Once I'd evened up the odds some, then maybe. I rode out toward dusk, heading south out of town. I'd check in at the ranch house, maybe get some supper, then settle down somewhere in the woods overlooking the cattle and wait. The Colt lighting and lever shotgun were riding on either side of the saddle, and I was ready for action.

The steel dust was happy to get out of the stable and ride. I could tell William had been taking good care of him, but he was a horse that liked to be out on the trail. I guess I liked it that way too. A sudden sharp pain in my back, and I was thrown from the saddle. I heard the shot ring out on my way to the ground. I had the presence of mind to lie still, though the pain was nigh unbearable. Blood flowed into my mouth, and I knew they'd gotten a lung. A whoop and holler of triumph from the woods, then three of them came out of hiding and ran toward me. How they knew I was coming I didn't know, but they could have just been up on the hills, watching the town and waiting to see which way I'd ride out. Like a damn fool I'd stuck to the road. If I hadn't developed my current condition, I'd be in a heap of trouble, but I could feel the wound closing even as I let the blood slowly trickle from my lips, trying not to cough and hack it up. I could smell the men before they reached me. It had been a while since they'd bathed, but there was a light wind, and that explained why neither I nor my horse had caught their scent earlier. I could tell they were just men, not werewolves, which made my job even easier. One of them reached out and grabbed my horse's reins and was rewarded by a swift kick that sent him flying to land in a heap, yards away.

I leaped to my feet, catlike, and drew at the same time. One of the men froze, shocked to see me still breathing, let alone standing. The other was quicker and leveled his rifle at me just as I thumbed the hammer back and pulled the trigger. I felt a sharp jab in the stomach, just like I'd been punched unawares, and the other man fell back, a slug buried in his chest. I turned to the one who was still standing there, frozen, his eyes fixed on the bullet hole in my gut. I felt it closing, saw him watch in amazement. His jaw worked soundlessly. I snatched his gun away before he could react and threw him to the ground.

The sound of a hammer being pulled back alerted me, and I ducked at the same time I turned. The bullet whizzed by overhead, and I shot the third man twice, both bullets ripping through his throat. He died fast, but made a hell of a racket doing so. I picked the last man up off the ground and held him up in the air by his throat.

"Who sent you?" I growled.

"L-l-luna! He told us to do it! I swear, I didn't wanna but he made us!"

I bet. I'd planned on questioning him but realized I didn't

really need to know any more. It was already war, and I knew where to find Luna and his men. This one was unarmed and helpless now, but I knew by the gunpowder smell on him that this had been the one who shot me from the trees. I couldn't really hold that against him, as I'd done the same thing myself, many a time, just against a different sort. I set him down, and he crumpled to the ground, lifeless. While I'd been thinking, I'd crushed his windpipe and broken his neck. Guess I didn't know my own strength. Not wanting to complicate matters in town, I picked up the bodies and threw them far into the woods, surprised at how easy it was. The remainder of the ride to the ranch didn't take long, and I had healed up some time ago. Not a scar remained, just two holes in my clothing to remind me I'd been shot. The shirt had obviously been expensive, but I was glad that was the least of my worries.

Still, I suppose I had grown a little careless, what with my improved senses and other powers, and I resolved to use the same amount of caution I formerly had, when I had been fragile enough to be damaged by lead bullets. It was almost full dark now, and I was hungry. I fancied a visit to the ranch house and dinner – apparently getting shot works up quite an appetite – must be the healing that does it. I wanted to be in place well before any midnight visitors came, so with my stomach grumbling its feelings on the matter, I chose a likely spot and sat down to wait. My horse I had hidden well back in the brush, where the wind wouldn't carry his scent far. It didn't take long, just an hour or two before a sound perked up my ears. A branch broke somewhere in the woods, maybe two hundred yards to my left.

Ordinarily I wouldn't have even heard it, but now it sounded like a rifle shot. All was quiet for another fifteen minutes, then a furry shadow burst from the trees, running full tilt toward the dozing cattle. I let it take the first one, and as the cows broke and ran I kept my eyes on the woods for any sign that others were hanging back. I couldn't see anything, but I wanted to be sure. The werewolf was running about among the herd, slaughtering any that came within reach, throwing pieces all around. He wasn't feeding, just tearing them up and leaving them to die. I worked my way through the woods, but there wasn't a trace, save that of the one in the fields, still hard at work. I set down on his trail and waited. I figured he'd have himself a good feed, then saunter back through the woods, fat and happy. When he did, I'd be waiting, ready to test out my new silver bullets.

After some time, the wailing and cries of the cattle stopped. Then the sound of cracking bones and ripping hide reached my ears. It went on for some time. Say what you will, but the smell of the blood and the accompanying sounds made my stomach rumble. Lord, I was hungry. I brushed the back of my hands and sure enough, there was a thick patch of hair on each. That was when I realized I'd left the skin of medicine back in my room. Damn. I looked up at the moon, nice and full. Ordinarily it would have been a beautiful sight, but now it was something more. Like it called out to me – time to hunt, Thorn – time to chase. Oh, how I wanted to. A little shiver ran up my spine, and I tried to bury the thoughts. It was not only a very bad time to change now, but I didn't want to ruin my nice new boots.

I gripped the gun tighter and waited. It wasn't much longer before the huge black shape moseyed on into the tree line. I could see by the way he held his head he wasn't alert or watchful. He should have been. Just a little closer. A sudden gust of wind and the wolf snapped his head up, then sniffed the air. Time to move. Standing, I raised my carbine and fired.

It was dark in the woods, but I could see my sights perfectly, even the little puff of dust as the round struck between his ribs.

The wolf let out a howl, and I let go with a few more shots, peppering his heart and lungs with silver slugs. He collapsed on his side, twitching and jerking. He was still alive, but I saw him shrink, the hair falling off his body, until he was just a man, naked and bleeding in the bright moonlight. I stood over him, but didn't recognize his face. That was a bad sign. I thought there were only five of them left. If there were ones I hadn't seen, then I had no way of knowing how many of these things I was facing.

"You ... must be Thorn. They said ... they said you had silver bullets. Should have been ... more careful."

"What's your name?" I asked quietly. He didn't seem resentful about me shooting him and all, just peaceful.

He smiled then, the moonlight gleaming off a set of white, even teeth, stained by his own blood. "Jake. Jake Morley. I want you to know I didn't want this. Any of it. I rode for Luna for years. One day, he up and bit me, then explained what would ..." He erupted in a fit of coughing. When he was done, he continued. "He told me what would happen. You got to understand ... no choice. No choice but do what he says.

He has ... some kind of control. Like a body can't refuse but to follow his orders. I think you've killed me, and I have to say ... I thank you for it."

He was fading fast. I didn't have time for pleasantries. "How many of them are there?!"

"I guess ... about ..." And he died. His heels beat a tattoo on the cold ground, and he went limp. Great. I'd have to do some scouting, find out how many there were before making any further moves. Another glance at the moon told me I needed to get back to town, fast. I was shuddering and shaking by the time I made it back to my horse; the medicine was wearing off fast.

I didn't have much time. The wolves had almost gotten me last night, the Bear-Injun had said. I rode like the hounds of hell were chasing me and made it back to town in what had to be some sort of record. I ran up to my room with amazing speed and slammed the door hard enough to crack the frame. Snatching up the skin, I could see my hands were covered in thick, black fur. A look in the mirror showed the bones of my face had shifted slightly, my jaw jutting outward. My teeth looked longer and sharper.

Not wasting a second, I undid the leather tie and took a gulp of the bitter concoction. I'd just managed to close it up again when I sank to the floor, retching and clenching my stomach. It was over just as soon as it started, and I hoped it was something a body could get used to. It only lasted a moment, but that moment seemed awful long, if you know what I mean. I would see Liz before I went anywhere.

I walked down the stairs, looking cool and calm now, but a low hum of excitement seemed to vibrate through my very bones. I tried not to look up as I made my way over to Liz's place. I didn't need to wait and watch in the bushes this time. My sense of smell and hearing told me there was no one about. I knocked on her door and waited. I could hear her perfectly, and she was wrapping something up, and opening a drawer. She shoved something in it, and slammed the drawer shut. I could tell exactly where it was.

"Thorn!" She exclaimed, throwing open the door. I laughed and took her in my arms – just seeing her made all my worries melt away – until she punched me in the chest.

"I was so worried about you! Where were you last night?"

I didn't know how to respond to that.

"I waited, hoping you'd drop by, and when you didn't, I went out back behind the hotel and threw rocks at your window. I saw it was open, but you didn't come to the window, and I threw a lot of rocks. I looked everywhere for you, but you weren't to be found!"

She blushed again, in her way, when she mentioned coming to my window.

"What was so urgent?" I asked her. She hadn't struck me as the type to get upset if a man didn't spend every waking hour following her around like a lovesick puppy dog.

"I saw one of them! Around dusk last night, I walked outside to throw some things out, and there he was, in between some bushes. He ran off, but I caught a glimpse of him. I was scared, so I came to find you. Are you all right?"

"Yeah," I lied. "I'm fine. Couldn't be better."

"Thorn? You look ... taller."

"Well, I've uh, been exercising and things."

"Exercising, huh? If you say so ..." The look she gave me indicated she wasn't buying it, but it wasn't a subject I was prepared to pursue.

"You have the shotgun loaded?"

"Of course! I stayed up half the night sitting on the couch with it! So you didn't answer my question. Where were you last night?"

"I was, uh, out riding."

"Riding." This gal could smell horse manure when it was being shoveled, and as high as I was stacking it, I didn't think I could hold out much longer. I desperately wanted to tell her everything, but I admit I was afraid. Would she want to be with a monster, such as I'd become? What if she knew I turned into one of those things? Would she still want me to visit? There was another thing. The Injun had said he'd lived a long time. He didn't appear any older when I saw him than what he'd been when he became ... whatever you'd call him. If it was the same for me, you didn't have to be a genius to figure out what that meant for a relationship.

"Listen, Liz. I've got a lot going on right now, and as much as I want to, I can't tell you all of it. I wouldn't ... I wouldn't want you to think ill of me."

Her face softened, and she stepped closer. "Thorn, I think more of you than I think you know." She kissed me then, soft and sweet, and she smelled like wildflowers. I almost broke down right then and there.

"Why don't you have a seat, and I'll get you something to drink." Now that sounded right nice. Liz disappeared into her bedroom, and I desperately wanted to take a peek at what she'd hidden. I knew it was wrong, but I couldn't help myself. First, I tiptoed silent as a mouse over to her room. I wanted to be sure she was busy and I wouldn't get caught peeking this time. I leaned my head slightly so one eye could peer in. She had her dress off, and the sight of her in her petticoat brought a sudden rise in my pulse. I knew because it started pounding in my throat.

A newly familiar shudder ran through my nerves and I stepped back. The backs of my hands had sprouted hair again. Damn. Apparently it wasn't just anger that brought about the change. I flew over to the drawer in question and slowly pried it open. Inside there was a long rectangular object, wrapped up in a black cloth. With a glance toward her door, I began unwrapping it. The sound of bottles and jars opening and closing let me know I had a minute or two. It was another painting. It was of me. My face, to be more exact. It did me a lot more credit than the mirror did, but it was well done.

When a woman keeps painting your picture, that means she's got only one thing on her mind.

Or at least I thought so; I'd never had a woman, or anyone, put me in a painting before. A sudden surge of panic welled in my throat, and I wrapped it back up and replaced it just like I'd found it. The hair on my palms was gone again, so I arranged myself in her chair so as to look like I'd been waiting patiently, rather than snooping through her things like some kind of fiend. She came out in a very pretty dress, low cut and flattering. I'd never seen anything quite like it. Must be some kind of eastern fashion. I definitely approved. Her lips were painted a deep red, and her eyelashes seemed fuller and thicker.

Oh, stars. She sat down next to me rather than in the other chair, as she'd done before. The chair was just wide enough to hold us both, though tightly. Suddenly, the room felt awful hot. She handed me a drink, and I gave her what I figured was a very awkward smile and gulped it down. She took the glass from me and set it down on the table. Firmly.

"How do you like my dress?" She asked it sweetly, fluttering her eyelashes. Now, I had more than a few thoughts about that dress, but not one of them seemed like the kind of thing you say to a respectable woman.

"It's, uh, it's nice ... ," I stammered.

"Nice?" She looked at me with an eyebrow arched. She'd been doing that repeating thing a lot tonight. I wasn't sure why.

"Yeah, you look, uh, very pretty."

"Oh? Well, thank you." She looked pleased now, and shifted in the chair. It seemed to bring her closer. Her face was awful close to mine, her lids half closed. My throat was very tight.

I reached out a hand to stroke her hair, so soft and fine. She closed her eyes. I saw my hand was covered in fur again, and snatched it away. Damn, and damn again! Her lids flew open.

"Why are you sitting on your hands?"

"Uh, no reason, I just uh, I hurt them today ..."

"Oh, well, let me see then."

"No, really, that's okay, I ..." I wished I hadn't left the gloves in my room.

"I have to be going now. Really. I have some ... sheriffing to do. Thanks for the drink, Liz!"

I rose quickly, gave her a peck on the cheek, and started for the door. She stared after me, dumbfounded. I hated being a werewolf. The moon was bright and full outside, and even though I'd taken the medicine, a part of me still wanted nothing more than to go out and run in the woods and call to the bright sphere in the sky. But that would not do. I had enemies about, and they would surely be out there now, perhaps waiting for me to leave town, thinking I'd have no choice but to change, and they could hunt me down and kill me. A few minutes later I was in my room with three bottles of whiskey. I guzzled one to no effect, but the second and third brought about the desired result, and at some point, I don't remember when, I drifted off into sleep.

CHAPTER 10

By dawn, I was out on the trail, having al-ready taken my medicine. Blech. It still tasted awful, but the experience wasn't quite so bad as before. I was regretful about having to run from Liz's place last night with my tail between my legs, and about the fact that I had a monster living inside me. Or rather, that I'd turned into a monster.

I'd sat my horse for some time outside the schoolhouse, trying to work up the nerve to just go in and lay it on the line for her, what I was, what I'd become. I figured if she re-ally cared, then maybe she'd be willing to deal with it, and I should just go in and explain what happened to me. I didn't. Today would be a good time to scout out Luna's ranch, which I hadn't seen as of yet.

Not intending to make the same mistake twice, I left town to the east, then immediately rode like hell into the woods and took a long, serpentine pattern, working my way north toward the Crescent Ranch. It was risky, but now was the best time to go have a look-see. Luna and his wolves would be sleeping after a long night under a full moon, and with any luck they wouldn't know I'd taken another of their number last night. I was near where I figured the ranch to be when I smelled smoke. With it came the sour scent of unwashed clothes and bodies. My sharp ears picked up the noises of men talking, laughing, and the occasional sizzling of hot metal against flesh.

Leaving my horse well back in the trees, I crept closer. Three men were branding cattle with a running iron, cattle with an unfamiliar brand on it. They were reshaping the brand, making it look like a crescent. Rustlers. There was a cabin behind them and a corral where three horses stood, cropping grass.

There were maybe fifty head of cattle, one or two of them with the Circle C brand on their flanks. I didn't doubt for a minute these were Luna's hands, and I didn't yet know how many there were. I doffed my boots and hat and injuned my way over behind the cabin.

Finding a rope, I coiled it into a lasso and crept closer to the men, busy with their work. I would have a little fun and hopefully get the information I needed. There were some brush and trees in between the corral and the fire, so I gently removed the planks from the fence and led out one of the horses. I should have just enough rope. Tying one end to the still-saddled horse, I led it around to the edge of the brush. I swung the lasso in the air and let it go, catching one of the men around the waist. A hard slap on the horse's rear sent him a-running, and the man in the rope dragged along with him at an incredible speed. I ducked back behind the brush before the others saw me.

This was fun! A peek through the leaves showed me they had their guns out, looking all around and clearly confused. I stayed low and ran on cat-feet around to the other side of them. Finding a handy log, I whipped it at the back of the taller one's head, and he hit the ground in a heap. The third man, lean and unshaven, turned about again and again, his pistol pointing all over the place.

"Who's there? Speak up, or I'll shoot!" I sure wasn't going to say anything, but when I didn't, he was as good as his word. The rustler took potshots here and there in the woods, which was entertaining until one of them ricocheted off a tree right above my head. Playtime's over. I took careful aim with the carbine, and at this distance it was an easy shot. The heavy slug blew a hole in his gun hand you could see daylight through. He cried out, and I entered the clearing.

"Mighty fine day, isn't it?" I said, the rifle over my shoulder.

"Yuh bastard! Look what yuh did ta my hand!" As if I didn't know, he held it up. It was probably ruined, but I figured he was getting off pretty easy. Most would have either shot them on sight or held a hemp party in their honor. I didn't care for his tone, so I took a few long strides, seized him up, and slapped him twice across the face, hard. That got his attention.

"How many hands does Luna have?" "Gosh, don't squeeze so hard! I dunno, ten maybe."

"Just ten?"

"Well, ten that do any work anyway. Four of 'em just seem to sit around the ranch house during the day, 'cept at night they ride out sometimes."

"You've got a new job. There's a posse coming. All the ranchers in the valley are on to you boys, and they're gonna string you boys up from the nearest tree and leave you to hang. I'm just the advance party, sent to figger out how much rope we're gonna need."

His eyes were wide and scared. "Your new job is to go back to the ranch and tell those boys to sit tight 'til we get there. I don't want to have to chase them all over the territory, so you make sure they know to sit tight and not go anywhere, got it?"

He nodded vigorously, but I knew he'd do exactly what I wanted him to do, and by nightfall, there wouldn't be a single hand on that ranch to ride a fence line or rustle cattle. 'Ceptin' the werewolves of course, I didn't plan on them leaving no how. I drove off the other two horses and let the crippled rustler go off afoot. I wanted plenty of time before he reached the ranch, so I could set back and watch the results. It wasn't long before I reached a hilltop overlooking the Crescent.

The main house and bunkhouse were set into a draw between two fingers, and I could see herds of cattle stretching off for quite some distance. There were more, far more than I think I've seen on just about any ranch in my life. Apparently, rustlin' paid off pretty handsomely. Until now. I was going to destroy this place and the evil it held. I was no saint, but these monsters were draining the country dry, sapping the hard work of innocent, good men. I may play fast and loose with the rules, but I had no pity for men such as these, whether or not they were monsters.

Folks may not think highly of me, bein' a bounty hunter and all, but the men I shot and occasionally brought in still breathin' were evil and had committed heinous crimes against their fellow man. I was just the bigger snake in the field.

I would do my job now, only this time, it was personal. An hour passed, and I could see the rustler I'd shot hurrying up to the bunk house. Not five minutes later, men poured out in all directions, grabbing their horses and scattering toward the hills, riding like the devil himself was behind them. I had a good laugh at that, but regretted my choice of hiding places when I saw Luna and two others stumble out from the main house to see what the ruckus was all about. I was far away on a hilltop, but if I'd been closer, one good shot from my carbine could have ended it all, right there.

Disappointed, I set my mind to getting a good understanding of the layout. Luna had chosen prime land, with streams running through it from down off the hills and mountains, a good year-round water supply that also kept the grass growing green and tall. The tall hills would keep the cattle pretty close in, and provide little pockets of shelter for them to winter in. Yes, sir, this was a fine ranch. I was well hidden, and so I dozed off for a while. When I awoke, it was near dusk, and I could see the sun setting behind the ranch house, right over it behind the mountains.

It was a beautiful sight. Maybe when this was all over, I could take Liz up here and show her. For now though, I had work to do. There was no way to approach the ranch without being seen, 'less I come up behind it. It took a few hours, but by the time the moon was high in the sky I was on top of the ridge just behind the ranch house. Whoever was still there was fair game, as far as I was concerned. From what the rustler told me, there were only four of them left, besides Luna, and with my new silver bullets, I was sure I could take them all. Leaving my horse, I worked my way with all possible care down to a position back in the trees, but commanding a view of both structures. The moonlight was good, and it called to me as before, but not as strongly, being on the wane. I could see everything as clearly as if it were daylight. There was a fire burning inside the house, and I could hear men talking. They were a good hundred yards away, but I could pick them up easily, and I counted the voices.

One ... two ... three. Maybe the other two were just being silent, or asleep, but the hair on the back of my neck stood up. Could this be ...

A trap. I knew it in an instant, but it was already too late. The forest around me exploded as two huge shapes rushed me from either side. I leaped away just in time and fired as I went. A sharp whimper of pain, and then they were on me. Claws raked my side, but I smashed a muzzle with the butt of my carbine, and with my new strength it had some effect. Teeth bit down hard on my thigh, and the lightning was knocked out of my hands. I ripped both the Colts out of their holsters and let fly. Thumbing the hammers back as fast as I could, I poured silver into each beast until the hammers clicked empty.

One was dead, but the other was still fighting. Claws slashed my face, but I could feel it healing even as my head turned back around, and I kicked out as hard as I could. That knocked the wolf back a step, and I palmed my derringer and stuck the two barrels right in his eye and emptied it. He dropped down, smoke rising from the socket. I didn't waste a second. I figured Luna and the others would be on their way here already, and my guns were empty. I gathered my carbine and ran up the hill as fast as I could. The brush thundered behind me, and they were hot on my heels. In my current situation, there was no way I could fight off the three of them. I'd taught myself to reload on the run, but I couldn't afford to slow down for a second or they'd have me. I whistled, and heard strong hoof beats pounding down the hillside toward me.

The steel dust appeared in the moonlight a second later, and I jumped on as he rode by. I had my shotgun out before we ran smack dab into the wolves, and I sprayed buckshot all around me, temporarily blinded by the flash. I heard a series of yelps and whines, but didn't know how well I'd hit them. I kept going down the hill, past the ranch house and through the field. I was jamming cartridges into my lighting as fast as I could, but nothing chased me across the field. They had failed. I hoped they were hurt pretty bad, but wasn't going back to find out. I'd taken two more of them and ran off their hands, and that would be enough for one night. As I reached the woods on the other side of the field, glowing eyes of green and blue watched my progress, then melted back into the trees.

They'd be enraged now, and I didn't think they'd give up the chase. I didn't want to draw them back to town where they could kill me in my room, and I knew nothing would stop them now. Turning the horse's head north, I rode hard and fast, well away from where they'd be expecting to find me. Twice I doubled back and waited, but nothing came up the trail. I rode the most confusing route I could find, gradually working my way back to the town, traveling north, then east for a while, and changing course every so often. If they weren't behind me, they might be trying to get ahead of me, and I didn't want them to be able to predict where I'd show up. I was pretty slick in the woods, but not slick enough, I guess. Riding up on a ridge, I caught a scent of wolf. Drawing the reins tight, I waited, straining my ears for the slightest sound. There was nothing, but I knew they were out there.

"Thorn, can you hear me?!" It was Luna's voice, his human voice, deep and resonant. I declined to answer.

"I know you can. You're a good man, Thorn. We could use someone like you. I'm down a few hands now, but I don't hold it against you. We just got off to a bad start, that's all. Why don't you come on out and we'll talk some."

Perhaps he meant it, but I wasn't buying into his game either way. I'd been listening to where his voice came from and thought I had a pretty good idea. He stayed silent, waiting for a reply. When I did, it was with the eloquence of my Colt lightning. The shot cracked through the woods, and I heard the bullet scream off and sharp thwack as it impacted with a tree somewhere. Oh, well. At least I'd made my point pretty effectively.

"If that's the way you want it, Thorn. We'll get you, one way or the other." Heavy bodies crackled through the brush near where I'd heard the voice. I must not have missed by much. A few shots with the lightning to see them off proper, and I reigned up my horse and headed in the opposite direction, as fast as I could ride. I didn't weave or try any tricks, just rode as hard as the steel dust could handle, which was hard indeed. We made it into town together unscathed but for my shirt, which was ruined, again.

My flesh was in much better condition, but the fast healing seemed to work up quite an appetite. I was of a mind to visit Liz, as a woman most always has the fixings of a meal, but after my abrupt departure, I didn't want to try that again until I could get this fur business under control. I made it up to my room without a sound in my stocking feet and reloaded my guns with more silver bullets, leaving the ones in my cartridge belt in place. There was an odd smell in my room, and I recognized it as that of the clerk. It was foul and musty, almost like a musk, and stank up the whole room. He'd been in here.

Perhaps it was just to change the sheets, or refill the water, though there was a maid for that. Maybe she had the day off, or had taken sick. At any rate, I wasn't gonna stay in the room tonight, as that would be the first place the werewolves would come looking. So opening the window to let it air out and leaving the stench behind, I took my weapons and bedroll to the stable with me. After fixing up my horse with a double portion of hay, barley, and a handful of sugar (I could smell where William had been hiding it) I crawled up into the loft.

Lying down in a big pile of hay, I tipped my hat over my eyes and went to sleep, the carbine in hand. I dreamed of a full, fat moon and the sounds and smells of the hunt. I was running in a primeval forest, untouched by man. Game was everywhere, and for the taking. I took a lot. I feasted on blood and raw flesh, still warm from the kill. The fear of my prey was most delicious of all though, its scent intoxicating. I ran down deer, elk, and antelope, and slew them all. Suddenly, my nose caught the most heady aroma yet.

I couldn't see my prey, but heard it as it dashed through the woods beyond, pitifully slow. The fear was rolling off it in waves, but I held back, filling my nostrils with it, basking in pleasures of the chase. I entered a small clearing, lit by the moon and stars, and gathered myself to pounce on my exhausted quarry. It lay in the grass, bleeding from scratches and panting. It turned its face up to look at me, the savage predator. My lips drooled with saliva and my stomach rumbled. I saw the face.

It was Liz. I jumped to my feet, and the first light of dawn was peeking through the boards of the stable. I panicked. Had I changed? Please, dear God, don't let the dream have been real! I was fully clothed, though, and there wasn't a speck of blood on me that wasn't my own from the night before when the wolves had slashed me. Thank heavens. Sweat covered my body – cold sweat. I felt greasy and my heart was pounding, but I sat back down and rolled and lit a cigarette.

This time I smoked the whole thing, even though it stank and tasted like ashes in my mouth. I needed to calm my nerves and think this one over. I wasn't no hand to interpret dreams, but I knew from what little I'd read from the Bible that sometimes they meant something, and I had a feeling about this one. It seemed to say I was a danger to Liz. I couldn't disagree. What if I turned on her, when her kisses had aroused the wolf living inside me. What would happen then? I knew from before that I wasn't entirely in control, and as much as I'd like to think I'd never hurt Liz, I didn't know that. I was a monster now, and no fit company for a woman like that to be takin' up with.

I confess my heart wanted to break, right then and there, but there was no doubt about it, I couldn't be around her anymore. I'd never felt anything like this for a woman, and the pain I felt now was also unlike anything else I'd ever experienced. I had to stay away, and that was that. Seemed to me that the best thing I could do was be about my business, take care of this thing with Luna once and for all, and go on the trail again, as far from Elk's Run as I could get. I'd leave this sheriff business to someone suited for it, and go back to the only thing I was ever really good at, bounty huntin'.

With all these thoughts in mind, I wandered over to my room, stashed my guns, and cleaned up a little. Putting on my last shirt, another black silk job, just as nice as the first, I walked over to my office. There was a stack of messages, telegrams and whatnot. I suppose I'd been neglecting my day-to-day duties, but I had more important concerns, so I let the pile sit. I'd been hungry before, but the thought of not seeing Liz again had put all thoughts of food far from my mind. I did heat some coffee and had a cup and a good think. It was time to end this thing with Luna, but I'd showed my hand last night and barely made it out alive. Still, I'd done some major damage, and evened up the odds a bit. Tonight, one of us would die. Bein' that I was a werewolf now, just like them, gave me a bit of an advantage. They couldn't shoot me to any effect, but I had silver bullets. They would have to change to fight, and I could remain a man, and gun them down like I'd done the others. Like varmints. Well, big, furry, lethal varmints anyway.

Curious now, I took a look at the stack of mail and read through it. Notices of bank robberies down in Idaho, requests for information on the whereabouts of wanted men, even a telegram from Denver giving the description of a masked man who'd robbed an undisclosed amount of silver from a train a couple miles from Elk's Run. I didn't figure to be much help with that, and the description was pretty vague. Not much I could do with it, no how. I crumpled it and dropped it in the wastebasket. Gradually, I became aware of a foul smell. It was a werewolf. I slipped the thong off my guns, but the scent wasn't strong enough for there to be one about. I sniffed, closing my eyes and letting my nose tell me where to look. In the drawer. There was an envelope, and sure enough, the scent on it was fresh, from last night. I was again glad I hadn't stayed in my room.

It read: "Thorn. You had your chance. Now we do this the hard way. I have Liz. Come to the ranch at dusk, and we'll let her go. If you don't show, I've had a mind to take me a woman for a while now, and this one's mighty purty."

I wasn't much of a hand for spelling, but even I could spell "pretty." There was something else in the envelope, a lock of fine chestnut hair. One whiff told me they did indeed have Liz. There was no point rushing over to her place. They had her, and I knew it. I resolved to go. It would mean my death, almost certainly, but I would go nonetheless, and try to take them with me. They had me dead to rights, and there wasn't much I could do about that.

I suppose if I was a hero I would have sprang into action, done something clever and brave, and saved the day. As it was, I set in the chair awhile, a dark cloud over my thoughts. I was fresh out of clever. A short cough brought me back to reality. Warren stood in front of my desk, holding his hat. "Sheriff." He nodded.

"What is it, Warren?"

"I come to ask for ... for a job." He looked a mite sheepish.

"You want to be a lawman?"

"Never thought I would, but my stake's run out, and the other night, helping you with those drunks, I ... I kind of enjoyed it."

I thought Warren would make a fine lawman. He was big, strong, and liked to fight. His mere presence would discourage a lot of the ne'er-do-wells, and though it was a far cry from how he'd started out, there was more than one bad man who'd turned over a new leaf and career on the right side of the law.

"I'd be a good deputy," he said quickly. "I'll follow orders, and the law."

"I don't think you're cut out to be a deputy, Warren," I

said, and his face fell. "I think you'd be much better as a sheriff."

He looked up quickly, just in time to catch the silver badge I threw in his direction. He was flabbergasted.

"I've got other cattle to herd, Warren, and you'll do a fine job. See the mayor this morning, and tell him you're the new sheriff. He's a greasy rascal, but you'll be able to get a good wage if you haggle some."

"Uh, just one more thing, Sheriff, I mean, Thorn ..."

I paused with my hand against the door. "What?"

"Just ..." He looked down, embarrassed. "Don't tell my brother, okay?"

I smiled then. "Don't worry, Sheriff, I won't."

CHAPTER 11

THE FIRST PLACE I WENT WAS TO MY ROOM, TO
gather my weapons. I took the Winchester with me. I would
load it up with silver bullets and have one more weapon to
use without reloading. I needed all the firepower I could get.

Upon returning to my room, I paused suddenly just outside the door. I could smell the foul scent I'd picked up on the
clerk, stronger than hell, and when I listened, I could hear
him breathing inside. He was opening drawers and shutting
them. Whatever the hell he was doing, it sure wasn't changing the sheets. I drew back against the wall, just outside the
door.

Suddenly it opened, and I grabbed him by the throat and
forced him back into the room. He had my carbine and shotgun in his hands, and I smacked them loose to clatter on the
floor. No one steals my guns.

"What the hell do you think you're doing?" I growled.
His eyes were scared, but then something in them changed,
and I saw raw hate. I also realized what I'd been smelling on
him. I was an idiot not to figure it out before.

"Hell with you, Thorn! Did you find out yet? Luna's got
your pretty little woman, and he's going to kill you tonight,
and there's nothing you can do about it!"

There might not be, but to ease my discomfort, I threw
the clerk against the wall, hard. He went down, but sprang
right back up again and delivered a punch to my gut that

would have hurt, in my former state. As it was I just punched him back, and he lay on the floor, dazed and bleeding. The cut over his eye healed up in an instant.

"What would Luna want with a little fish like you, anyway?" I demanded.

"Go to hell, Thorn! I was going to take your precious guns, and you'd be powerless! Luna gave me power, made me strong! He's stronger than you, and he's going to ..."

I'd heard that part already, and so I booted him in the face, which shut him up, at least for a second. Then fine gray fur covered his exposed skin, and he shrank out of his clothes. Before me sat a coyote, still wearing the tie. It looked kind of pathetic. He growled and snapped, savaging my kneecaps with his claws, and biting hard with small, sharp teeth.

It stung a little, but even in man form I was far stronger, and I tore him loose and grabbed him by the hind legs. I slammed him on the floor again and again, then tossed him from the window.

He knew about them taking Liz, did he? In my mind, that made him responsible, and he tried to take away the one advantage I had. He was mine. For all the damage I'd done him, he still hit the ground running, and I picked up the carbine and drew a bead. He was a fast little varmint, but it seemed easy to track him with the rifle. I gave him a pretty good lead and pulled the trigger. He went sprawling end over end and lay still. I was about to shoot again, just to be sure, but he changed back into a flabby, skinny clerk again, dead and still and I let him be.

He was just outside the woods, and sooner or later some of his kind, other coyotes I mean, would be along to give him the attention he deserved. I loaded another cartridge into the carbine and filled the Winchester up with my silver bullets. Digging out my medicine from my saddlebags, I undid the tie and held it up to my lips.

I paused. Hell with it. I tossed it out the window, where it spilled out onto the long grass. I would need all my strength for what lay ahead of me, and there was a good chance I wouldn't survive. Taking my guns and saddle, I went down to the stable, and had William get my steel dust ready. I had a few things to do.

I drew all my money from the bank and knew I'd never had so much at one time before. At least I'd die a rich man. A visit to the general store was next, and sure enough, they had jars of honey, though mighty expensive. I bought two. Crossing back over to the stables, William was out front, reigns in hand. I took them from him and swung into the saddle.

"William, take this," I said, handing him all my earthly wealth, tied in a bundle. "If I don't come back in a few days, it's yours. Get yourself some schoolin' and maybe write yourself one of those novels you like so much about your old pal, Thorn. Make me out to be handsome, will you? One more thing. You can ride a horse, right?"

He nodded.

"Take these jars, and this note," I was scribbling on a scrap of paper, "and ride out along the tracks, near the tunnel. Set it down somewhere, and open up the lids. Then ride fast back here, and stay put. Can you do that for me?"

He nodded again, solemnly. I knew he'd follow my instructions to the letter. I didn't know if it would work or not, but it was worth a shot.

"Good man. Take a hundred dollars out of there for

yourself, you've done a fine job for me, and I appreciate it."
He looked at the money, then back up at me.

"Mr. Thorn? You're coming back, right?"

"I don't know son, I don't know." I turned then, and rode out of town at a gallop. There was a chance they could be lyin' for me, but I'd deal with that if it came to it. I rode like it was my last ride, and maybe it was.

***

Despite all that lay before me, I was happy. I had a good horse, guns that shot straight, and the affections of a good woman. If a man needs any more than that, he's plumb spoiled, I say. If my life was going to end today, well, as that Injun said, it was a good day to die. I slowed some before I reached the Crescent. I didn't dare delay, for fear they'd hurt Liz, but I wanted to get a look at things before I rode down into the trap they surely had waiting. It seemed to me they held all the cards. I'd have to find some way to slip an ace in my sleeve.

Try as I might, no brilliant plan sprang to mind. There was no movement in or around the ranch house, but that didn't mean anything. They could be inside, with Liz, or they could be somewhere in the woods beyond, well hidden and ready to shoot me as I rode up. I wouldn't learn anything here. I would just have to ride up there and roll with the punches as they came. I'd done it before, just not under such dire circumstances.

Whatever would happen, I was determined that Liz should come out of this alive. I was expecting a shot or some kind of warning when I rode into the yard. I was fifty yards from the house, but there was no sign that anyone was around. I could tell by the smell they were there, though, so

I sat my horse and waited, my weapons bristling from the saddle in just about every direction. I had two Winchesters now, my Colt lightning, the repeating shotgun, two wheel guns, and my derringer in my sleeve, all loaded up with silver cartridges.

"Well, Luna, are we going to do this or not?" I yelled into the house. A dark chuckle reached my ears from inside.

"We are, Thorn, we are. Be patient will you? I've waited a long time for this now, and I'd like to savor the moment. Why don't you say hi to my new gal, she's awful purty!" With that he stepped out into the doorway, holding Liz in front of him. He had one of her hands behind her back and a wolfish set of claws at her throat. How he'd managed to change just one of his hands, and not altogether, I couldn't figure, but he'd had more practice at this than I, and it wasn't the first thing on my mind, anyhow.

The other two wolves stepped out from either side of the house. They were shirtless and unarmed. Guess they figured the bullets wouldn't do much good on me anyhow, and they intended to rend me limb from limb. "Drop the guns, Thorn. Now," Luna demanded and pressed his claws against Liz's throat. A small trickle of blood ran down over her fair skin. Now, dropping the guns didn't seem like a wise thing to do, but I couldn't see a way out of the matter. I might be able to make the shot, but Luna would be fast enough to kill her if I drew, and there was a chance of hitting her, too.

"Don't do it, Thorn! Don't let them kill you!" It was Liz, and she meant well, but I couldn't take her advice. I had gotten her involved in this, and I wasn't going to let her die for me.

"I'm sorry Liz, I have to. I'm sorry I got you into this."

"Don't do it, Thorn! I love you! Do you hear me? Don't worry about me, just kill them all!" I did indeed want to kill them all, but ... what was that she said? She loved me. I'd never heard that before from a woman. I think I grew another inch that very second.

"Aww, isn't that sweet," Luna's dark voice chuckled, "Two lovebirds. Well, it don't matter anyway. He'll be dead soon sweetie, and you and me, we'll get to know each other soon enough."

"Take your hands off her, Luna!" I was plenty mad now. Fine, I would do as they asked, and find another way to kill them all, guns or no guns.

I dropped the rifles, shotgun, and pistols to the ground and rode forward. I still had my derringer, tucked back up in my sleeve. It was only two shots, but if I got half a chance, I'd take Luna down with me. They all grinned, seeing me unarmed and helpless.

"Isn't that sweet, gal? He's giving himself up for you. He's done dropped all his weapons, and now we're gonna kill him."

"Go to hell, bastard!" Liz kicked and struggled, but she was no match for the werewolf's strength, and he just laughed and held her tighter.

"Don't worry, darlin', there'll be plenty of time for you to struggle later on, when we're done with your sweetheart. You know what she called us, Thorn? She called us "disgusting monsters." Now, that strikes me as kind of unladylike, don't you think? 'Specially because she ain't got no problem with you bein' one of us, and all."

He feigned surprise.

"Oh, could it be you haven't told her yet? Didn't you

show her what you really look like?" I was getting plenty mad now, both at seeing Liz in distress and with all the taunting Luna was throwing my way. Shivers ran up and down my spine, and I knew I was about to change. I hadn't taken my medicine. Liz was looking from Luna to me, confused. It was true. I was a monster now, just like them. And soon she would know it. Just to push me over the edge, Luna forced her closer and gave her a wet kiss on the cheek. Liz screamed. That was it. I felt the hair popping out of my skin turn to fur, and I leaped off the horse just in time to feel my bones stretch and shift, and by the time I hit the ground I was a huge, snarling wolf. And down one more set of clothes, not that it mattered much. The wolf in me wanted to attack, to rip and tear and pour out his rage upon his enemies, but I could only focus on the look in Liz's eyes.

She looked shocked. I was sure then I'd done the right thing in not telling her, for as much good as it did me. She would never want to be with me now, even if somehow I survived this. It didn't change my feelings for her, and I didn't blame her, not one bit. I just wished I'd left Elk's Run back before I'd mixed her up in all this. The two others changed then, even quicker than I had, and in the blink of an eye I was being circled by two snarling, ferocious wolves. Luna stayed as he was, laughing and enjoying the coming show. Liz looked terrified.

I was about to be ripped to pieces, and I knew it. The wolves snapped at the air, and inched closer. Maybe if I attacked now, took the first one down, I could ...

An ear-splitting roar made everyone, myself included, turn and look at the source of the noise. There, at the edge of the woods, stood the largest bear I had ever seen in my life.

It would easily make two of the one I'd killed before coming to this place, the one that tore me up so bad. He stood on his hind legs, a terrifying spectacle. My gambit had paid off after all. The wolves around me sank back, teeth bared and hackles raised.

"What are you waiting for?! Get him!" Luna shouted, and threw Liz to the side. He leaped off the porch, changing into a wolf as he ran at me. He was huge, far bigger than I was. I snarled and charged him. The other wolves ignored me, looking scared but running for the bear all the same. I lunged into the air, going for Luna's throat. He batted me aside easily, and I hit the ground hard. I rolled, just in time to avoid having my own throat torn out. He was fast.

Faster than me, it seemed. I leaped for him again, and we went end over end in a dervish of fangs and claws. He took a good chunk out of my hind leg, and I managed to catch onto his ear, tearing it. His claws raked me all over and my blood flew everywhere. I wanted to shout to Liz to get away, to escape, but all that came out was a growl. I fought wildly, desperately, but I was getting the worst of it.

I charged in again, but Luna rammed me with his shoulder, spinning me over, and it was a near thing moving out of the way as his jaws snapped shut inches from my exposed throat. I backed away, and we circled each other. We charged at the same time, but he was bigger and heavier, and bowled me right over. I landed on my back, and he was on me in a flash. He went for my throat. I was a goner. Two sharp reports rang out, and he whimpered and rolled off me. Liz stood right next to us, my smoking derringer in her hand. Luna lunged for her, but I bit down hard on his foreleg and his teeth snapped shut, barely nipping her arm. I clawed and scratched, and we rolled across the ground, me taking the worst of it, but managing to move the fight away from Liz. He sunk his teeth deep in my shoulder, and I couldn't dislodge him until I raked my claws across his eyes. That made him let go, in a hurry.

We circled each other again, each looking for an opening. I was getting my tail handed to me, and I'd already lost a lot of blood. We were both healing up as we moved, but I a little slower. He'd have me soon, if I didn't do something quick. I considered things, for the briefest of moments. I'd been wild, fighting like an animal instead of a man. Luna had experience, and he had cunning, and he was using both to gain the advantage. I had to do the same, or I'd be dead in a few moments. Clawing at each other was useless. The wounds healed up right away, and weren't very deep. I made as if to run at him again, mindlessly, and he lowered his shoulder to meet me, trying to knock me over again. My paws were still very much like hands, and that's how I used them.

I raised up in the air, made a fist, and pounded down on Luna's head like a sledgehammer. He sat back, dazed and surprised. I rushed forward, slamming huge paws into his head and gut, and he didn't know how to react. His talons sliced at me, but didn't do much damage. I had a fistful of his fur, and the other fist I was pumping into his jaws as fast and hard as I could. Some teeth fell out, and I grabbed him behind the head and threw him over my hip. He landed hard. Leaping on top of him, I sank my teeth into his throat, shook my head back and forth, and tore out his windpipe and some other things.

He staggered away, but I could see the wound was already closing, but slowly. I didn't know how much of this it would take to kill him, but there was one way that seemed sure. Seizing him by the head, I stood on his back and pulled and wrenched upward. The strength seemed to rush through me, and in a second his head popped free, spraying blood and gore all around. The body quivered and shook but didn't grow a new head, or seem likely to. It was over.

The big Injun, Andio ... uh (I give up) stood triumphant over the scattered remains of the other two wolves. He looked like he'd been done for a while. "Not bad, white man. You ver' bad at pictures. But I understand. Is good that woman help you. You need it. Ver' funny!" Yeah, funny. The note I'd sent with the honey had paid off. I wanted to be sure he'd smell the honey immediately and come running, but I guessed he'd probably read it only after gulping down both jars.

I didn't know if he could read English, so I'd drawn crude stick wolves, surrounding a stick figure with long hair, and a crude map. I'm no hand at art but was glad I'd been able to make myself understood. I shuddered to think of the outcome if the Bear-Injun hadn't showed up. I looked down at my hands, soaked in blood. Hands. I was a man again. I turned to look for Liz and saw she was okay. She was standing just a few feet away in the sunlight, the wind blowing her curly hair. She looked beautiful, even drenched in blood.

"Well, at least now I know what you look like naked." she said and smiled. She didn't look at all displeased, though she wasn't meeting my eyes.

"Liz, I'm sorry ... I--"

"Hush," she said and put a finger to my lips.

"You should have told me, Thorn. I love you, and I don't care if you turn into a wolf. You're not like the others, and they're gone now."

I was buck naked and covered in blood. Liz took another step closer and pulled my head down to kiss me. She must love me indeed. I admit I was lost for a good long while there, but I came up for air suddenly, remembering something. I grabbed at her arm and saw the bite. It wasn't bad, but I knew what would happen now.

"Liz, you've been bit! Honey, I have to tell you ..." I rushed over my words, stammering, but she put her fingers to my lips again.

"I know," she said. "The others were talking about it, while they were waiting for you. I'll deal with it, no, we'll deal with it together. Who knows? It might be fun! I'm just glad we're okay. You're going to stay now, aren't you, Thorn?"

Wow, what a woman. I looked around at the ranch, at the woman I held in my arms. This was a fine place. We could move in here, as Luna was dead, and the way I figured it, I'd won it fair and square. A visit to the lawyer would fix things up pretty easy, and it would be a good place to raise young'uns.

"Ha, ha, your woman never lets you talk, she always shush you! Ha, ha. You should beat her, white man. Make her listen. Ver' funny."

Pointedly ignoring the big man's suggestion, I took Liz into my arms and kissed her again, long and hard.

Colin Webster is a U.S. Marine veteran with plenty of experience in life or death situations and combat with firearms. He is intimately familiar with the weapons and armaments of the late 1800s. Colin has published *Blood on the Mississippi* and *Blood and Tequila*. Colin lives in New Bern, North Carolina, where he works as an independent security consultant.

White Feather Press Books by Colin Webster

Blood and Tequila

Blood on the Mississippi

Blood and Silver